Summerland

Rory O'Brien

The Merry Blacksmith Press

2015

Summerland

© 2015 Rory O'Brien

For information, address:

The Merry Blacksmith Press
70 Lenox Ave.
West Warwick, RI 02893

merryblacksmith.com

Published in the USA by The Merry Blacksmith Press

ISBN—0-69258-800-0
978-0-69258-800-0

In Memory of My Parents

The Newport Season

THOUGH THE WEATHER IS NOT FAVORABLE, the Newport season is fairly launched. Most of the cottages are opened, the occupants remaining comparatively quiet, as is usual during the early summer months. This period is devoted to rest, the later weeks being more especially appropriated to entertainment and recreation. Such being the case, people who do not comprehend the situation complain every year, about this time, that Newport is dull and dreary. These critics seem to be under the impression that the cottagers come here to exhibit themselves to citizens and strangers, and that so long as they take enjoyment in their homes in comparative quiet, they must be in an unhappy frame of mind. So the story goes out every year that things are not so lively as usual; that they are, in fact, exceedingly dull. But it is safe to assume, each year, that no more of our summer people have gone to Europe than is customary, that there is no greater number of families in mourning (and therefore not so situated as to give entertainments), and no larger show of empty houses. As a rule in these particulars, one Newport season is about the same as another. Places made vacant are quickly filled. While some may go, others are sure to come. Newport has a fixed and permanent character not enjoyed by other watering-places. New cottages are being built every year, and new interests awakened, and the summer of 1893 gives no sign of either greater or lesser prosperity than has heretofore been enjoyed. It has no booms and is scarcely subject to serious declines after the manner of some other resorts; about the only change is the steady growth of numbers, increase of cottages, and greater love for the old town that has come to command the world's admiration.

– Newport Journal & Weekly News
July 1st, 1893

Chapter I

MISS BROOKE WAS SHOWN INTO the séance chamber, and smiled at how perfectly the scene matched her expectations of it.

Madame Priestley, the medium that all of Newport was already talking about, had taken one of the largest and finest suites at the Ocean House, one of the largest and finest hotels in town. The suite had a spacious double-parlor, richly furnished and paneled in black walnut, with the inner chamber curtained off from the outer by heavy velvet portières. Pale white candles flickered in the corners, providing the only illumination and casting long shadows on the dark walls. The scent of a few rosy joss sticks smoldering somewhere drifted through the room.

Miss Brooke's quick count showed over a dozen people gathered there that evening, standing and sitting around the room, some alone and others clustered into little groups of three or four and conversing in whispers. All of them had received the same invitation, on stiff cream-colored paper, written in a firm, precise hand. Half of Newport was anxiously hoping for such an invitation, and once the summer people had settled themselves into their cottages along Bellevue Avenue the demand for a sitting with Madame Helene Priestley would be even greater. More than any concert or ball or champagne dinner, this marked the opening of the season and, for the moment, Miss Brooke, the lady reporter, was one of the fortunate few.

Some familiar faces, eerie in the candlelight, nodded in greeting as Miss Brooke surrendered her damp wrap to a dry-voiced servant and accepted the proffered glass of sherry. She steered Walter toward the window seat opposite the door. Here, standing just inside the velvet-draped archway, she snapped open her fan of embroidered Chinese silk, newly purchased for the occasion, and looked calmly around the room, while rain splashed against the window behind her.

Walter, her unimaginative brother and unenthusiastic escort for the evening, whispered in her ear, "So, who else is here?"

"Well, that's Mr. Rathbone and Mr. St. Anne over in the corner."

"The lawyers? What would lawyers be doing at a séance?"

"For that matter, what is a reporter doing here?" Miss Brooke replied. "I believe that's Mr. Blackington, the banker, over there. And there's Reverend Hopkins. But who's the other clergyman he's speaking with? Do you recognize him?"

"No, I don't."

"Interesting. I think I may—oh, dear." Miss Brooke stopped short and bit her lip slightly. But she smiled again and said, in her warmest manner, "Good evening, Mr. Carson. I had hardly expected to see you here."

"Good evening to you," said the oleaginous Mr. Carson, crossing the room to join them at the window. Carson was Miss Brooke's hated rival from another newspaper, a man with a thin beard and no scruples whatsoever. He sipped at his sherry and said, "Always a pleasure to meet up with our celebrated girl reporter."

"Lady reporter," she corrected him smilingly.

"As you say. So then, you've come in search of good copy, too?"

"I have come because I was invited to what promised to be a most interesting evening."

"Interesting?" Carson snorted. "Rubbish. Probably an evening of black thread and hidden assistants. Look around this room right now and ask yourself this—which one of them is in on it? Which one?"

"In on what, exactly?"

"The whole thing!" Carson hissed. "The whole foolish business. Somebody here is her confederate, and I, for one, am not going to be caught napping, Miss Brooke."

"I am quite sure you are not, Mr. Carson."

The lady reporter and her brother stood sipping their sherry after Mr. Carson oozed off to buttonhole another unfortunate across the room.

"He may have a point, you know," Walter said quietly. "I mean, you don't really think there may be something real in all of this, do you? Séances? It's the nineteenth century, for Heaven's sake...."

"Mr. Carson has never had a point in all the time that I have known him. And there is certainly a good story in all of this, whatever else there may be."

"Well, all right then, but—ah, good evening, Reverend Hopkins." Walter's demeanor changed on the instant.

"And a good evening to you," the lugubrious-faced Reverend replied. "Well, this surely is a fine night for a séance, wouldn't you say?"

"You mean the rain? Yes," Walter said. "If you don't mind my asking you, Reverend, who was the other minister you were speaking with earlier? I didn't recognize him. Is he new?"

"That was the Reverend Mr. Barrows, Madame Priestley's brother—or half-brother, I should say. A very unusual fellow from the First Spiritualist Temple of Philadelphia. I shall look forward to speaking with him some more."

"A Spiritualist minister?" Walter was scandalized.

"Oh, yes. There are quite a few of them now, quite a number. Spiritualist churches have been springing up like mushroom of late, and the congregations in some of the older churches are growing by leaps and bounds. I haven't seen quite so much interest in this sort of thing since just after the war... A few of my own flock have recently approached me, seeking guidance in such matters."

"Here?" Walter's sense of scandal deepened. "In Newport?"

"Yes. I was discussing it with someone just this afternoon, in fact."

"Well, I must say that... the idea of all of this being treated as some kind of faith just seems not quite right to me somehow. Spiritualist churches, spiritualist ministers." The unimaginative Walter shook his head. "What's next?"

"We must remember that our own faith began among the lowly, with clandestine, candlelit gatherings in the catacombs, taking the sacrament in secret. 'God moves in a mysterious way; His wonders to perform.' Well, I really must introduce you to Reverend Barrows." Reverend Hopkins squinted across the dim room. "I don't see him just now. I hope he turns up—we were having a fascinating discussion of funerals. I have to officiate at one tomorrow," he said sadly. "And, not surprisingly, the Spiritualist position on such things is quite different from what I'm used to. Well, I'm quite sure he'll be back."

The Reverend left Miss Brooke thinking that if what he said was true—that speaking with the departed was part of a new revelation, the cornerstone of a new faith—then séances made for a very strange sacrament indeed.

The dry voice announced, "Mr. Richards."

Benjamin H. Richards came into the room, refused an offer of sherry, and seated himself deep in an armchair not far from Miss Brooke's window. Richards was a dour-looking middle-aged man with long, mutton-chop sideburns; he wore a sober black suit, and a Masonic charm on his watch chain glinted in the candlelight. He was a beefy, square man and nothing in his appearance or deportment would have suggested that he was a police detective—in fact, that he was Newport's only detective, with a reputation stretching from Boston to New York.

"No surprise to see him here, I suppose," Walter said quietly. Mr. Richards was known to have consulted a number of clairvoyants and spirit-mediums in some of his more difficult cases. He made no secret about it, and his rate of success was high.

Richards gave the lawyers a curt nod, and Miss Brooke edged a little closer as Mr. Rathbone crossed the room to meet the detective.

"So what are you expecting tonight, Richards?" the lawyer asked.

"I'm not quite sure," was the quiet rejoinder. "But I've done some checking up, and I've heard some wonderful things about this woman."

"So have I."

"And so what are you expecting?"

"Ask me again later."

Miss Brooke overheard two couples she did not recognize conversing in hushed tones.

"Yes, we sat with her last season in London," a big blustery man with three chins was saying. "Our summer cottage was not yet ready, so we simply had to summer abroad. We did find quite a few lovely antiques for the cottage—paintings and things. Perhaps we can show you them sometime. At any rate, we did sit with Madame Priestley. She was extraordinarily popular over there, wasn't she my dear?"

His decorative little wife nodded dutifully and gave her husband an affectionate pat on the arm.

"Yes, yes—well, there was some talk of her being received by the Queen, but I'm not quite sure what ever came of that."

"We have been received by the Queen," the other woman beamed. "Three years ago. I wore these very pearls."

"Our daughter married a peer," her husband explained. "And that required no little effort on my part to arrange it, I don't mind telling you, sir," he mumbled to the other man.

His wife made little deprecating sounds with her tongue.

"Yes, well, I don't know if Madame Priestley ever was received or not," the blustery man went on. "But we did manage to arrange a sitting with her, and we were not disappointed, were we my dear?"

Another dutiful nod and affectionate pat.

"I have never been to a séance before," said the woman with the pearls. "But I have been told that I am of a deeply mediumistic character, and that I would make an excellent medium, should I care to try!" Her eyes grew wide as she said this.

"Yes, I can see that all quite plainly. Isn't it so, my dear?" Nod, pat. "I'm quite sure you would make an excellent medium—We'll have to see what Madame Priestley has to say about it!"

All four of them burst into loud, foolish laughter.

Miss Brooke made the Reverend Barrows's acquaintance a little while later, when Reverend Hopkins brought him over and made introductions.

He was a small, round-faced man, the Spiritualist clergyman, with tiny wire-framed spectacles, a gentle voice and a thoughtful manner, moving slowly and watching carefully. He wore a respectable frock-coat, baggy trousers, a high clerical collar and a small, plain silver cross. He bowed and his clear blue eyes twinkled with the light of the candles.

"Miss Brooke, Miss Brooke, it is a pleasure to meet you at last," he said with a broad grin. "My sister has been very, very eager to meet you, and we are both most pleased that you came."

"We were honored by your invitation, sir," Miss Brooke replied. "May I ask how you and you sister are both enjoying Newport?"

"We both *adore* Newport, though we have only been here a few short days! It is, I must confess, an even pleasanter place than England—a place which we both felt a great fondness for—but, unfortunately, the climate was disagreeable to me; I am of a somewhat... delicate... constitution." He smiled. "But Newport is so lovely! Only this afternoon, I took a stroll and the mansions simply take one's breath away!"

"Yes, but our summer people prefer to call them cottages," Miss Brooke smiled. "Though there certainly are many mansions in Newport."

"'In my Father's house are many mansions,'" Reverend Barrows quoted, laying a pious hand on his breast. "But tonight, my sister wishes to repeat an experiment she performed before the court of Czar Alexander, when we were in Russia a year ago. You will assist us? Ah, good. Thank you.

"I had a writing tablet," he went on, patting at his pockets and making a quick search through his coat. "Ah, here it is. And here is a pencil. Now, would you please be so kind as to write down some small piece of personal trivia—a name perhaps, or a date, or your favorite song. Something which carries some small personal significance or meaning for you, something that neither my sister nor I could possibly know. Do not let anyone see what you have written, and certainly do not tell anyone. Tear that sheet off and hand the tablet over to your brother, who will please do the same. Fold up your slip and keep it with you—you may have to produce it again later." He handed her the tablet and the pencil, chuckling good-naturedly and saying, "My sister is really most excited about this evening."

Madame Priestley herself did not appear until nearly midnight, when the heavy portières were drawn aside and she slipped into the room like a dignified shadow.

She was a woman of singular appearance, and as unlike her half-brother as could be imagined; where he was short and round and ordinary, she was tall and straight and striking. She had dark eyes, finely-sculpted features, and a knowing smile. Her thick dark hair fell loosely to her narrow waist, accented by a long streak of dramatic white she made no attempt to conceal. Her gown was a simple one of dark gray silk, almost black, with a few touches of brocade and an onyx cameo at her white throat. Her age would have been impossible to place; Miss Brooke would have guessed closer to thirty than forty, with those old eyes in a young face.

She was the most beautiful woman in the room, and all eyes were drawn to her. The nervous expectation that had hung heavy in the room all evening jumped a few degrees, as though Madame generated some strange electricity.

Madame Priestley had left America a few years before, an unknown, and had now returned with a name—and a name to conjure with. Within weeks of her arrival in Europe, reports began to filter back to New York drawing rooms of the marvelous American spirit-medium who astounded her sitters, baffled scientists who came to test her, and made believers out of skeptics. She read the minds of peers, levitated tables with the gentry, and contacted the shades of departed aristocracy. Many hailed her as the modern Witch of Endor. News of her return to America and her plans to summer at Newport caused a minor sensation. Newport did not admit social climbers to its ranks, the cynics sneered; let her go to Bar Harbor or Saratoga for a couple of years and then see if Newport would have her. Only last season, one such thwarted social climber, snubbed by the summer colony, had discharged her staff, torn up the lease on her expensive summer home, and shot herself with her husband's old Army revolver. And polite society did not lose any sleep over her.

But her story would not be Madame Priestley's. As she stood before her guests, Miss Brooke knew that all of Newport—Astors, Vanderbilts, and all the rest of the Four Hundred—would come forward to make their oblations at her altar.

"My dear guests," she said in her smooth contralto, "the spirits wait for us, as we wait for them."

Reverend Barrows began his speech as the sitters took their places around a large table in the next room. He took a candle in one hand and a worn Bible in the other, and read from the Book of Samuel.

"'Now Samuel was dead, and all Israel had lamented him, and buried him in Ramah, even in his own city. And Saul had put away those that had familiar spirits, and the wizards, out of the land. And the Philistines gathered themselves together, and came and pitched in Shunem: and Saul gathered all Israel together, and they pitched in Gilboa. And when Saul saw the host of the Philistines, he was afraid, and his heart greatly trembled. And when Saul inquired of the Lord, the Lord answered him not, neither by dreams, nor by Urim and Thummim, nor by prophets. Then Saul said unto his servants, "Seek me a woman that hath a familiar spirit, that I may go and inquire of her." And her servants said to him, "Behold, there is a woman that hath a familiar spirit at Endor." And Saul disguised himself, and put on other raiment, and he went, and two men with him, and they came to the woman by night: and he said, "I pray thee, divine unto me by the familiar spirit, and bring him up, whom I shall name unto thee." And the woman said unto him, "Behold, thou knowest what Saul hath done, how he hath cut off those that have familiar spirits, and the wizards, out of the land: wherefore then layest thou a snare for my life, to cause me to die?" And Saul sware to her by the Lord, saying, "As the Lord liveth, there shall be no punishment happen to thee for this thing. " Then said the woman, "Whom shall I bring up for thee?" And he said, "Bring me up Samuel." And the woman said unto Saul, "I saw gods ascending out of the earth." And he said unto her, "What form is he of?" And she said, "An old man cometh up, and he is covered with a mantle." And Samuel said unto Saul, "Why hast thou disquieted me, to bring me up?" And Saul answered, "I am sore distressed; for the Philistines make war against me, and God is departed from me, and answereth me no more, neither by prophets, nor by dreams: therefore I have called thee, that thou mayest make known unto me what I shall do...."'

"The first séance in recorded history, my friends, recorded in the greatest of all histories, the Holy Writ! It shows us and teaches us the wisdom of seeking the advice and the succor of the spirits.

"And in our own time, dear friends, two little girls, two dear little children clasped hands with those reaching out across the void! I am speaking, of course, of the sainted Sisters Fox, Margaret and Kate, who first heard the spirit raps some forty-five years ago—the mysterious raps that were the signs and messages from the Happy Summerland where the enlightened spirits dwell! And how far we have come in those forty-five years. How much we have grown!"

Reverend Barrows proved to be a forceful, even powerful, speaker, preaching with sincerity and conviction. Miss Brooke could easily see him making converts and swaying unbelievers in the pulpit of the First Spiritualist Temple.

Every one of the sitters startled when a loud *rap* sounded from an empty corner.

"Teddie is here," Madame Priestley said, quietly and gravely.

"Teddie is my sister's spirit-guide, her control," Reverend Barrows whispered. "A drummer boy who crossed over at Bull Run. He is a little, mischievous child, but he is in touch with spirits of an altogether higher order."

Another *rap* from the opposite corner of the room now startled the circle.

"Teddie has bought others with him," said Madame.

Again, Miss Brooke could feel that nervous expectation run through the room, could almost taste it. The hairs on the back of her neck prickled, and she heard the blood rush in her ears. It had grown warm, nearly unbearably so, and perspiration stood out on the foreheads of a few of the gentlemen, including Walter.

From a small satin satchel, Reverend Barrows produced a pair of school slates in wooden frames, measuring perhaps eight inches on a side. All four sides were blank, and he stacked one slate atop the other with a small stick of white chalk between them. He then asked for the nearest sitter, a gray-bearded, professorial man, to tie them securely with a length of black silk ribbon he took from around his sister's narrow waist. The man tied a couple of tight knots, and the slates were passed around the circle for examination. Each sitter being satisfied that all was as it seemed, the bound slates were placed in the middle of the table, next to the single white candle that feebly lit the room.

The medium certainly was being cautious, thought Miss Brooke. She was being very careful to show that everything so far was fair. There were some—and no doubt Mr. Carson was among them—who would have found this very show of fairness to be somehow suspicious.

The candle on the table wobbled slightly.

"Teddie has brought many others with him tonight," Madame Priestley said. "Many others... and they know all. There are no secrets to be kept from the spirits...."

"I would ask each of you to recall the writing that you did earlier," Reverend Barrows instructed, taking his seat at the table and gesturing for all to join hands. "Recall it to your mind and concentrate... focus your whole attention upon it."

Miss Brooke thought of the folded slip of paper, tucked deep in her bosom.

She had been separated from Walter, who sat opposite her, sandwiched between the woman with the pearls and Reverend Hopkins's wife. Reverend Barrows had quietly insisted that the seating around the table alternate—lady, gentleman, lady, gentleman—and so she found herself between Mr. Richards, the detective, on one side, and the gray, professorial man on the other.

The bound slates were directly in front of her, only a few inches away.

Madame's leaned back in her chair and inhaled deeply, rhythmically, for many long minutes. Slowly, her head lolled to one side and she lay still. Her breathing became shallow, and then stopped altogether.

The sitters exchanged uncomfortable glances when she did not move.

Richards leaned forward, with a quick look over to Reverend Barrows. "Madame—" he began.

With a shriek, she suddenly pitched forward, nearly banging her head on the polished tabletop. She gasped for breath, as a nearly-drowned diver coming up for air. Her red lips peeled back to bare clenched white teeth and her eyes remained tight shut as she heaved in and out of her Paris gown. She snapped back upright to sit ramrod-straight in her chair.

"One of you..." she said rasped, "one of you is thinking of a title... it is... it is not very clear to me."

Miss Brooke felt Mr. Richards's hand tighten on hers.

"You," the medium said, her eyes half-opening to stare at Richards. He nodded slightly. "A title... a book... moon...."

"Concentrate," Reverend Barrows urged him. "Concentrate."

Richards screwed his eyes shut.

"*Moonstone... The Moonstone*...." Madame Priestley said with a visible effort, leaning forward heavily before falling back in her chair and slipping deeper into trance.

Mr. Richards's amazement found no expression other than a dumb grin. "I was thinking about that book just this morning," he murmured.

"The Carruthers matter," Madame said, giving the detective a meaningful though blind glance. "Speak to me about that... later... I have a date... a very unclear date...." Her voice faded.

"Will the person thinking of a date please concentrate their whole attention upon it," Reverend Barrows whispered earnestly.

A slow minute ticked by before the medium spoke again.

"Nineteen years ago," she said with certainty. "Nineteen years. March. No, April... April the seventeenth, 1874." She looked vaguely at the professorial man who still gripped Miss Brooke's hand. "It is the day your daughter crossed over."

The man nodded anxiously and asked, "Is she here?"

The medium's unfocused eyes swept the room; then she closed her eyes and shook her head.

Across the table, the man's wife was sobbing uncontrollably.

Madame Priestley's pace quickened as her trance seemed to deepen; she went around the table, meeting the apprehensive gaze of each sitter without seeing them. Mr. Carson, she declared from the depths of trance, was thinking of turtle soup. He explained, with some embarrassment, that it was a favorite dish prepared by his mother. Walter Brooke had posed a question about the future of the Newporters base ball team, and the spirits assured him of their success. Reverend Hopkins's Bible quote was easily revealed ("If God be for us, who can be against us?"), before Madame came around the circle to Miss Brooke.

"It is a name," she said in a faraway voice. "A woman's name. I do not think that it is someone you know personally but… I have the initials N. B.—The first name is Nancy… Nellie. You are thinking of Nellie Bly."

Miss Brooke felt faint.

Some fifteen minutes later, the spirits signaled the end of the séance by a final series of loud raps, a violent jarring of the table, and by releasing their medium from her trance. She was pale and drawn, and delicately dabbed spittle from her lips with a lace handkerchief. Her brother went to bring her a glass of water from a pitcher on the marble-topped sideboard. Although she had been unable to reveal the contents of two folded slips, it did not impress her sitters any the less.

When she had finished the water and caught her breath, she said hoarsely, "There are still the slates."

"Yes," her brother agreed. "The slates. Miss Brooke, I believe you are closest."

Trying to keep her hands from trembling either too much or too obviously, the lady reporter picked up the set of child's slate gingerly. She untied the silken knot and opened them carefully, almost fearfully, as though they might burn her.

Chalked across the surface of one slate was a childish scrawl, *Teddie.*

And across the other were scribbled over a dozen names— *Arthur, Horace, Emily, Hannah, Charles, Rosannah*—many of which the sitters recognized as belonging to family, friends, and old sweethearts long since dead and buried.

And with that, the séance was over.

Miss Brooke and Walter came out onto the Ocean House's wide verandah, glad for the cool air after the closeness of the séance room, and found Mr. Carson smoking a cigarette and steadying himself against one of the bronze Chinese dogs that stood sentinel at the hotel's entrance. He was quite obviously shaken, and jumped slightly when they approached him.

"Well, what did you think, eh?" he asked in a quaking voice. "Damn good show, wouldn't you say?"

"I've never seen anything quite like it," said Walter.

"No, neither have I," Mr. Carson replied, puffing at his cigarette. "The Happy Summerland. Makes you wonder, doesn't it?"

He peered out into the balmy Newport night.

"I don't suppose either of you recognized any of those names, did you?" he asked, flicking cigarette ash in a way that was calculated to show nonchalance. His hand shook slightly.

Miss Brooke and her brother exchanged questioning looks, then she shook her head.

"No, Mr. Carson, I'm afraid we didn't." She smiled. "It's almost a disappointment, really."

"I see."

"Did you?"

"Yes," he said, after a long pause. "Yes, I did. Well... good evening to you both."

He walked away on uncertain legs.

Chapter II

THE BELLS TOLLED LONG AND HOLLOW as the pallbearers carried the glass-top casket down the steps of Trinity Church to the waiting hearse.

It was a lavish funeral, with expensive and extravagant trappings. A pair of mutes flanked the Church door—two somber-faced boys no more than twelve years old, whose sole duty it was to stand like melancholy little statues and remain silent. The glass-sided hearse, already heaped high with lilies and roses, was drawn by four glossy horses adorned with long plumes waving in the breeze. For tokens, the numerous mourners were given gloves, long silk scarves studded with jet, and a few close friends received locks of the deceased's hair in lockets or other ornate keepsakes.

Behind the mourners stretched a long line of carriages and coaches. The best of Newport society had come to pay their respects, and everyone who should have been in attendance was. Arrayed in all their mournful finery and packed into family pew-boxes, they conducted themselves as though at a fashionable but gloomy ball.

Prayers were said for the dead woman as the casket passed by those gathered there; a few reached out to touch the cold glass sides, and their hands came away chilled. Rarely was the summer whirligig of balls and parties and gossip halted by a funeral, but for the moment the summer colony put such things aside mark a loss.

A small plaque on the lid of the casket was engraved, *Mrs. James Hornbeck*, and beneath the name the single word *Resurgam*.

Colonel James Hornbeck stood a few feet away, watching as the casket was reverently placed into the hearse. He was a tall, broad man who yet retained the stiff military bearing he had acquired so long ago. He wore a flawless Prince Albert and held his silk hat in one hand. His lined and aging face was as still and unflinching as flint as he nodded his gratitude to each one of the mourners, but he spoke to no one. He was Colonel Hornbeck, and he would not unbend himself an inch. Not even now.

His wife, Amelia, had been the last scion of an ancient Newport family, the Presburys, who had made their fortunes in the days of the Triangle Trade; her ancestors had been sea captains and vestrymen here at Trinity. They had met at a cotillion and he asked "May I have this dance?" And they watched the sun rise together. They married the day before young Hornbeck had gone to take command of his regiment, with her silhouette on a silken cord around his neck and a rose from her garden pressed in his Bible. Hornbeck men always answered the call, he said, always did their duty. He was decorated a number of times before limping home from Chancellorville with a Confederate bullet in his leg. Upon his return to New York, Amelia had bought him a silver-headed cane and they spent their first summer at Newport. A few years later, when cottages along Bellevue Avenue were fast becoming the fashion, he built her a mansion that she named Blithewood House, and the Colonel put away his sword to become a member of Society. In New York, he had a brownstone on Fifth Avenue, a pew at Grace Church, and a box at the Metropolitan Opera; in Newport, he had a mansion along Bellevue, a pew at Trinity, and a shaving-mug at Merker's barber shop.

If ever a man loved his wife, people said, then that man was James Hornbeck.

The couple had two children, twins, both grown and married now. James Hornbeck II had married a steel heiress from Pennsylvania; this had been a great relief to his father, as young

James's first choice had been an actress. That little debacle had cost the Colonel a tidy sum and a few sleepless nights before it was brought to a satisfactory conclusion, leaving young James free for his steel heiress. For his daughter Rachel, thank heavens, the Colonel had been able to find a banker from a respectable Boston family, and the proper arrangements were made.

Rachel leaned heavily on her father's arm now, with brother James standing close behind. Her full mourning bonnet and voluminous crepe veil hid her tears, though she raised one gloved hand to dab at her eyes. At her breast was a simple oval brooch with a lock of her mother's hair clasped inside.

Everywhere the eye turned was *black*—black horses with black plumes, black gloves and black scarves, long staves and canes wrapped in black, black crepe and silk, black satin and lace, black armbands and veils, black suits and gowns. Rachel was swathed entirely in black, wiping her tears away with a black-bordered silk handkerchief, black veil billowing in the warm breeze, and she, of course, was not the only woman in the cortège dressed in such a manner. It was as though an enormous murder of wealthy crows had descended on the churchyard.

Colonel Hornbeck's sister Sarah—Mrs. Jonathan P. Newland—had come immediately from New York when the sad news reached her. The Colonel wished that she had stayed home; she made him nervous. Sarah still dressed every day in full mourning, widow's weeds seventeen years after her husband's death. She was like that, and the Colonel only hoped that she would not throw herself across his wife's casket, as she had done with her own husband's years ago.

"Look at her," Sarah cooed, looking at her sister-in-law. "She looks as though she's sleeping. Only sleeping, James...."

But Colonel Hornbeck could not bring himself to look at his wife's dead face.

The funeral-goers climbed into their coaches and carriages, and the cortège slowly made its way through the narrow, unpaved streets. All along the route, curtains and shades were drawn as they passed houses, and men stopped to remove their straw hats and derbies respectfully. Onlookers stayed out of the street—it was bad luck to cross in front of a funeral, and bad enough luck to even see one.

At length, the procession reached the cemetery on Warner Street. A couple of the undertaker's men were on hand to guide them to the grave.

Amelia and her Colonel had loved to take long strolls through this cemetery, hand in hand. Often, they spent the entire afternoon in the shadow of their favorite tree and lingered over a picnic lunch. They had brought the twins here when they were younger, and little James liked to play hide-and-seek with his sister among the gravestones and marble angels.

Oliver Hazard Perry was buried here, along with his brother Commodore Matthew Calbraith Perry, both Newporters. The Commodore's daughter Caroline had married the socialite and Rothschild banker August Belmont, also interred here. Belmont's crypt, with its huge caryatid-supported arch, grand sepulcher and sweeping benches, dwarfed the simpler graves of his wife's father and uncle. He had even donated a chapel to the cemetery, in his usual ostentatious way, that was dedicated to the memory of his daughter. The stained glass and mosaic steps were beautiful.

August Belmont had been gone for three years now, and Hornbeck remembered that funeral clearly. He had no idea then that Amelia's would follow so closely. It hardly seemed fair; Caroline Belmont was still alive and well....

Amelia's grave was one of two marble sepulchers in a grassy plot surrounded by a wrought-iron fence; many of her forebears, the Presburys, were buried nearby. On the north side of the circular plot, opposite the gate, was a mournful marble angel as tall as a man, wings tightly furled and beautiful faced turned heavenward. In one hand the figure carried a smooth escutcheon of white marble, engraved with the words *Memento Mori*.

The family entered the plot with the minister, Reverend Hopkins, while the rest of the mourners gathered outside the iron railing, watching. Reverend Hopkins spoke of the comfort of the Resurrection and, in the distance, Trinity began to ring the death knell for Amelia. But the Colonel did not hear.

She had loved to come here, Amelia—they both had. Like so many of their generation, they had no aversion to graveyards and cemeteries. They were restful places. The grave had been laid out almost two years ago and, when it had been completed, they came and picnicked under the angel's gaze. Later, they had gone to leave flowers on the Presburys' more modest graves.

The casket was carefully placed in its sepulcher, and the lid was lowered. The Colonel just heard the faint *click* of the spring lock as it engaged. Amelia had been firm on that one point: there must be a spring lock that allowed the tomb to be opened from the inside.

Reverend Hopkins was sprinkling holy water over the grave, over the mourners.

Hornbeck stood staring at the smooth cover bearing his wife's name, then nervously glanced over his shoulder to the matching grave, his grave. It was there waiting for him, with his name sharply chiseled into the cold marble.

The funeral was over now, and the assembled company went quietly back to their waiting carriages.

He felt strangely cast adrift, lost. For days and days now, he had no other thought than this afternoon, this funeral, that everything must be perfect and flawless. He owed her that; he demanded that. Now that it was over, however, he felt only uncertainly. He realized, with a sudden shock, that he had not thought any further than the events of this afternoon, that he had not given a thought to a single moment *after* the funeral.

He knew the rituals and the mourning customs, knew what was expected of him. He would wear a black armband for a year, as would his son. Rachel would be in full black for a year as well, and her jewelry could be of jet, or simple pieces ornamented with her mother's hair or portrait; the day before, her maid had taken Rachel's diamonds to the jeweler to be reset in hard black enamel. In her second year, she would be allowed certain shades of gray, white and—if she felt daring—pale lavender. None of the family was to leave the house for a month, save to attend church, and would avoid balls and other celebrations for at least a year.

The Hornbeck ball at Blithewood House had been a highlight of the Newport season for many years now, but there would be no ball this summer.

Hornbeck felt Rachel's arm around his shoulder, and Sarah tugged gently at his elbow. Time to go. They reminded him of the small gathering for a few intimates back at Blithewood House—there were still tokens to be distributed: rings and memorial portraits. These details, which seemed suddenly so trivial and foolish, needed yet to be seen to. It was expected.

As the family coach rattled down Bellevue Avenue, the Colonel realized that while he knew what was expected of him, what was required—the rules were firmly established as though carved in marble and the military, with its strict regulations and hierarchy, paled in comparison to Newport society—he had no idea what to do without Amelia.

Blithewood House was a sprawling, Queen Anne edifice built on the cliffs overlooking the Atlantic; most of the estates along the east side of the Avenue commanded ocean views. The exterior was painted gay shades of yellow and blue and red, with a sweeping double-decker verandah and a formal rose garden. There were gables and balconies and a stone turret the Colonel had had copied from an Alpine castle. Inside the imposing house were long, echoing corridors lined with suits of armor, high-ceilinged rooms furnished with French furniture, and woodwork stained the colors of honey and coffee and chocolate.

Blithewood House had been built twenty years before, when Newport was still a quaint resort on an island a few hours away by steamer. It was a quiet place where one went to get away, but now it had changed and Newport was the queen of watering-places.

Every season, as old New York descended on Aquidneck Island, things became more exclusive, more arrogant, and more of the old charm was lost. Compared to some of the extravagant and almost decadent mansions now being raised along Bellevue and Ochre Point, Blithewood House was hopelessly old-fashioned, even small; some of the rooms were still without electricity, and the household staff was less than half that employed by some of the other estates.

But it was *their* house....

The few guests gathered in the drawing room, sipping their drinks and saying over and over again what a lovely ceremony it had been. Mr. Rathbone, the family lawyer, was there; he had handled Amelia's will, and Dr. Collins was there, too. In one far corner sat a pair of old men the Colonel had known since his Army days. They both wore faded Union uniforms, now just a little too small for either of them. Rachel and young James sat with their aunt on the horsehair sofa, graciously accepting the sympathies of those who approached to offer them.

Hornbeck himself stood with one elbow propped up against the white Carrera marble mantelpiece, swishing his brandy in a cut-glass snifter. Scores of calling cards were carefully arranged on the mantel, all with the top right-hand corner turned down, a sign that the caller had come to express condolences. All the best families had sent their respects, usually via their liveried footmen and not in person.

At the far end of the drawing room hung a portrait, a painting by John Singer Sargent done years ago, when the family was wintering in London. The Colonel wore a silk-lapeled frock coat and his gray beard was well-trimmed. Amelia wore a Worth gown of dark velvet and brocade, with one hand on the Colonel's shoulder. Young James was a clean-shaven version of his father, and Rachel was swathed in a fur-lined cloak; the English climate had been too much for her.

Thankfully, the guests did not stay long, not much more than an hour. Glasses were drained, a few tokens and bequests were given, and his friends departed. They were all kind people who understood.

The rest of the family withdrew as well, to their guest rooms upstairs. Rachel and her husband spent many summers at Newport, and young James and his wife were having their cottage built farther down the Avenue, but they were staying upstairs until its completion. There was enough room for all of them, and Aunt Sarah, and many more besides.

"If there's anything you need," Dr. Collins said, solemnly shaking the Colonel's hand.

"Yes," Mr. Rathbone seconded. "Anything."

"Of course," the Colonel said. "Of course."

A few hours later, when it was quiet, Hornbeck went upstairs to his wife's room, down the hall from his own.

Amelia had always been very particular about her things, and any new maid quickly learned their proper arrangement. Although not by any means a harsh woman, she had once dismissed a careless abigail for failing to dust the top of her vanity mirror sufficiently thoroughly. Such slatternly behavior would not be tolerated at Blithewood House.

Just this morning, a trio of maids, overseen by the housekeeper had very carefully gone over the room and put everything in order. They dusted, they polished, they smoothed, they fluffed, folded, and saw to it that there were fresh flowers in the vases. No object, no matter how small or seemingly inconsequential, was out of place—not a silver-backed hairbrush, not a perfume bottle, not a cameo, not a stickpin. Everything was as the mistress of the house would have it. When they were finished, after a couple of hard hours, the housekeeper and her maids left silent and respectful, like vergers in a church. This room was sacred now, sacrosanct.

Standing in the doorway, the Colonel was once again haunted by the feeling that had followed him all day long: that if he were to turn around, Amelia would be standing there smiling at him as always, as though she had never been gone for a moment. Earlier in the day, he had heard footsteps coming down the stair. Amelia, he had thought... but of course it had not been. It was Rachel, who then wondered why her father looked so startled to see her.

His old war wound ached, and he limped to a wicker chair over by the open window. The wound bothered him when it rained. The sky was clear, and a warm breeze fluttered the heavy silk curtains, but it still ached.

He sat there until long after sunset, when the shadows gathered around him.

The letter from Madame Priestley would arrive a week later.

Chapter III

THE FALL RIVER LINE'S PASSENGER STEAMER *Pilgrim* arrived in Newport from New York twenty minutes late on a humid and misty Thursday morning. The Line's steamers, with their brightly-painted twin paddlewheels, were some of the fastest and most luxurious ships afloat. In addition to the high-vaulted ceilings and thick Oriental carpets, each vessel boasted a fine orchestra; passengers dined and danced to the tune of "After the Ball," "My Sweetheart's the Man in the Moon," and the always popular "Daisy Bell."

One of the few wakeful passengers onboard was Mr. Martin Morrison. He glanced at his watch—half past three. Passengers would not disembark until seven. Newport was dark and wet and quiet, except for a few balls far down on Bellevue Avenue that were just beginning to break up.

Morrison had arrived in New York from London earlier that day, and had immediately booked overnight passage on the *Pilgrim* amid the general rush. The name *Pilgrim,* he thought, suited the passengers better than the ship. He took the cheapest single room available, not wishing to put his employer to undue expense, and had spent the entire trip, including the ten-day voyage from London, reading in his little cabin. He devoured every Newport guidebook he could find and, when he reached New York, collected more and studied them aboard the *Pilgrim.* Now, when he closed his eyes, a map of the town unfolded itself like a chessboard in his head, and he could name nearly every street and building he saw. He has always been meticulous in his preparations.

He snapped his watch shut and spread out on the bunk. He had not traveled like this since his days with the Foreign Office and, tired as he was, he could not sleep. He was held awake by a certain nervous excitement—the same anticipatory tingle that had always felt when about to begin a new job, a new game.

A porter called him at a quarter to seven, rapping sharply on the door. Mr. Morrison rose, shrugged into his checkered jacket and, collecting his traveling-trunk and valise, reached for his bowler— or his derby, as they called it here.

Steamers of the Fall River Line docked at Long Wharf, one of dozens of wharves jutting out into busy Newport Harbor. A train was just pulling into the nearby railroad yards. A row of cabs waited for some of the eight hundred or so passengers the luxury ship carried—tourists, day excursionists, bankers and businessmen, honeymooners, a few millionaires… and Mr. Morrison.

Morrison was a thin, ordinary-looking man with a face no one ever noticed or remembered; he was simply a plain blond Englishman with a thick walrus mustache and a nondescript manner. He could have been anything at all except what he really was—in a silk hat and monocle, he could pass for a peer; in a tweed cap and rolled-up sleeves, a laborer; in a straw hat and bow tie, he would be indistinguishable from any other summer tourist.

A chorus of shouts went up. "Cab, sir?"

Morrison piled into a hansom, stacking his trunk and valise beside him. Through the little trapdoor in the cab's roof, he called up to the driver, "Is there a boarding house nearby? Some place cheap but decent?" The guides had listed several, but it was always best to get a local opinion.

"I know a good place right on Thames Street, sir," the man said without hesitation. Morrison smiled—in Newport, apparently, Thames was pronounced phonetically: *Thaimz*. The guidebooks had failed to mention this.

"Take me there, then."

They went up Long Wharf, past the rows of little shops and run-down flophouses and saloons not yet opened for business, and a few that were. The wharf was just beginning to awaken; a few fishermen were leaving their houses, loaded down with nets and poles and gear, their wives waving from the windows. Others stood leaning in open doorways, puffing at the first cigar of the day and sipping coffee.

"First time in Newport, sir?" the cabman asked.

"Yes."

"Well then, sir, let me be the first to welcome you. Give you a bit of a tour as we go along, at no extra charge, of course. Newport, Rhode Island, founded 1638, one of the most prosperous cities on the Colonies, back when we was Colonies, you understand. Occupied by the British during the Revolution...."

He paused for a moment, choosing not to regale his English fare with the horror stories his mother had thrilled him with growing up: tales of British pillage and plunder, of the cold winters when the Redcoats had torn down half the houses in town for firewood. Mr. Morrison, on his side, nodded politely and said nothing; he had grown up hearing stories of some heroic ancestor who took the King's shilling and never returned to England, having died at Yorktown defending the Empire.

As the cab rounded the corner onto Thames Street, the driver pointed out a square brick building hung in red-white-and-blue bunting.

"That's City Hall on the corner there, sir, built as a market house back in the Colonial days, and that's the courthouse there at the top of the Parade opposite. It's the old Colony House, and the Declaration of Independence was read from its steps, over one hundred years ago. Well, this here is Thames Street, where most of us live," he said, as the cab rattled over the cobblestones. "The rich folk live over thataway," he waved vaguely toward the southeast beyond.

Thames was a busy street, lined on either side with steep-roofed Colonial and turn-of-the-century houses, with only a scattering of newer buildings. Nearly every house had a shop on its first floor, with a plate-glass window proudly proclaiming each merchant's name and specialty in foot-high letters: cobblers, tobacconists, stationers, photographers, barbers, and tailors all crowded together. This was a bustling working-class neighborhood, hung in more patriotic bunting and flying flags; Independence Day was only a few days past.

The street was filled with people just beginning the day; men opening their shops, others off to work. Some whizzed by on bicycles. Newsies hawked the morning edition, and sandwich board men advertised cheap breakfasts and good cigars.

"That's Merker's barber shop there, sir. The only barber in town fit to cut the hair of them down on Bellevue. The gents, they all got their own shaving-mug in the cupboard there, with their initials. You look close enough, you'll see Vanderbilts and Astors and all the rest of them in there... Now, I don't quite know if you can make it out from where you're sitting, sir, but on your left you can see the spire of Trinity Church, just peeking over the rooftops there. George Washington, father of our country, took Communion there. Sat in pew number eighty-two."

"Sorry, but could we stop here for a moment?" Mr. Morrison interrupted his garrulous cabman.

The cab pulled up in front of a little shop. A large wooden Indian in full headdress stood by the door and the sign swinging in the early morning breeze read:

William J. Martin
Tobacconist, News Dealer & Stationery
Temperance Drinks of All Kinds
And
Milkshakes

Mr. Morrison bounded up the steps and into the shop. A young man behind the counter asked how he could help.

Morrison bought an armload of newspapers. Newport published six, including, *The Newport Mercury,* the oldest paper in the nation. He also purchased a pouch of tobacco, a box of Havanas, and a copy of the town directory. He declined the offer of a milkshake.

It turned out that the boarding house's proprietor was married to the cabman's sister. This went a long way toward explaining the man's lack of hesitation in recommending a place to stay. It was a pleasant clapboard house, opposite the wharves, and in need of a new coat of paint. The owner showed his new boarder upstairs to his room while his wife called, "Thanks again, Jimmy!" from the front steps.

The room was a good-sized, airy one on the third floor, with small-paned windows looking out across slate rooftops to the harbor. Morrison had been billeted in far worse places in his day. It was simply furnished and lighted by a single oil lamp on the table; there was no electricity in the house, and little in this part of town at all. There was another boarder across the hall, and an earth closet down in the cellar.

"And will you be staying with us long?" he asked.

"I'm not quite sure yet," Mr. Morrison replied. "I shall have to see how things go for me here—but you may depend on me for a week at least."

The owner, a fat man with alcohol on his breath, looked pleased and withdrew nodding and smiling and closing the door after him.

Mr. Morrison waited until he heard the landlord going downstairs before he locked the door and began to unpack. He sorted his things and placed them in the drawers of the modest wardrobe or hung them in the little closet. In his trunk, nestled between his suits and shirts, was a locked box of polished steel. The key dangled from Mr. Morrison's watchchain.

The box held his old service revolver—a six-shot Adams with a good, God-fearing six-inch barrel and a box of cartridges. He locked the box in the bottom drawer of the wardrobe and slid this key deep into his pocket.

When he finished unpacking, he sat by the open window in his shirtsleeves, smoking cigar after cigar and working his way through the stack of newspapers. There—buried amid reports from the World's Columbian Exposition in Chicago, articles about the annexation of the Hawaiian Islands, and long gossipy columns on Lizzie Borden, the Fall River spinster acquitted of the murder of her father and stepmother only a couple of weeks before—Morrison found what he was looking for: a pair of notices concerning Madame Priestley.

"For those who considered interest in the mysteries of the séance-chamber to be something of our parents' and grandparents' day," the first one ran, "it can only be said that those mysteries have returned and taken rooms at the Ocean House. A few spirit-mediums of greater or lesser repute are passing their summer here, mingling with the usual cottagers and summer colonists. We have seen mediums come and we have seen mediums go, and it will be interesting and perhaps instructive to see how this latest crop—and one of them in particular—is received."

The second was in a different paper.

"Newport has long been home to the unusual, and even to the fabulous, and this season seems to be no exception. Only a few nights since, this writer was invited to attend a séance where many startling and amazing 'manifestations' were to be seen. The medium, Madame Helene Priestley, has arrived here recently from abroad, and it is our understanding that the demonstrations she offered our European friends were of no less startling a character. It only remains to be seen how her career shall progress through the season."

Mr. Morrison spent another hour or so perusing the papers and carefully thumbing through the city directory before changing his clothes and setting out on a long walk.

Newport has the advantage of being small, and so no place in town was very far from any other place—at least in terms of its geography. In other ways, however, places in Newport could be worlds apart, as Mr. Morrison discovered. In walking up the gentle hill from Thames Street to Bellevue Avenue, he passed from the heart of the old Colonial town to the gilded playground of the summer colony.

Nearly all of Newport's most select shops and expensive stores were clustered along the northern quarter of the Avenue; Worth had a boutique here, and Hodgeson, the society florist, was only a few doors down. Hodgeson primarily handled the flowers for balls and weddings and the occasional funeral. Here was the Reading Room, once the most exclusive club in town, and the Casino, the club that replaced it. These were all new buildings, none much more than thirty or forty years old; no peeling-paint clapboards here, but beautiful modern Stick Style and Shingle Style structures lining the street.

The rest of the Avenue stretched away to the south, running down the eastern side of town, where the ocean beat against the cliffs. The Astors and Vanderbilts had their estates there, along with the parvenus and tycoons trying to marry their daughters off to titled foreigners. More huge cottages were being built in this neighborhood by the burgeoning summer colony, each striving to outdo the others in ostentation and pretense. It seemed strangely fitting to Mr. Morrison that the sun rose over the mansions, and set over the wharves.

He arrived in time to see one of the most important of all Newport rituals: the daily round of afternoon calls. Dressed in all their finery and with a stack of calling cards in a shiny case, the wives and daughters of Bellevue spent the late afternoon riding up and down the Avenue, visiting. A light phaeton seemed to be the preferred vehicle, the carriage's low sides affording the best view of the women's gowns and dresses. They were driven by stiffly perfect coachmen in bottle-green jackets and tall silk hats, and a pair of liveried footmen rode on the rear of the carriage. Millionaires' wives only received callers one day a week, the rest of the afternoons being spent in making their own calls. So cards were left by the footmen, the ladies themselves never leaving the phaeton, and the round of visits went on.

Morrison stood across from the Ocean House as the carriages clattered by in clouds of dust. Bellevue was unpaved and the wealthy ones who lived along it had every intention that it should remain so. The city made periodic attempts to pave Bellevue, but they were always blocked by the summer colonists, who would not allow their domain to be interfered with. After several fractious years, the city had settled for a water truck making its rounds up and down the Avenue, spraying water, replacing the dust with mud. .

Despite its name, the Ocean House was a mile from the water, and not a single room had an ocean view. Its advertisements claimed, quite rightly, that it was situated in the most fashionable part of town and afforded its guests an opportunity of seeing the distinctive features of summer life in Newport not to be found elsewhere. It was a wonderful building—a five-story Gothic hotel, painted bright white with green shutters. It was a hotel worthy of London, thought Mr. Morrison.

Morrison walked up the sweeping verandah and through the doors guarded by hulking bronze dogs. The lobby was huge, lit by big electric chandeliers and scattered with potted plants and deep armchairs. A number of rich loafers sat and smoked and paged through the New York papers. Shouts of gamblers went up from the low-stakes casino off the lobby; it offered gentlemanly games such as cards and dice. Those seeking more interesting wagers would have to look elsewhere.

He glided unobtrusively over to the long reception counter, straw hat in hand. Smiling vacantly at one of the clerks and pretending to be fascinated with a pile of the hotel's pamphlets—*Newport and Its Advantages as a Summer Resort*—he glanced over at the guest book. He had to look twice before he found the name he wanted.

Reverend Barrows & Madame Priestley—Suite 507.

Morrison pocketed one of the pamphlets and crossed over to the little Western Union alcove on the other side of the lobby. The girl at the window sat by an electric fan and was absorbed in a dime novel. When she noticed Mr. Morrison standing and waiting politely, the novel was thrown, with embarrassment, below the counter.

He dispatched a pair of telegrams; the first one was to an old friend and opponent in London, someone he had known since they were at Sandhurst together. It read simply:

NQB3
– M

The second was to his client in Surrey.

ARRIVED NEWPORT SUBJECTS HERE STOP
EXPECT NO DIFFICULTIES WILL WIRE AGAIN STOP
--M

Not a bad day's work, Morrison though, as he headed back down the hill. But these were only the opening moves of the game, and he knew from long experience that there was often no predicting how the rest of the game would play out.

Chapter IV

A HANSOM PULLED UP in front of the strangest brownstone in all of Manhattan and its passengers, a well-dressed young couple, stepped out.

The woman, in long gray silk evening gloves and a big, ostrich-feathered hat, smiled up at the driver pleasantly. She opened her tiny reticule and fished out a half-dollar.

The cabbie leaned forward expectantly.

The lady's husband, knowing what was to come next, thrust his hands deep into his pockets and looked away down the block. He wished that she wouldn't do this sort of thing, but he had long ago resigned himself to the fact it was, after all, in her blood.

She reached up to the driver on his box, standing tiptoe. The half-dollar glinted in the cab's sidelights. The man reached out his hand to take his fare but it was gone… vanished.

"Oh, dear," the lady flushed. "I'm afraid this is always happening to me."

Her husband, a few feet away, rocked back on his heels and tried not to notice.

The cabbie, however, certainly had noticed, even if he was not entirely clear about what had just happened.

The coin had been in the woman's hand, then it was gone. He blinked hard two or three times.

"I think I have another," the lady said contritely, dipping her hand back into the bag. A moment later she was daintily holding another half-dollar.

She tossed it up to the bemused cabbie. His hand shot out to catch it and he grabbed at… air.

And the smiling lady's hand was empty.

He glanced down at the street, thinking that perhaps the coin had landed in the gutter. But he had not even heard it hit the ground.

The husband smiled weakly when the driver glared at him.

"Now just what the hell is going on here? Are you people going to pay your damn fare or not?"

"There is no reason for that kind of language in front of my wife," the husband protested. "Now, Hope—"

"Hush, Jack," the lady said, still smiling her sweet smile. "I am afraid we have tried our friend's patience a little too hard."

With that, she took a couple of steps up to the horse's head, patting him along his sleek brown flank. She scratched him affectionately between his long ears before quickly and deftly pulling a silver dollar from one of them. The horse flicked his ear and swished his tail, but otherwise took no notice. A second later, a cube of sugar appeared at the lady's fingertip, a welcome treat for the horse. .

Hope placed the dollar gently in the driver's hand, and closed his fingers over it, saying, "Thank you."

"You're most welcome, ma'am…" the man stammered uncertainly. As she turned and walked away, he opened his hand to see if the dollar was still there, and was relieved and a little surprised when it was.

The husband simply shrugged at him and followed his wife up the steps of the brownstone as the cabbie bit the coin several times.

The door was opened by a very correct, elderly English manservant named Edward. Edward had known the lady since she was a girl, and now bowed politely as she bounced past him.

"Hello, Edward!" she said, sweeping into the house.

"Good evening, Mrs. Westlock, and to you, Mr. Westlock."

"And where is my uncle?" Hope asked, pausing for a moment to study her reflection in the large hall mirror. The gilt frame was adorned with dozens of grinning and grimacing devils' heads. "He said he had something very important to discuss, but he wouldn't say what. You know how mysterious he can be."

"Only too well," was Edward's pained reply. "However, the Professor awaits you in the parlor. Dinner shall be served promptly at seven."

"Thank you, Edward," Hope called over her shoulder as she headed down the long hallway to the parlor.

Along the length of the passage Hope's uncle, Professor Erasmus von Hellmann, had arranged a number of trophies and artifacts from his younger days. He had been famous once, not long ago, as a master magician and illusionist, exposer of spiritualists and worker of wonders. The very name of von Hellmann had promised a packed house and an audience waiting to see, as the posters declared, *"FAKE MEDIUMS EXPOSED!!!"*

And so, in little nooks and pigeonholes and on small shelves in the hall were a papier-mâché skull whose jaws clattered upon command, a wand alleged to have belonged to Dr. John Dee, the famous Elizabethan necromancer, and a crystal ball said to have been scried into by Cagliostro. There were sets of Chinese linking rings and bouquets of feather flowers. In a glass case were some of the oldest books on magic, among them the anonymous *Hocus Pocus Junior* of 1634, and the even older *Discoverie of Witchcraft* of Reginald Scot, dating from 1584. There were posters and lithographs as well, advertising performances by the Professor, or his friends, or sometimes even his rivals. There was one proclaiming *"Maskelyne & Cooke—Royal Illusionists and Anti-Spiritualists at Egyptian Hall— England's Home of Mystery"*, and another emblazoned, *"Les Soirées Fantastiques de Robert-Houdin"*, and still another: *"Von Hellmann & The Uncanny Esperanza—Fake Mediums Exposed!"*

Von Hellmann was certainly talented enough and knowledgeable enough of the mediums' methods that he often joked that he could easily have gone into that line of dubious business himself. But instead, he set out to expose every spirit-medium he could find, and he had effected some startling unmaskings. He had caught Forbes, the slate-writing medium, with a piece of concealed chalk, and had found out Robertson, the levitator, when his spirit guide proved to be a midget swathed in a length of mosquito netting. He had lost track of how many suits and counter-suits had been filed against him in the courts, and he had been called as an expert witness in a number of cases involving mediumistic fraud. One wag had even dubbed him "The Conjurer of the Courtroom."

But all that was behind him now; he had not gone after a medium in years. He was too old, he declared, as his seventieth year approached, to go chasing after charlatans and performing grand illusions and card tricks. He left that to younger minds and nimbler fingers. So he retired to live among his props and his memories, and the name von Hellmann ceased to terrify the Spiritualists, if it was ever heard at all. Recently, he had begun to drive the final nail into the coffin of his career: he was writing his memoirs.

As Hope entered the parlor, however, she could only wonder what her uncle was being so mysterious about.

She found him perched on the edge of the sofa, peering into an old scrapbook through oval pince-nez balanced on the end of his long nose. The old man chuckled to himself as he turned the pages, and Hope noticed that he was looking over a bunch of newspaper clippings, some going back thirty, forty, even fifty years, detailing some of his more famous—and infamous—investigations and exposures.

"Hope!" he cried, as she shut the door behind her. He tossed the scrapbook aside and grinned warmly as he rose from the sofa. "I've been waiting for you both. And good evening, counselor," he called to his niece's husband. "I am so happy you came."

Anyone who met Professor Erasmus von Hellmann often remembered him as standing a good six inches taller than he actually was. He was not a short man, but a striking and magnetic one who dwarfed those around him, even at his age. The thick dark hair of the old days was gone, replaced by a long white fringe flowing past his shoulders like a heretical monk's tonsure. His face was long and narrow, and his white goatee, at once shaggy and immaculate, only added to his already charmingly infernal appearance. His eyes were quick and clear and dark, and Hope knew from the light in her uncle's face that he was being mysterious about something of importance—almost personal importance. She had not seen him like this since before his retirement.

"We have much to discuss," he said. "But first—have you been working on anything?"

"Yes," Hope replied. "The coin trick you showed me last summer. The one you said you got from the clever Frenchman."

"I had quite forgotten I showed you that. You will have to show me later," von Hellmann smiled eagerly. Turning to Jack Westlock, he asked, "And how are things in the courts, counselor? Don't you have a couple of trials coming up?"

"Robbins the poisoner and Fredericks the vitriol-thrower," Jack replied wearily. "I've been running myself ragged trying to put those two cases together."

"He certainly has, poor dear," his wife seconded.

"I want hanging for Robbins and good ten-year stretch for Fredericks. That girl was quite a beauty...."

Hope cleared her throat a little sharply, and then smiled at her husband the same way she had smiled at the cab driver.

"Counselor, if you would be so good as to touch the bell for Edward," von Hellmann chuckled.

Hope could not divine what was on her uncle's mind over dinner; he seemed anxious and impatient, but not irritable. He was in high spirits, full of laughter and fond memories of past exploits. He was even being nice to Jack, much to her surprise. She could not count how many times her uncle had told her that she could have made a much better match than a lawyer. No excitement, he insisted, boring—and no real talent, either. In fulfilling his avuncular duties, he had offered to make her a number of fine introductions, but these were usually to sword-swallowers or contortionists in heavy Chinese makeup.

But tonight he chatted pleasantly with Jack, and laughed at his jokes. Whatever it was, Hope thought, it was good news.

It was half-past eight and Edward, silent as a ghost, was pouring coffee before von Hellmann finally came to the matter for which he had summoned them.

"Do you remember Professor Townsend, Hope?" he asked.

"From Harvard?"

"The same. I have just received a letter from him. He writes that he and his wife are attempting to spend a quiet summer in Newport, staying with a relation, I believe, but their rest has been disturbed by a spirit-medium who goes by the name of Madame Helene Priestley."

"And how exactly has she disturbed him?"

"You know Townsend—the very mention of a medium is enough for him. He's too eager to prove his foolish theories, always looking for that one medium who'll convince everyone."

"I thought you liked Professor Townsend."

"I *do* like him. He's a good egg but... credulous. He's as bad as Crookes used to be in England."

The two men had known each other ever since they had served together on the Wraeburn Committee for the Investigation of Psychical and Spiritualistic Claims. Townsend was a distinguished author, lecturer, philosopher and believer; von Hellmann an illusionist and conjuror and unrepentant skeptic. Both had the respect of peers and public, and their arguments had raged long and loud. During the Committee's four-year lifespan, no decisions were ever reached, and the thousand-dollar prize for genuine occult demonstrations went unrewarded. Afterward, the magician and the philosopher settled into a strange and rivalrous friendship.

"I haven't heard from him in over a year," von Hellmann went on, drawing Townsend's folded letter from his pocket. "And now this. He says that this Priestley woman is the real thing. He was at a séance a week ago—she gave one for a bunch of bankers and journalists and policemen and whatnot—and they all went away quite impressed."

"So, when do you leave?" Jack Westlock asked.

"In a couple of days," von Hellmann replied, with his devil's grin. "And actually... I was hoping you might come with me."

"How wonderful!" Hope cried. "I haven't seen you hunt mediums since—well, since before we were married, Jack. I'd love to, again."

"Well, Jack. What do you say?"

"I might be able to get away for a few days—maybe a week, no more. Messrs. Robbins and Fredericks are expecting me, you understand, but I suppose I could catch you up on the weekends. I know a few fellows who leave the city to join their wives in Newport on Thursday and arrive back in Manhattan Monday morning. So I guess I can leave Hope with you." He gave his wife's small hand a squeeze.

"It's settled then," von Hellmann proclaimed, banging his fist on the table. "We leave as soon as is convenient. I am told that Newport boasts a couple of fine theaters, and I'm sure either one of them would be only too happy to have the great Professor Erasmus von Hellmann and his assistant, the Uncanny Esperanza, grace their stage. It's settled then," he repeated, sipping his coffee and nodding pensively. He murmured into his cup, "And we'll show them there's some life in the old boy yet."

And his eyes glinted with the fire that burns heretics.

Chapter V

COLONEL HORNBECK SPENT THE LONG WEEK after the funeral slowly discovering how much of Blithewood House was Amelia's, and how little of it was his.

He had built the house for her and she was its sole mistress. The corps of servants answered to her and carried out her wishes to the letter. She conferred with the housekeeper, Mrs. Frost, going over the household accounts and instructing her in engaging and discharging members of the staff. She planned the parties, the balls and the dinners, including Rachel's coming-out cotillion some summers ago. She decided whose invitations to accept and, perhaps more importantly, whose to decline. She determined when it was time to redecorate a room or expand her husband's wardrobe, and chose what style she liked best for both.

For his part, Colonel Hornbeck signed the checks and retired to the Casino, or the Reading Room, or his yacht. Such was the way in Newport. It was a woman's town, the menfolk agreed; best to let them run things as they wished and turn up in fancy clothes when they wanted you to. Many husbands didn't even spend the week in town, but in New York; they would catch the Friday night steamer, be sociable for the weekend or retreat to the safety of their clubs, and board that same steamer, now Manhattan-bound, late Sunday night.

Hornbeck was sitting in Blithewood House's formal little rose garden—Amelia's garden, of course. Keeping up a proper garden in Newport's salty air was something of a challenge, but Amelia had worked hard at it with the able assistance of Louis, the French gardener. The result was lovely: eight kinds of roses, huge bushes of flowering purple hydrangea—Newport's favorite flower—a path of crushed seashells, thick English ivy crawling up the side of the house... lovely, but now suddenly lonely.

He was slowly becoming accustomed to her absence. He no longer expected to see her coming into the room or telling the butler to have the carriage brought around. The habits of a lifetime, of a marriage, were only just beginning to slacken, and while he no longer expected, he had found himself hoping....

"Father?" Rachel broke in on his thoughts. "Father?"

"Hello, my dear," the old man said a little weakly, straightening himself up in his chair. "I was almost dozing."

"I thought you might be. I've brought you some lemonade." She set the tall glass down on the lawn table at her father's elbow.

The harsh black of full mourning made Rachel seem pale, tired around the eyes, but perhaps it simply accentuated what was already there. It pained Hornbeck to see his daughter this way; she was not yet thirty, too young to be so bereft. He was too aware that this is how he would see her for at least the next year, decorum exacting its price.

"This just came for you," Rachel said a little nervously, holding out a letter,

It was in a small envelope of stiff expensive paper, written in a precise, copperplate hand and sealed with black wax. Hornbeck tore it open almost with annoyance.

Ocean House

Blithewood House
Bellevue and Cliffs

My Dear Col. Hornbeck –

> *It is my hope that you shall excuse the forward nature of this note, but I felt that it was very important that I communicate with you.*

Please accept my deepest sympathy for your loss, but also be assured that, although your wife has crossed over, she is not gone; not lost, but gone before.

Indeed, for three nights past, your dear wife Amelia has visited my sister's dreams, and impelled us to speak with you. She urges you not to grieve overmuch, and reminds you that you may have this dance with her forever, as she first did so many summers ago.

My sister is most eager to meet with you. You may be aware that she has been able to place many yet among the living in touch with those who wait beyond in the Happy Summerland of the spirits.

We wait to hear from you at your earliest convenience, and we wish you much happiness. Remember, there is no death, and there are no dead.

I am,

Very Sincerely Yours,
Reverend John H. Barrows, D. D.

Hornbeck folded this missive up and struggled to his feet, leaning heavily on his silver-headed cane. The old war wound in his leg had suddenly begun the throb painfully.

"What is it, Father?" Rachel asked. He seemed so small and frail just now.

"I don't know," he replied distantly. "I don't know... yet."

They went back into the house together, arm in arm. He was visibly shaken by the letter, and Rachel began to worry. But he would say nothing to her as they crossed the broad lawn.

Once inside, Hornbeck withdrew to his oak-paneled office, seating himself at his massive antique writing desk. His usual letterhead had been replaced by mourning stationery: black-edged paper, simple envelopes with a two-inch black border, a few long sticks of black sealing wax, all neatly arranged upon the desktop.

He wrote a note to Reverend Barrows, declaring that he would be only too happy to receive the Reverend and his sister on Friday, the day after tomorrow. He would have the Hornbeck carriage sent to meet them at their hotel promptly at seven-thirty. He sealed the letter and rang for the footman.

"Take this to the Ocean House immediately," he said when the man appeared. "Quickly now—go!"

As the footman left him, closing the oak door quietly, Hornbeck drew out his pocket-watch, a large seventeen-jewel Swiss affair on a solid gold chain. Amelia had given it to him on their wedding day, and it still kept perfect time.

Opening the glinting cover, he gazed at the inscription inside. *To my Colonel. You May Have This Dance Forever—June 1st, '68.*

The answer to the first question he had ever asked her, at that cotillion so many years before.

For the next two days, Hornbeck was a holy terror to his company of servants—he wanted everything put in order, everything put in place. The staff, who had only just begun to recover from the stress and strain of the funeral, worked diligently. Henry, the butler, reminded his employer that an underbutler had been recently discharged and the vacancy had not yet been filled. Supplementary servants would also be required, he added, if the rest of the family intended to stay for much longer.

"You handle it, Henry—I trust you," Hornbeck said dismissively. "Get whatever reinforcements you think you need."

He had no sooner excused his butler than Sarah swept indignantly into the room and planted herself firmly in the big red leather chair opposite his desk, the chair reserved for visitors.

"James," she said, with the quiet intensity she reserved for her most indignant complaints. "James, I am greatly disturbed by your plans."

"What's wrong, Sarah?" he asked, already knowing her answer.

"This... medium, this necromancer coming tomorrow night."

"What about her?"

"James! How can you invite such a person into your house? Into Amelia's house? It almost seems...."

"It almost seems like what, Sarah?"

"Blasphemy!"

"Stop talking nonsense."

"It isn't nonsense, brother. You do know what kind of people these spiritualists are... Scandalous! Free Love! Socialists! Suffragettes! For Heaven's sake, James, think of Amelia!"

"I am, for Heaven's sake, thinking of Amelia," Hornbeck explained patiently. "This woman says she can contact her, and if that's true... don't you understand, Sarah? If she can actually contact Amelia, it changes everything."

"And what does that mean?"

"I don't know. Not yet. But I must find out. I must know."

"But it's so dangerous," Sarah protested, shifting uncomfortably in her seat and smoothing her skirts. "We are told not to seek out those with familiar spirits."

"She sought me out. She claims that Amelia contacted her."

Sarah would not be mollified.

"Such people should not be invited into a Christian home, James," she insisted. "You cannot even begin to count the risks. Whatever would Amelia think?"

"Don't you understand that it is precisely *because* of Amelia that I have invited them?" He stopped. He could feel his temper rising. Sarah had the ability to annoy him like no other person could. Quietly and calmly, he asked "What would you give to speak to Jonathan again?"

Mention of her husband's name brought Sarah up short.

"Try to see it from where I stand," he said.

"I know how much you loved her...."

"No, you don't. You couldn't."

"I don't think she would want this," Sarah said firmly, wringing the folds of her skirts with nervous hands.

"Apparently, she does," Hornbeck said tiredly. "Sarah, I am not a fool, and I'll thank you not to treat me like one. I will not argue about this with you any further."

After a long and uncomfortable silence, Sarah asked delicately, "Do you think this woman really is... in touch with her?'

Hornbeck considered his reply carefully before answering.

"You've heard about mediums and their supposed powers as long as I have, of course," he said. "But I never thought much about it—never had to. But now.... I must find out. I must see for myself."

Silently, he added, *By God, I hope she is.*

The medium and her brother arrived at a quarter to eight, as heat lightning flickered and flashed across a painterly sky and a sudden summer downpour threatened. They were shown into the drawing room and received by the family.

"A pleasure to make your acquaintance," Hornbeck said, kissing Madame's hand. "May I present my sister, Mrs. Newland; my son, James Hornbeck the Second, and his wife; and this is my daughter, Mrs. Christie, and her husband."

Hands were shaken and polite murmurs made before Colonel Hornbeck stepped back to regard his visitors.

They certainly were an odd pair, this brother and sister, standing together arm-in-arm. Hornbeck found himself looking back and forth between the minister's round boyish face and the medium's straight patrician one. He wore simple black, a little rumpled, with a high clerical collar contrasting sharply with Madame Priestley's décolleté Parisian gown. Her long hair was arranged artfully, and she carried a square velvet bag in one gloved hand.

What a striking woman, Hornbeck thought, and those eyes! What wonders and terrors those eyes must have gazed upon in their time, visible only to her and to no other, That, perhaps, explained why her hair and begun to whiten in that singular fashion....

Wine was served and the guests made cordial small talk: the men about yachts and horses, the women about houses, fashions, and scandals. It was nearly half an hour before young James asked the question that had been on everyone's mind.

"Madame Priestley," he said cautiously, "if I may make so bold as to ask, how long have you been blessed with these... abilities... we have heard so much of?"

A small smile played on Madame's full red lips before she answered.

"Since I was a small girl, I always seemed to be aware of those things which were unknown to others," she said in her low voice. "I have always been sensitive, and not a few people described me as mediumistic from a young age. I was much troubled by nightmares and dark dreams, and it was not until many years later that I learned these dreams were attempts by those beyond to reach out to me, to one they felt could help them be heard."

"So my sister, you see, did not choose the spirits," Reverend Barrows said. "The spirits, instead, chose my sister."

"By the time I was of age I was conducting two or three séances a week, attempting to place the bereaved in touch with those they had loved."

"And collecting no fee," Reverend Barrows said, giving his sister's hand a squeeze. "No fee! We were adamant about that. We were doing God's work, and helping our fellow travelers. And we still are, we still are!"

Hornbeck glanced over to his own sister, but Sarah would not meet his gaze.

"And what about you, Reverend?" young James went on. "Are you also so gifted?"

"No", was the modest reply. "It would seem that whatever small gifts I might possess lie in an altogether different direction." He gave a broad grin. "But I must admit that I have always felt a strong connection to my dear sister—a connection so strong that I might describe it as almost preternatural."

"Rachel and I have often felt that same way, haven't we Rache?" young Hornbeck said at once. "Felt that we were linked, as twins so often do. Once, when we were children, I was out playing—just out back there, with our governess Mrs. Hawkes. You remember Mrs. Hawkes, don't you Rache?"

"Of course I remember her," was the sour reply. "A horrible old woman who used to drink when she thought Father wasn't looking."

Colonel Hornbeck arched an eyebrow, but let it pass.

"I was running around in back," young James continued, "and I ran toward that line of trees you can still see through the windows. And when I came under the shade of the trees, I startled a pair of rabbits—little brown ones, and one of them had a sort of white star on its forehead, stretching back between the long ears. They saw me and they *bolted*!" He laughed at the memory. "Must've frightened the life out of 'em."

"So old Mrs. Hawkes called me back and brought me inside, not at all pleased that I had wandered out where she couldn't quite see me. And when I came into the morning room…."

At this point Rachel took up the story.

"I was there with my sketchbook and pencils. I always thought that drawing was a fine way to pass a morning when I was a girl. Well, just as Jimmy came into the room, I was finishing a sketch of a rabbit with a star on its forehead! I had never drawn a rabbit before, and I certainly never drew one again." She blushed slightly. "To this day I do not know why I made that sketch; I simply did. And I have wondered about it a great deal since."

"As have I," her brother agreed.

"We did some table tipping one night in college," Mr. Christie said, a little uneasily. "Five or six of us, when we should have been studying. That table moved clear across the room and I swear not one of us was doing it. We spent the next few nights trying to do it again, but we couldn't." He took a sip of his wine. "Apparently, the spirits are fickle."

Colonel Hornbeck had remained silent during this talk of spirits, half-lost in an old memory he had nearly forgotten until just now.

The day of the disaster at Chancellorville, he awoke from a restless night and called out to Frankie for coffee. One of the countless boys who served in the camps, Frankie was a freckle-faced, gap-toothed lad of about thirteen who poked his head into the tent and said, "Yup," as he had every morning for over a year. A moment later Frankie handed in a hot tin cup and the Colonel stood there in the humid dawn wondering what the day would bring. Outside he could hear the rest of the camp slowly waking up. He sipped his coffee and reached for a map.

He dropped the cup when he remembered that Frankie's head had been blown off by Confederate artillery at Fredericksburg a week before.

The Colonel was roused from his melancholy reverie by the low voice of the medium.

"There is a spirit in this house tonight," she said. "I can feel her very strongly."

A heavy silence settled over Blithewood House after Rachel and Sarah withdrew to their upstairs rooms, leaving Rachel's husband and young James to sit with Reverend Barrows over whisky and cigars. The only sounds Colonel Hornbeck heard was the rustling of Madame's silken dress whispering down the long hallway leading to the library, and his own anxious breath.

Closing the library door behind them, Madame lit a stout white candle before extinguishing the hissing gas jets in the room one by one. She then placed the candle on a little three-legged table in front of the grand horsehair couch, and motioned Hornbeck to seat himself at the other end. A light rain splashed against the windows and she folded her hands atop her square velvet bag.

The memory of the past few days flashed through his mind like a nervous ghost. Had it been only two days? Three, perhaps, since her brother's note had arrived? It seemed as though he had awaited her arrival for weeks, possibly months, and now that Madame was here, in his house, sitting on the couch with him, he realized he had no idea of what to expect next.

What if Madame could contact Amelia? What would it mean if she could? How would it change not only his life, but her death as well? Would Blithewood House still be a place of mourning, and would he still be a widower and bereft? A taste came into his mouth that he had not tasted since the War, when he knew that tomorrow would be utterly different from today, in fearful and yet-unknown ways.

"There is an old belief that the tears of the grieving wet the shrouds of the departed, making them uncomfortable and unhappy; while simply a quaint folk custom, it does remind us the departed do not wish those left behind to mourn for them. What so many call Death is not the end, but simply a crossing over… I know that your Amelia does not want you to grieve, for she is near you always.

"Please, sir, focus your gaze on the flame of the candle and listen to the sound of my voice for a moment," she continued. "You needs must clear your mind and banish all negative thoughts and troubling influences. Be at your ease, Colonel, for only then can we meet with success. Bear in mind that we do not summon the spirits, we do not command them to appear to us. We can only create the proper atmosphere and they come if it pleases them to do so. I can make you no promises tonight, do you understand?"

Hornbeck nodded, staring at the flame.

A moment later, Madame said, "I can feel her here. I can feel her presence very strongly."

Hornbeck opened his eyes and looked around the room a little skeptically. There was nothing but long shadows and the bright afterimage of the candle flame blurring his sight.

"You will see in time."

"When will that be?"

"I cannot yet tell. But it will happen when the time is right for it to happen. You must be patient, Colonel, and you must have faith."

She opened her bag and drew out a pair of slates and a small piece of chalk.

"It has been found by greater and more gifted souls than myself that when the conditions are most favorable, the spirits may be coaxed to leave us messages."

She placed one slate atop the other, with the chalk between them; the wooden frames allowed enough room for the chalk to roll freely along the blank inner surfaces. Reaching up, she took a wide silk ribbon from her hair, and a few loosened tresses tumbled down over her bare white shoulders. She bound the slates together, knotting the ribbon securely and placing them next to the candle. She set her small hands on either side of the slates and nodded for Hornbeck to place his hands on hers.

They were silent for a long moment.

Madame leaned back and breathed in deeply.

"Spirits," she said, "spirits, we reach out across the void this night, holding out our hands to our departed sister Amelia—Amelia, we are here, we wait for you, we are eager to make contact with you, Amelia. James has missed you so, Amelia. Will you not offer him some measure of comfort from the Summerland, Amelia? Some small sign?"

The windows rattled in the warm, wet breeze.

"Can you hear us, Amelia?"

Silence and long flickering shadows.

"We wait for you… we invite you… we entreat you…. Please answer us…."

"Amelia—?" Hornbeck glanced around him again. He could feel his heart racing, could feel his hands quiver atop the medium's.

He could almost feel someone looking over his shoulder.

Amelia?

Amelia…?

Resurgam…

Amelia!

He thought the table wobbled slightly.

He thought—just thought—he could hear a faint scratching sound, as of chalk against slate.

"Oh, my God."

The medium was still speaking. "Come to us Amelia. The way is open for you and we wait patiently."

The table very definitely wobbled, teetered. The candle nearly tumbled to the carpeted floor, but Hornbeck's big hand shot out to catch it, scarcely noticing the hot wax spattering his fingers. His other hand clutched at the slates, which evaded him and slid to the floor.

Hornbeck froze. Waiting.

And everything was still and quiet.

"I believe," Madame said distantly, "I believe she has left us."

"Are you certain she was even here?" Hornbeck demanded.

"Quite. But she has departed for now."

"Will she return?" he asked in a small voice.

"Now that she knows the way, I have no doubts… but open the slates."

With one strangely steady hand and the other strangely trembling, he clumsily retrieved the slates and pulled the silken knot loose, tossing the ribbon away. He paused for a moment before opening them, unsure he would find anything and even less sure that he would believe what he might find.

Then he saw the writing—two scribbled names.

One slate read *James.*

The other, *Amelia.*

His tears ran down his face like the rain outside the window.

Chapter VI

MR. MORRISON SPENT HIS DAYS lounging in the lobby of
the Ocean House, sometimes screened by a potted palm, other
times apparently absorbed in a newspaper or a novel, and at yet
other times seeming to doze lightly as he waited to meet someone,
but always watching.

Thankfully, in the busy lobby of a large hotel, a man with
Morrison's forgettable features could go almost unnoticed. To
ensure this, he changed his suit at least twice daily, during the
quiet times when he slipped back to this Thames Street boarding
house. In the old days, he thought ruefully, he would have a
partner or two to work with, and they would have watched the
hotel in shifts. It not only made less work for each, but lessened
the chance of discovery. A large part of Mr. Morrison's chosen
career had been built upon his ability to blend unobtrusively, and
his life had depended upon it more than a few times.

He watched the summer people come and go, ebbing and
flowing like the tide on one of the rocky beaches nearby. They left
in the morning, sometimes returned for lunch, and were not often
back before midnight. He saw cunning, well-dressed young men
trying to catch the eyes of oil and steel heiresses, and railroad and
banking magnates trying to catch the eyes of cunning and well-
dressed young women. He saw husbands and wives bid their lovers
goodnight before going upstairs to their rooms, and several times
saw the spouses do the same a few moments later. He began to
recognize the faces of men going into the little casino to test their

latest system, and of the men who always came out rich because they cheated at cards. He knew the grifters and the burglars by sight, and occasionally acknowledged them with a curt nod; they greeted him in return, taking him for one of their own.

And, of course, he saw Madame Priestley and her brother.

She seldom came down before noon; most of her morning was spent receiving visitors and supplicants. Anyone who entered the lobby swathed in full or even part mourning was certainly there to see Madame. Her afternoon were spent in making calls of her own, usually to teas or garden parties along Bellevue; in a short time she had become a popular guest. Her evenings were reserved for séances, either in her own suite or, more and more frequently, at one of the many mansions.

Her brother passed most of his days roaming the beaches and seeing the sights, a smiling summer tourist. Morrison saw the two spend little time together, except when a carriage rolled up to whisk them down the Avenue for a private séance at a millionaire's cottage.

As was the case tonight.

The carriage arrived toward dusk, just as it was beginning to cloud over. Morrison saw Madame Priestley retrieve a small velvet bag from the Chubb safe behind the hotel counter before she and her brother entered the carriage. He followed them in a hansom to Blithewood House, one of the large houses fronting the sea, and then walked back briskly to the Ocean House, returning just as it began to rain. They would be away for most of the evening.

He walked quickly through the lobby, looking neither right nor left. He went up the broad, carpeted staircase to the spiritualist's suite. She had apparently requested a set of rooms, arranged off the main corridor. This worked to Morrison's advantage as he knelt down and peered closely at the door's lock. It was a fairly simple one.

He had dressed in a plain dark suit and soft hat, and from an inner pocket he drew out a neat morocco case. He had purchased the case and its contents in a low shop in the Old Nichol, just off

Bethnal Green Road in the East End of London. It was an excellent set of lockpicks.

He defeated the lock in under half a minute and closed the door quietly behind him.

Morrison had spent much of his life in hotels, moving from assignment to assignment, from case to case, but only rarely had he stayed in a place this grand. It was a handsome suite, with an airy front room paneled in black walnut and tastefully furnished. A pair of Gothic arched window-seats, draped in heavy velvet brocade, looked north and east, the curtains muffling the sounds of the busy streets below. A broad portiered archway led to the more intimate little parlor, with the bedrooms arranged off this inner chamber. Here was a large round table with high-backed chairs gathered around; this was where the séances were held. The two gas jets by the fireplace were left burning low in this room, and the feeble light reflected in the lustrous dark woodwork.

The rooms still smelled faintly of incense and candlewax— there had been séances here nearly every night he had watched, and Morrison had seen so many enter resolute and even skeptical, only to depart shaken and uncertain.

He began his searching the bedrooms, starting with the brother's.

The dark paneling, stolid furnishings and hunting scenes hanging on the walls showed this clearly to be a man's room. The bed was hastily made, and a linen nightshirt and a cotton dressing-gown tossed carelessly on a chair at the foot of the walnut bedstead.

A large oil lamp stood close by on a table by the bed; stacked up by the lamp was a small, worn Bible and a few dime novels, along with visitors' guides and *The Official Bulletin of the Newport Casino*. The Reverend Mr. Barrows's bedtime reading certainly was an interesting mix, and Morrison could only wonder what sort of dreams the man must have had.

He set out on a methodical search of the room, the kind of search he had conducted countless other times in countless other rooms.

He found nothing of interest as he went through the drawers of the Reverend's bureau—just the usual socks, underclothes, starched handkerchiefs and stiff collars. The broad mahogany top was littered with small nothings such as brushes, a silver shaving mug, and tooth powder. Morrison made sure to leave everything as he found it.

In the filigree wastepaper basket, among the opened envelopes, discarded scraps and bits of blotting paper, Morrison found a crumpled slip with a name and address written on it: *Arthur Lake, 104 Church Street.* He copied this into his pocketbook before carefully replacing the paper. Church Street, thought, was just off Thames and not very far from his boarding house.

In the fancy wardrobe, buried in back and hidden by black suits, shoes, and worn traveling bags, Morrison discovered a small, locked wooden box with brass fittings. This, too, fell to the Old Nichol tools. Inside, wrapped in a dark oilcloth, was a six-shot .44 Winchester, the Frontier Bulldog.

Morrison let his breath out slowly as the big gun sat in his hand, cold and heavy. He had brought his Adams with him that night, tucked into an oversize pocket his tailor had created specifically to hold it. He felt its reassuring weight resting against his ribs, and wondered what kind of clergyman would feel the need for a gun, and why.

He glanced over at the pile of dime novels on the bedside table—Nick Carter, Old King Brady, Deadwood Dick, and volumes of the New York Detective Library already falling apart with rereading. He shook his head and rewrapped the pistol with great care and gently replaced it in its box.

The last thing he found in the room was a fat wad of hundred dollar bills, some seven thousand dollars in total, tucked between the plump mattresses.

Making sure he left nothing disturbed, Morrison passed through the séance room into the spiritualist's bedroom. The door's hinges creaked slightly, no doubt a result of the damp summer.

This was a richly furnished and feminine room: pale walls and courtly portraits, fine French furniture and a huge wardrobe for the many gowns and hats a season at Newport required. A wet breeze fluttered the lace curtains. Madame's bed was neatly made, all her things arranged precisely on her vanity table. This seemed a little unusual, as Morrison knew (via a five-dollar bill to the concierge) that Ocean House maids were forbidden to enter the suite, and the brother and sister kept no servants of their own. It was uncommon for a lady of society to look after herself.

Morrison launched into the same routine here as he had in the other room—searching under the bed, under the thick Turkey carpet, rummaging thoroughly and carefully through all the drawers of the wardrobe, making sure Madame had hidden nothing among her petticoats, corsets, or her long Paris gowns. He spent a full forty-five minutes checking through everything, and when he was finished he went over the room again.

This is what he had expected; he did not think that the spiritualist would be so careless as to leave anything incriminating or even suggestive in her suite. Indeed, he had seen her come down to the lobby to retrieve her bag from the safe in the manager's office. Anything suspect would be kept there, including—in all likelihood—they very thing Morrison had crossed an ocean to recover.

Once again making sure he left everything as he found it, Morrison stepped back into the séance room. He stood in the doorway for a few long moments, staring at the thick stumps of the burned-down candles in the center of the round table.

His thoughts wandered, and he caught himself wondering what exactly went on in this room, night after night, when the sitters formed a circle and joined hands in the dark. Did the dead speak? And what did this spiritualist do; what signs and wonders did she show to make believers out of the doubters? How did she convert them to this strange faith whose strange claims could be proven by the light of a candle? What lay hidden in the shadowy corners of this room?

But he pushed those thoughts away after only an instant; they were not part of what he had come to do. It was not his job, spirits were not his concern, and matters of faith did not fall within his purview.

He turned his attention back to the room; eight chairs were drawn up to the table, with a few more standing back against the walls. Another arched Gothic window seat, hung in heavy draperies, looked eastward. A pair of framed landscapes were displayed on plaster walls painted to resemble veined marble.

Between the doors that led to the two bedrooms was a small fireplace, the marble mantelpiece of which was piled high with letters and visiting-cards. Most of the stationery and cards had broad black borders. Half of Newport seemed to have visited this woman, and the letters mostly described bereavements and begged genteelly for Madame Priestley's help.

Stuffed into the already-full letter rack between an advertisement for Madame Donovan's Worth boutique and another advertisement for the services of a Jeremy Mumford, a Thames Street photographer specializing in spirit photographs, Morrison found a note that gave him a chuckle.

> *Blithewood House*
> *Bellevue and Cliffs*
> *July 16th, 1893*
>
> *My Dear Rev. Barrows –*
> *Col. Hornbeck presents his compliments to both you and you sister, and would be only too pleased if you both would favor him with a visit on the day after tomorrow. A carriage shall arrive for you at seven-thirty in the evening. Until then, I am,*
>
> *Very Sincerely Yours,*
> *Col. James Hornbeck*

Morrison replaced the letter and glanced at his pocketwatch—nearly midnight. The spiritualist and her brother would be returning from Blithewood House soon. Time to depart.

But dammit, he thought, all this work tonight with so little to show for it. He was no further ahead than he was when he first picked the suite's lock. But there was nothing more to be done for now.

What had he learned? That the Reverend Barrows had a large pistol, and possibly thought of himself living the life of a dime novel hero, had he not been called to serve? He had a large cache of money hidden in his mattress. His sister, on the other hand, was coolly efficient, and too clever to leave anything worth finding in their rooms.

A few of the letters on the rack were slightly askew, not exactly as he had found them. While it was unlikely that they would be noticed, he took no chances. He took a step back into the other room...

And heard the sound of a key being fitted into the suite's lock.

"I think we shall be hearing from Colonel Hornbeck quite soon, my dear," Reverend Barrows's voice came from the other side of the door.

"I believe we shall," his sister replied in her low, serious tones.

The window seat opposite the door—Morrison barely had time to throw himself behind the brocade draperies before the door swung open.

"But why is it so wet here?" Reverend Barrows grumbled. "America's premiere resort, where it rains two days out of three. I do wonder—"

"Sshhhhh," Madame cut him off with a sharp hiss for silence. "Sshhhh..."

"What?"

"Someone..." she began in a faraway voice, "someone has been here."

"*What do you mean?*"

"Someone has been here—while we were out."

"Good God—are you certain?"

"I can feel it. Can't you?"

"No—I don't know," was the choked reply. Morrison could hear the fear in the man's voice, and he realized that the Reverend Mr. Barrows was afraid of his sister. "But who?"

"I don't know" she said irritably, and then said what Morrison, holding his breath behind the curtains, had been dreading to hear. "There—look at the letter rack. Some one has been here and gone through the letters."

Very gently, Morrison eased the Adams out of his pocket. He'd had to shoot his way out of such situations before. His fingers held the grip tightly and he waited.

"Good God!" the Reverend cried. Morrison heard him storm across the suite to his room, the thick Turkey rug doing nothing to muffle his panicked footfalls.

Morrison heard the sound of the wardrobe being thrown open, of drawers being opened and slammed shut. He heard a lock spring open as the Winchester was checked, and a breathless voice mumbling over and over again, "All right—all right—all right."

Madame Priestley was silent in the front room, arms folded and head tilted a little to one side. Morrison could just see her through the half-drawn curtains. She was only a few feet away, with her back to him, seeming to listen to the rain outside. A few dark ringlets curled loosely over the nape of her smooth neck.

Reverend Barrows came back into the room, flustered and sputtering.

"I think somebody may have been in my room, but I can't be sure. Good heavens! What shall we do?"

"Go get the manager—find the hotel manager and tell him what has happened. Bring him here."

"Good—excellent. What about you? Aren't you going to check your room?"

"I have nothing for anyone to find," the spiritualist said flatly.

"All right—I'll be right back, then."

He dashed out of the suite, leaving the door ajar in his haste.

Morrison was alone with Madame Priestley.

She stood there in the room for a few tense minutes, barely a yard away from his hiding place. He moved back, pressing himself flat against the wall behind the drapes. He heard her turn, dress whispering silkily as she did, and he could almost feel her staring out the window, watching the rain stream down the panes.

He froze. Any movement would be reflected in the window and then he was done for. He stood perfectly stiff.

After a moment she breathed deeply and sighed, as though she had finally reached a conclusion, or satisfied herself of something. She turned again and went quietly into her room; Morrison heard the creak of the hinges as she shut the door behind her.

Morrison counted three and stole from the little alcove, slipping the Adams back into its pocket. He crept across the room and out into the hall.

Coming down the broad staircase to the lobby, he passed the excited Mr. Barrows and the sleepy night-manager on their way up to the suite. He nodded politely to them and walked on, hands thrust deep in his pockets.

Chapter VII

PROFESSOR ERASMUS VON HELLMANN, in a white linen suit and wide-brimmed Panama hat, stood on the corner of Thames and Pelham Streets, soaking in the early morning sun.

They had arrived the day before, the Professor, Hope and Jack, and Edward, checking into the Ocean House. *And why not?* the magician had asked. Not only was it one of the finest hotels in town, but it was where *She* was staying. He had not seen the medium yet, but he knew there was more than enough time.

The young people had gone off shopping and sightseeing today, with the imperturbable Edward in attendance. They were in good hands, leaving von Hellmann free to reacquaint himself with the town.

And Newport had changed considerably since his last visit, more than twenty summers before. Everyone, it was said, came to Newport either sooner or later, but it had been a smaller, quieter, less self-conscious place then. The summer people tended to be writers and artists and intellectuals from Boston and New York, and their cottages really were cottages.

He smiled as he recalled one warm night when he'd been invited to entertain at a gathering of the Town and Country Club. This little club's membership of fifty or so included Oliver Wendell Holmes, Henry Wadsworth Longfellow, and Julia Ward Howe, among others. Von Hellmann had spent a pleasant evening astounding some of the best minds of the day with card tricks and sleight of hand, and little illusions with rings or handkerchiefs or watches; he'd even included a few minor spiritualistic mysteries in the program.

That sort of salon was gone now, vanished like a half dollar and replaced by the Brenton Point Golf Course, the Casino, and the mansions. Money and prestige now determined membership. The old faux finishing style, in which plaster walls were painted to resemble marble, exotic woods or silken wallpapers to "fool the eye," had given way to the actual, costly *vrai* materials themselves. Times had changed.

And yet not so very much; von Hellmann felt the new summer colonists, raising these monstrous houses and styling themselves the aristocracy of the New World, were still heavily involved in fooling the eye.

He made his way down crowded Thames Street, flowing with the others along the bustling street, heading toward a photographer's studio he'd noticed the day before. Of all the colorful posters and sandwich boards, stenciled plate glass windows and bright signs swaying in the salty breeze, this one, modest as it was, had caught his attention.

There it was now—next block up.

> *MR. JEREMY MUMFORD*
> *Photographic Studio*
> *303 ½ Thames Street*
> *ARTISTIC PHOTOGRAPHS*
> *India Ink, Crayon & Pastel Portraits*
> *& Spirit Photography*

Von Hellmann bounded up the steps spryly and found himself in a large shop, bright and sunny, presided over by a portly man in pince-nez, presumably Mr. Jeremy Mumford. He wore a velvet vest, and his aesthetically long hair curled onto his collar. As von Hellmann entered, he took his velvet-collar frock coat from a peg and shrugged into it, saying cheerfully, "Good morning, sir. Come for a sitting today?"

It took von Hellmann a moment to place the voice.

He smiled and said, "Hello, Jerry Chace."

It had been decades since they had first met—the man had been a spirit photographer then, too, going by the name of Chase. The magician has set his sights on him and eventually revealed him for the double-exposing fraud he was. Chase's flourishing studio had closed up and he had disappeared; von Hellmann hadn't thought about him in ten years. Yet now here he was again, playing the same game under a new name. Only this time, with his clothes and his hair, he was passing himself off as an artist and an aesthete the way other Newporters passed themselves off as royalty in marble castles and palaces.

The man in the pince-nez blanched.

"Von Hellmann?" he gasped. "Oh, Christ—What—have you tracked me down after all this time? Come to finish me off, you sick old man?" He pointed a shaking finger. "I have a gun in the next room you bastard—"

"Calm down, Jerry, calm down. I only came to have my picture taken; you remember how vain I am. And now here's my old friend. How serendipitous."

"What the hell do you want?"

"Such language, Jerry. What would your other clients think? No, I simply want a pleasant chat with an old friend," von Hellmann chuckled, turning a contemptuous eye on Chase/Mumford. "You've done pretty well for yourself, haven't you Jerry?"

And Jerry had done pretty well—the studio was small but well-appointed. He had a variety of furniture on which to pose his sitters—horsehair sofas and overstuffed armchairs. Two dozen hand-painted backdrops were available, along with appropriate props ranging from drapes and plants to Roman columns and a large papier-mâché boulder to lean against pensively. His camera was an expensive tripod-mounted Normandie, all mahogany with brass fittings and a leather bellows. In back of the studio, through the flowery curtains, was the darkroom.

"So," Jerry said a little nervously, picking at imaginary lint on his vest, "what would you like to talk about, then?"

Von Hellmann realized with some satisfaction that the man was still afraid of him.

"I'd like to ask about another member of your peculiar tribe, Jerry. The woman calling herself Madame Helene Priestley."

"So it's her you're after," Jerry's face lit with relief. "I should have known you'd come after her. She's good."

"Have you seen her work?"

"Oh, yes; the wife and I sat with her a week ago. She came in for a portrait. She's been a very busy woman since her arrival."

"You and the wife? You really have done well since last we met. But tell me, Jerry—what do you think of her? Your honest opinion, as an insider?"

"She's genuine."

Von Hellmann chuckled dryly. "You don't believe in genuine mediumship any more than I do, Jerry, and for the same reason— we've spent too much time around these people. We've been to too many séances to believe, Jerry."

But Jerry folded his arms and stood firm.

"If you came here to add another notch on your belt of exposed mediums, you better turn around and go home now," he said. "Come to think of it, I haven't heard of you catching anyone for years; actually, I haven't heard anything at all about you. So that's it, then—going after her is just another publicity stunt for you, isn't it? You figure you'll ruin her like you ruined me, and... oh, but you haven't changed, you old bastard."

Von Hellmann smoldered. Realizing he wasn't the target had made the photographer brave.

"So what about the rest of the Newport spook racket? You're the only spirit photographer in town; what about other mediums?"

"There have been half-a-dozen mediums here the past few seasons; it's getting popular again. But I think Madame Priestley has sent the others packing; she's the biggest name in town right now, and everyone lost their regulars to her."

"And what of the Newport blue book? Is she in possession of that by now?"

According to skeptical legend, every town had a blue book—a compendium of notes about the various sitters who had consulted the spirits and what was known about them, and this was passed among the mediums active in that locale. Such a reference ensured that the spirits could supply a sitter with the correct information regardless of which medium it came through. Any new information gained, of course, would be added to the book for the next operator.

"There's no blue book here."

"Oh, Jerry. How can you have gotten so far in your line of work while being such a poor liar? Ah, well; are you going to take my portrait, or aren't you?"

"Of course, sir. I think that that armchair there best becomes a man of your years. I trust that you'll agree? Good! If you would be so kind…."

The smirking spirit photographer got a large Ripley dry-plate and loaded the Normandie. He filled the flashgun with powder and magnesium and told the magician to hold still.

When the exposed plate was sitting in its developer, von Hellmann asked, "Don't you think that Mumford is a little too close to Mumler, Jerry?"

"That's the whole point—Mumler was a man ahead of his time. He took his camera and gave the world proof of spiritualistic claims. A great man. God damn genius."

Mumler was a Bostonian who had discovered the faces of "spirit extras" in his portraits, and a new craze was born. The grieving thronged his little studio, hoping that Mumler's camera could catch their lost loved ones in black and white. The widowed Mary Todd Lincoln paid him a visit, and her portrait showed the assassinated President standing solemnly behind her, his hands resting on her shoulders. Charges of fraud were leveled against Mumler, when certain of his extras were recognized as very living Bostonians. He resurfaced in New York City some time later and was again dragged into court. The defense paraded a seemingly-endless stream of clients who insisted they would not be fooled by the simple double-exposure technique described by the prosecution. Von Hellmann appeared for the prosecution, as did his old friend P. T. Barnum, who had declared the photographs to be "humbugs." Although acquitted, Mumler vanished shortly after the trial was over.

"Well, this really has been most enjoyable, Jerry, but I have another appointment to keep at the Casino. If you'll excuse me, I will be going."

Jerry nodded and promised to have the finished portrait sent on to the Ocean House.

Later, when it was ready, he sat back to admire it. It was a fierce portrait of von Hellmann, seated in the armchair and staring defiantly back at the camera. *"From the Studio of J. Mumford, Thames Street, Newport, R. I."* ran the curlicue script beneath. It was a good photograph; one of his best.

Standing behind the magician was the wispy form of Madame Helene Priestley.

"Yeah, he'll like this. The old bastard."

Some fourteen years before, James Gordon Bennett, Jr., publisher of the New York *Herald*, had dared his friend Captain Henry Augustus "Sugar" Candy to ride his horse through the Newport Reading Room, then the town's most exclusive men's club. The dare was accepted and Candy and his horse gleefully scattered the members who had gathered that day looking for nothing more exciting than a newspaper, a game of dominos, and perhaps a glimpse of a well-turned ankle passing by. Colonel Hornbeck had been among the clubmen routed that day.

The club was outraged and Candy and his horse both promptly expelled. Bennett retaliated for his friend's censure by building the imposing Casino, just up Bellevue Avenue near the Ocean House. Within a couple of months, the Casino had eclipsed every other club on the island, including the Reading Room, as the place to be seen, the place to be a member. McKim, Mead and White had designed the lavish club, with an arched entrance, a gabled façade, and cool verandahs around the horseshoe piazza. There was a semicircular gazebo for morning concerts, grass courts for lawn tennis, and elegant clubrooms for reading, billiards, cards, dining, or lodging. Strangely for a place named the Casino, gambling was forbidden. And, unlike the Reading Room, women were allowed as members.

Von Hellmann came through the archway, purchased his one-day membership for a dollar, and paused for a moment to listen to the open-air orchestra just finishing up its morning concert. A shacker brought him a tall orangeade, the shackers being the young boys who catered to the members' every whim. They were usually curly-headed lads from the neighborhood, and were the only townsfolk who ever entered Casino grounds; all others stayed away, shunning and being shunned; the only other exceptions were the reporters who lounged and slouched about, eavesdropping and hoping for a good story.

Von Hellmann passed the lawn tennis courts, and the great grandstand, which had been bought from his old friend Barnum. It was a huge and ugly old thing, but Tennis Week was fast approaching and, as one of the most important weeks in the Newport calendar, the best of Newport society would soon be taking their seats there, and no doubt losing their gloves and parasols beneath it as people always did.

He found Professor Townsend at a table, looking a little thinner than he remembered, the long beard not as black as it had once been. Still, von Hellmann was winded from the uphill walk from Thames Street, and was sure he did not look as young as Townsend remembered either.

"Good morning, professor," von Hellmann said.

"And to you, professor," Townsend replied, warmly shaking hands. "How have you been?"

"I have been absolutely splendid. And where is Mrs. Townsend?"

"She's up there," Townsend pointed up to the second floor. "In the Ladies' Reading Room today. She sends her regards and says that, while she will be happy to see you, she is convinced you and I will spend our afternoon together reliving old adventures and reviving old arguments, and she wanted a more peaceful day than that."

A waiter brought them their lunch and, afterwards, the two men retired upstairs and sat on the front balcony overlooking the Avenue. Across from them was the Old Stone Villa, Bennett's home, with gas-lit, glass-eyed owls atop the gateposts. It had been built back in the 'fifties and was rumored to be haunted.

"I should have known you'd come straight here when you got my letter," Townsend said, swishing his whiskey-and-soda around in its tumbler.

"Of course you should have. A genuine medium is not to be missed."

"You don't believe in genuine mediums."

"I believe that I have never yet sat with one. It would be impossible and foolish to declare all mediumistic phenomena to be fraudulent, sight unseen—"

"Nonsense. That's just what you've always done. You can't hide behind rhetoric like that. I know you too well..." Townsend caught himself and sighed.

"Reliving old arguments," von Hellmann said quietly.

They sat together in silence for a few long minutes before either of them spoke again.

"Tell me about the Priestley woman," von Hellmann said at last.

"She arrived from England in June, and started to hold séances almost immediately. I had heard of her before—a colleague of mine sat with her a few times, and he was very impressed. And so was I when I finally saw her. She was the talk of the town by the time the season started. She's a kind of safely controversial figure to have around—it makes your social rivals jealous that she's telling fortunes at your afternoon tea and not theirs. There have been a few doubters, of course, but everyone so far has been impressed by her.

"I've conducted a few interviews with her sitters afterwards—I have over a dozen signed affidavits from people swearing that she's put them in touch with dead friends and relatives she could not possibly have known, and told them things while in trance only known to the sitter and the deceased. Half a dozen of those I've interviewed say that she has materialized spirits they recognized as people they knew in life. They recognized the faces, von Hellmann."

"People always see just what they want to see."

"Yes," Townsend replied with a harsh look, "Yes, they do."

"I've been in touch with Maskelyne," von Hellmann continued, ignoring the professor. John Nevil Maskelyne was Britain's premiere conjuror; he and his partner Cook had been declared the "Royal Illusionists and Anti-Spiritualists." Like von Hellmann, he was no stranger to the courtroom, and had been involved in countless suits and counter-suits during his long career. "He tells me that the Priestley woman and her brother left England quickly and quietly. No one seems to know why."

"Interesting," Townsend said.

"So what is she doing now? Still having séances at the hotel?"

"No. I thought you would have heard. She and her brother had to leave the hotel."

"Why?" von Hellmann asked with a wicked smile. "Did she hear I was coming?"

"Her rooms were broken into and ransacked a couple of nights ago."

"Ransacked! How interesting! Tell me the whole story."

"One of the members here is a Colonel James Hornbeck—I've known him in a vague way for years. His wife died suddenly a few weeks ago and nobody's seen much of him since. Well, he invited Madame Priestley to his home for a séance—a successful one too, by the way—and while she and her brother were out someone went through their suite."

"Do they know who? Or why?"

"No idea. Reverend Barrows—that's the brother—seems more shaken by it than his sister."

"So where did they go?"

"Hornbeck invited them to stay with him as his guests."

Von Hellmann frowned. That would make her harder to get to.

"Is she still giving séances for others?"

"Oh, yes. In fact, from what I hear Hornbeck insisted that she should continue sharing her gift with any who needed her. She gives readings in the afternoon, when her time isn't taken up with too much else."

"How much does she charge?"

"She charges nothing. She accepts donations and gifts, and donates half of everything she receives to various charities."

"Do you remember Carter? The levitating medium? He used to make generous donations to the Temperance League, the Orphans' Fund. He was a fake, too."

"You could never conclusively prove that."

"I could never conclusively prove that to *you*."

"Reliving old arguments," Townsend chuckled dryly.

After a moment, von Hellmann asked, "So what do you think of her? Genuine mediumship or…?"

Townsend pondered his reply carefully.

"There are one or two things she has done which I'm sure can be accomplished by trickery; the sort of thing you have demonstrated time and again. But of course while these things *can* be produced by trickery it does necessarily mean that they *are*."

"The existence of wigs does not disprove the existence of real hair, as you have often observed."

"Quite. So while I feel that some small number of her effects can be the product of trickery and quite possibly may be, at last I must say the majority of what she does is absolutely genuine."

"She only cheats *sometimes*."

"And not very often, at that. No one has caught her, but I have seen her do some things that I have seen you do, too, and I must take that into consideration. And yet most of what she does remains inexplicable by normal means."

Von Hellmann considered what Townsend had said. Townsend was not a stupid man, no foolish dupe waiting to be deceived. And his claim of "mixed mediumship" had been heard before, back during their time on the Wraeburn Committee. After the first few times, von Hellmann began to regard it as Townsend's trump card.

"Well, we'll see, won't we? Listen, Townsend, this woman hasn't offered to contact Michael, has she?"

Michael was Townsend's son, who had died some years before.

"No... no she hasn't. I think he may have come through during our first séance with her, but he didn't stay. No." He fumbled with a napkin for a moment before saying, "She has made contact with Josephs. Remember Josephs?"

"From the Wraeburn Committee? I had no idea he was dead."

"Back in '86. His heart."

"Never liked him," von Hellmann said nonchalantly. "Still, bringing back a psychic investigator—good theater."

More silence.

"So what do you plan to do now that you're here?" Townsend asked.

"Well," von Hellmann replied thoughtfully. "I was thinking about inquiring at the theaters in town and seeing if they could fit me in somewhere. It would feel good to be in front of an audience again. It's been years. And of course, I want to investigate Madame Priestley."

"You want to expose her."

"That all depends on her. Can you provide me with an introduction to her patron, this Hornbeck?"

"I can," Townsend sighed. "But for God's sake don't make me regret it afterward."

"I told you, that depends on her. You said she gives readings in the afternoons?"

"Between two and four, when the dowagers are going up and down the Avenue. She will answer any three questions written on folded slips. She did it for me last week, and I don't see how it could be anything other than genuine."

Chapter VIII

"**I HOPE YOU HAVE BEEN ABLE** to make yourself comfortable here," Colonel Hornbeck said to Madame over breakfast.

"Very comfortable, thank you," said Madame, sipping delicately at her steaming tea. "You have a lovely home. And it is very kind of you to open it to us so generously."

"It's a bit old-fashioned by Newport standards. Nobody builds wooden houses anymore—now everything is marble. Like Marble House and that *thing* Richard Morris Hunt is building over on Ochre Point... but those are both Vanderbilt houses, and one never knows with them. Yes, Blithewood House is fairly old fashioned, but it was always more than enough for us...."

"She is still here," Madame said quietly, breaking in on the Colonel's unspoken chain of thought. It was not this first time that morning she had done so. It made Hornbeck a little uneasy. "Can you not feel her?"

And yet it was also somehow reassuring; indeed, the mansion seemed less gloomy, less like a house buried in mourning since Madame and her brother had arrived three days before. Paradoxically, Madame's presence was at once intimidating and soothing.

"Sometimes I think I can—other times I'm not so sure. And still other times, I think my mind must simply be playing tricks on me. When... when can we try to contact her again?"

"I am afraid that my sister has not yet fully recovered from the outrage at the hotel," Reverend Barrows interposed, smiling.

"It may be a week or more before her powers have regained their strength. Reaching out across the void in a weakened condition could be very dangerous, couldn't it, my dear?"

His sister smiled and sipped her tea.

"But do not worry, Colonel—my sister shall soon be able to repay your gracious hospitality."

"Think nothing of it. You are my guests, and I ask for nothing in return save the pleasure of your company. I am only sorry that you have suffered such an unfortunate occurrence here in our dear old town."

"I hope my afternoon readings did not cause you any inconvenience yesterday," Madame said.

"None at all."

"I would like to continue; in just a few short weeks in town I have found a number of souls in need of advice and guidance. I feel that I must help them, even," with a sideways glance toward her over-protective brother, "even in my weakened condition."

"The morning room remains yours, if it still suits you," Hornbeck said.

"It suits me very well, thank you."

"Good."

Henry, Hornbeck's discreet butler, glided silently into the room, bringing a silver salver with a pale cream-colored card upon it. It was the card of Detective Benjamin H. Richards.

"Ah, excellent. Show him in, Henry."

Richards and his uniformed sergeant were brought in promptly, the bulky detective dwarfing the other man. Normally, a working man such as Richards would never have been allowed into so much as the front hallway of any house along Bellevue, but Hornbeck was keenly aware that circumstances here were highly unusual. The sergeant drew out a pocket-book and pencil and Detective Richards, with a brusque greeting, went right into the reason for his visit.

"In the three days since we received your initial complaint," he began, "We have scoured the hotel for any clue as to the identity of the person or persons who entered your suite. I regret to say that we have found nothing. My men have interviewed everyone from Mr. Weaver, the manager, to the half-dozen negroes who clean the floors on Sunday mornings. No one remembers seeing anything at all out of the ordinary."

"Mr. Weaver assured me that this was the first time any such thing has happened at his establishment," Reverend Barrows said. "He offered profoundest apologies and offered to extend our stay at no charge... but my sister and I could not remain in such a place after what happened."

"I understand," Richards said simply. "I have both your statements here in my pocket; I came this morning to ask if there was anything you wish to add or amend? Perhaps in the past couple of days you have recalled something which you had previously forgotten?"

The brother and sister looked at one another and shook their heads.

"I am sorry, Detective Richards," Madame said. "I can add nothing to what I have already said."

"Nor I."

"I see. Well then, tell me—have you yourselves formed any theory?"

"None."

"Has anything of this sort happened before? Perhaps when you were traveling elsewhere?"

"Never."

"And surely you have made no enemies since your arrival in Newport?"

"Really, Richards—" Hornbeck protested.

Richards silenced him with a hard look. "These questions must be asked, sir."

"I should hope we have no enemies here," Reverend Barrows answered. "Newport has been so kind to us both. Still, there are always those who hate and fear that which is beyond their understanding. We have been plagued by such ignorance before, my sister and I. Helene has been accused of witchcraft and necromancy and blasphemy and a thousand other things in her mission. Many of the same charges leveled against Copernicus, Galileo, and so many other seekers after truth. We must simply accept that some are not sufficiently *advanced* to understand our work, but we hope that someday they will be."

"Every year the town attracts a great number of summer colonists, and unfortunately there comes with them a certain element which is not so welcome—or advanced," Richards smiled. "We have our pickpockets and our cat burglars, and the Ocean House is one of their favorite... haunts... if you'll forgive the term, Madame Priestley. The guests are wealthy and sometimes careless. I think you nearly fell victim to one of them—but you have been more cautious than some of the other guests and kept your valuables in the safe. My men are attempting to trace the movements of some of our more... well-known... cat burglars. We shall spare no pains."

"Thank you, Detective," Hornbeck said. "Please keep us informed of your progress. Good morning."

"Good morning," Richards said with a curt nod.

As Henry closed the door behind the detective and his sergeant, Hornbeck begged his guests' pardon; turning quickly to his butler, he said, "Henry, the presence of guests makes it all the more important that those vacancies be filled quickly."

"Yes, sir. I have filled the maid's position, and I have an interview in fifteen minutes with a man who I think will do very well as an underbutler."

"Excellent, Henry."

"There is one other thing, sir, if I may."

"Yes?"

"Eileen informed me this morning that she saw a ghost in Mrs. Hornbeck's room."

"What?"

"Yes, sir. Eileen was coming down the passage toward the room, with the intention of giving it a good dusting, when she says she caught a glimpse of a figure in the doorway. The figure withdrew, and Eileen claims she could see the edge of a dark gown swirl around the corner of the doorway. Upon rounding the corner, Eileen informs me that there was a female figure by the window, and then it was gone."

"Do I know Eileen?" Hornbeck asked.

"I believe not, sir."

"This is a most exciting and unexpected event." Reverend Barrows exclaimed. "Colonel Hornbeck, might I suggest that you sleep in your wife's bed tonight, should she return? It might be prudent to sleep there for several nights."

Hornbeck pondered the thought for a moment before turning to Madame Priestley. She nodded slowly and seriously, saying, "It can do no harm."

"Very well. I start tonight or tomorrow. Now Henry, you have your interview. You may go."

"Thank you, sir."

Being the butler of a well-established Newport household certainly did have its perquisites, Henry thought as he made his way down the servants' staircase and into the kitchen. He had a small oak-paneled office with an electric light and an electric fan, the finest bedroom in the servants' wing, and, having the imprimatur to engage and discharge members of the staff, he commanded more respect from them than was ever accorded to the Colonel. Indeed, their employer only knew his people by their first names, if even that. Henry remembered how it had once taken the Colonel nearly five weeks to notice one of the underbutlers had been replaced.

Henry also remembered the abrupt dismissal of the underbutler whose position now being filled; he had been expelled the morning after Amelia Hornbeck's sudden death.

The applicant was waiting in the sunny kitchen, smiling and chatting cheerfully with the cook and munching on one of her famous muffins. He was a plain-looking man with a thick walrus moustache and an English accent. He exchanged greetings with Henry and the two conducted the interview in the butler's office.

"Well, I must admit that being British is a point in your favor," Henry said, closing the door behind him. "Colonel Hornbeck believes, as do so many others, that Europeans have better manners than we Americans."

"Some of my countrymen do, and some certainly don't," was the smiling reply. "On my side, I don't judge Americans so harshly."

"Now then, your two letters of character are very good. You were underbutler five years in Surrey?"

"Yes, sir, with a very good family, too. And before that I was in London for several years, serving in the household of a retired barrister. When that gentleman passed away I moved on to Surrey. You may notice that the first letter of character is actually written by the barrister's son, who knew me quite well."

"So it is. But tell me, what made you leave Surrey for America?"

"I have been in service since I was fifteen, sir. First as a hallboy, then as a footman; the other footman was a bit taller than me, and mismatched footmen look ridiculous, I'm sure you'll agree. So I was moved up to vegetable cook and, afterwards, roast cook. Doing well there, I was trained as a valet to Mr. Whitcombe, the barrister. I am sure you know as well as I how long one can expect to wait for a vacancy to open in a household; I felt that I had reached an impasse of sorts in England, and so I decided to try America. I, of course, gravitated toward Newport because we hear such wonderful things about the place, even in Surrey."

Henry smiled to himself. Moving from house to house was a common way for a man in service to advance. The applicant was right, of course—waiting for a vacancy in your own house could take years, and who wanted to spend all that time carrying coal and cleaning up after the other servants?

"I think you will do nicely here, sir. Let me quickly outline your duties: you shall be responsible for keeping most of the other domestics on schedule, in addition to ensuring that the deliveries are made and merchant-appointments are kept. You shall be sent to the tailor and the laundry once or twice a week and also, in all probability, the cobbler as well. You shall see to it that the morning newspapers are ironed before being given to Colonel Hornbeck—he has a minor mania about that. You are given Wednesday afternoons off, in addition to every other Sunday. The Butler's Beach is an excellent way to spend a free day, take my word. And no flirting—under no circumstances will it be tolerated." Henry consulted the letters of character for a moment before concluding, "I hope that this is all clear and satisfactory, Mr. Morrison?"

"Oh, quite, sir. Thank you, sir."

Chapter IX

A FEW SUNNY DAYS LATER, Hope Westlock was shown into the imposing entry hall of Blithewood House by a liveried footman. The footman took her card and explained that Madame was currently engaged with another sitter; perhaps the lady would wait?

Hope accepted the proffered lemonade and spent a few moments lounging on the big horsehair sofa, hanging her long duster on a convenient hook.

She had been to readers and advisors before, countless times, watching how they operated. They were people who told you to proceed with caution and trust your own judgment, or that it would be wise to put things in order before moving on, and above all remember that communication was crucial in this matter, as with so many others. The list of bland platitudes and outrageous guesses Hope had heard through the years went on and on, rivaled only by the parade of characters who offered up advice from Beyond. Her personal favorite came from a tarot card reader whose Brooklyn timbre belied her supposed Gypsy origins. For an extra fifty cents, the Canarsie seeress had offered to tell Hope her lucky numbers.

She had seen this sort of person for years, and had had her fortune told by means of astrology (by the stars), cartomancy (by the cards), chiromancy (by the lines of her palm), and tasseography (by tea leaves). The many varieties of divination, Hope thought, were many times more fascinating than the nonsense rattled off by the supposedly enlightened readers. But she drew the line at entrails—no hepatoscopy for her. Professional interest only carried one so far.

Uncle Erasmus often joked that the pair of them should set up as mediums. They would, he insisted, be the best damn operators in the entire racket. He insisted, with a hearty laugh, that they would out-fox the Fox sisters.

A pair of society matrons emerged from a room off the hallway, one silent and the other giggling like a schoolgirl. They were escorted down the hall by the waiting footman, who saw them out and then brought Hope's card in to Madame. A moment later he reappeared and guided her into the bright morning room, quietly announcing, "Mrs. James Westlock of Manhattan."

The medium dismissed him with a curt nod and the two women regarded one another a little coolly. Madame was a formidable beauty, Hope noted, elegantly but simply dressed in a crisp white shirtwaist and dark mannish necktie. Something like recognition flashed across her fine features before she greeted Hope with perhaps a note of caution in her low voice.

"Very pleased to meet you, Madame," Hope replied. "I have heard so much about you."

"I must ask you not to speak—to say nothing. I beg your pardon for my abruptness, but I do not wish your words to cloud my intuition. If you will come over here, please."

She brought Hope over to a pair of comfortable chairs by a small octagonal table near the French doors leading out to the rose garden. Upon the table was a pale scented candle, a brass bowl, a few slips of creamy writing paper, a pen and an inkbottle. She took a seat, smoothing the lines of her long skirt and motioning Hope to take the other chair opposite.

"If you will take one slip of paper, you may write down three questions you wish to have answered, matters on which you seek advice, or a point about which the future is in doubt. Fold the slip once each way to ensure that I could not possibly see what you have written."

Madame turned her head away as Hope wrote her three questions. The first was, "*Does my husband truly love me?*" Her second question, written below the first, was "*Will we finally go to Europe this winter?"* For her third query, she wrote, slyly, *"Will my uncle be successful in his endeavor?"*

She folded the slip as she had been instructed, noting with the experience born of long practice that the slips folded down to a perfect size for palming and dexterous switching. So far, she has seen all of this before, many times.

Madame took the folded slip and held it in her hands, fingers laced tight. After a moment of concentration, she handed it back to Hope with the request that she burn the little piece of paper in the candle flame and toss it in the brass bowl. The two women were silent as they watched the paper curl and blacken and be consumed.

"Your first query involves another person, I believe a man, and you seem to have some doubt in your mind..." Madame began after another moment of concentration. "Yes, if I am not very much mistaken--"

She was interrupted by a knock at the door. Reverend Barrows entered, smiling apologetically for the intrusion. He crossed the room and handed his sister a folded sheet of paper.

"I would not have disturbed you, but this seems important, and would not wait," he said. "I knew you were anxious."

Madame read the paper over, wrote a few words toward the bottom, folded it back up and returned it to her brother, quietly saying, "We will speak more later, I am with a sitter now. Thank you, John."

"Of course. I apologize for disturbing you." Reverend Barrows said, bowing respectfully as he withdrew.

"A small personal matter," Madame waved a dismissive hand. "We will not be disturbed again, Mrs. Westlock. To return to your questions. Yes, I see some doubt clouding your mind... regarding... regarding... I cannot quite make it out. I think, however, that your doubts are unfounded. I see great love and happiness surrounding you; I even see joy. I can only urge you to put your mind at ease about this matter. May I ask what the matter is?" Madame asked in a confidential tone.

"My husband," Hope replied.

"You cannot possibly doubt his love for you," Madame said reassuringly, giving her hand a little sisterly pat. "While he may seem occupied elsewhere, perhaps absorbed in his work, you are never far from his thoughts. I can se that quite clearly. You have nothing to fear in that direction."

"Thank you," Hope said, trying to seem a little nervous and uncertain how Madame could know this.

"There are still two more questions," Madame went on. "One of them regards future plans, plans perhaps postponed or deferred from an earlier date. I have the impression of travel, or traveling. There is some question of whether this will or will not come to pass..." She smiled a little, and her eyes seemed to focus on something that was not there. "I almost think... yes, I hear French. I want to gather my coat around me; I'm so cold. We are in Paris, in wintertime. And I hear Italian and now the sun is warm upon my face and my hair...." Madame blinked hard a couple of times, seeming to snap herself out of a light trance. "I feel that you will finally get to Europe this winter. I saw you on the banks of the Seine, and in the shadow of the Colosseum. I saw someone else there with you—not your husband but a friend of yours, a woman. I believe I heard you call her Adrienne. Who is this, please?"

"Adrienne is a friend from school..."

"She lives now in Europe with her husband Paul. And their son. In Rouen?"

"Reims."

"I see. You have been hoping to make this trip to see her for some time?"

"Yes, but my husband's business..."

"The law takes up so much time."

"How did you know that?"

"It is my gift," Madame replied simply. "But you have one more question."

"Yes..."

Madame's face darkened as she meditated upon Hope's third query.

"This question regards someone close to you..." she began. "There is a plan or endeavor an older man is about to undertake... I see great difficulties ahead for him... a very sore trial, indeed. The outcome is... unforeseeable—I am afraid I can see nothing." She winced as from an unseen jab. "No, what little I can see is quite impenetrable and gloomy. This man must be very careful in what he is about to do. He may find that he is not equal to the task he has set for himself. He may be overwhelmed." She shook her head sharply. "I am sorry do be so dismal, but the outlook in this matter is not favorable."

"Well, I thank you for your insight, Madame; it has proved most interesting," Hope said, gathering up her things and going to the door. When her hand was on the cut glass doorknob, Madame caught her by the elbow.

"You must tell your uncle to be very, very cautious in what he does," she said a little harshly. "I think that perhaps he does not fully comprehend what he may be up against."

"She said *what*?" Professor von Hellmann demanded, almost choking with laughter.

"I've already told you. Twice," Hope replied.

"Flapdoodle," her uncle chortled. "Tell me again how you think she accomplished all this."

"Simple. The paper I wrote on was folded down small enough to be switched with ease. When I gave it to her to hold for a moment, to sense the vibrations or whatever she wants to call it, she switched it for a blank dummy slip, handing that blank back to me. The blank was burned while she opened and read my slip in her lap."

"And the brother interrupted you."

"He brought her a note, which she read over, folded up and gave back to him. No doubt my slip was surreptitiously placed into that note, which was then removed from the room. There was no evidence left to discover, and Madame was clean."

"And written in that note he brought to her?" von Hellmann asked, with the air of a teacher addressing a favorite student.

"Was written a few pieces of information gleaned from a letter in my duster, which was left on a hook in the hall where Reverend Barrows would have easy access to it. The letter, as we discussed, was addressed to my fictional school friend Adrienne, telling her I hoped to finally make it to Europe this winter, and I looked forward to seeing her and her husband Paul and their boy."

"A very smooth system they have."

"It has the added bonus of making her look very busy and in demand—even in the middle of a reading, she must stop to finish up other business."

"Excellent," von Hellmann declared. "Very excellent indeed."

"Of course you've proved nothing, really," Jack Westlock put in. "You think you've followed what she did—and you very likely have—but can you prove it? No. And does her cheating at these readings mean that she cannot contact the spirits? Also, no."

"Ah, counselor, *advocatus diaboli*," von Hellmann smiled. "The classic medium's defense; one kind of cheating does not imply another kind. Still, how else could she have come by the contents—the fictional contents, remember—of a letter in Hope's coat in the hall?"

"By her psychical powers, of course."

"So she uses her psychical powers to cheat? By reading my letter psychically?" Hope asked.

"I have seen far more ridiculous defenses raised in my courtroom. You can't prove otherwise."

"Your point is well-taken, of course, but I only sought to sound out the enemy, to see what we could see. Hope has done wonderfully, of course, and Madame Priestley's arsenal is stocked with nothing more than tricks I showed your wife when I was bouncing her on one knee."

"But she has a way about her," Hope said. "A weird piercing gaze. When she told me you should be careful… " She flustered a bit. "I was really struck by that. She can be frightening, Uncle."

"Spooked you, did she?"

"A little."

"Isn't it unusual for a reader to give a client such a grim prediction?" Jack asked. "I thought the usual modus operandi was to always predict better times ahead, to keep them happy so they would return with more money and a dozen friends."

"It usually is," von Hellmann replied. "But clearly, Madame is playing a different game, and taking the opportunity to give me a warning. But don't worry, my dear, we'll soon put her out of business." He patted her shoulder. "I have been speaking with Professor Townsend, who has been speaking to the man who runs the theater at the Casino."

Hope brightened. "A show?"

"A show. Two weeks' engagement, starting next Friday. Which reminds me—Edward?"

He was never far. "Yes, sir?" he asked tiredly.

"Here's a list of apparatus and equipment I need you to fetch from the city. You'll leave tomorrow."

"Yes, sir."

"Now," the old magician said, rubbing his thin hands together excitedly, "when Edward returns, we'll need a few afternoons for rehearsals and then we'll be ready. I'd like to do our old second-sight routine, if you feel quite up to it, Hope."

"Certainly."

"Splendid. A few card and coin manipulations, a couple of illusions, second sight, and then for the finale spiritualistic mysteries revealed—Fake Mediums Exposed!"

His laughter echoed down the long hallway of the Ocean House.

Chapter X

MR. MORRISON'S FIRST WEEK as underbutler at Blithewood House was spent in learning his office. He arose at six in the morning and saw to it that the other domestics were awake and at their duties. He made sure that the breakfasts were prepared correctly, the day's schedule planned, and the newspapers ironed. The rest of the day was spent in running errands, having others run errands, and making sure that those errands were run properly. He dealt with the gardener, the tailor, and the launderer. He announced guests, waited table, and served tea, and ensured that Colonel Hornbeck and his unusual guests wanted for nothing.

His second week was spent in becoming better-acquainted with his fellow servants. First was Henry, he head butler, quiet and efficient. Then there was Henri, the French cook and his assistant, Louis, who were practically indistinguishable though not related; and there was Alice, the housemaid whose days were spent in endlessly polishing the family silver and gossiping. Edgar, the footman, wrote poetry and Fred, the valet, drank. These two were carrying on very quiet affairs with Brigit and Eileen, the pert parlormaids.

On his day off, Mr. Morrison went swimming at the Butler's Beach and rubbed his sore feet, his aching back, and his dry hands. Being underbutler was not easy.

He also spent his second week watching, listening, and quietly probing.

"Things are running so much better in this house now," Alice would say, working away at the silver with large box of Putz's

Pomade Metal Polish nearby. "Henry was so pleased to find a British man such as yourself to take the position—he'll tell you Colonel Hornbeck wanted an Englishman but don't you believe him. Henry said to me one day, 'the Colonel's gone and dismissed Arthur and Sadie, now where am I going to find another English servant like Arthur?' And now here you are. He hasn't found another to take Sadie's place, but we don't need that vacancy filled, now do we?"

"Arthur and Sadie?"

"Yes, Arthur Lake, the old underbutler, and Sadie Frost, Mrs. Hornbeck's lady's maid." She stopped polishing just long enough to sigh with her whole body. "They were dismissed—*sacked*, as he said. Just a few days after Mrs. Hornbeck died."

"And why were they given the sack?"

"Nobody knows for certain—the Colonel didn't seem too happy about it at all. Sadie and Arthur were *together*, if you follow me. And some houses here won't allow that kind of thing among the domestics at all. But Colonel Hornbeck never seemed to care, or even notice, really."

"I see. Perhaps the Colonel suddenly reversed his position on… entanglements among the domestics?"

"But why now? It's so strange. But there's enough around here that's strange, let me tell you. What do you think of our guests?" she asked, moving on to what seemed to be a matter of greater interest to her. "Unusual family, aren't they?"

"Yes. Quite."

"She impresses me—she's so clever, so deep. I don't know."

Alice shook her head, reaching for another big box of Putz's.

Morrison went to patrol the upstairs. He went down the long hallway, paneled in black walnut, and the broad oak floorboards creaked under his tired feet. The upstairs was quiet; the servants had come and gone, Colonel Hornbeck was off on his afternoon constitutional along the Cliff Walk, and Madame Priestley was in the morning room giving her readings. Morrison remembered with a smile that her sitter that morning was Detective Richards. He had not seen Reverend Barrows all day.

He opened the door to the guest suite and glanced around quickly, making sure that the maids had done their job. He had to at least pretend he was an underbutler, even though his job was something else altogether.

Morrison was almost disappointed that no séances had been held since he arrived in the house. He didn't know if he believed in spiritualistic claims or not—he wasn't even sure he cared. For the moment, it simply wasn't his concern. He thought of himself as a practical man. He had an assignment in front of him and he applied his energies to that. Let the scientists and the philosophers argue things out; he couldn't waste time.

He was quietly frustrated in that assignment; after over two weeks he had nothing to show for it. He had managed to go over Madame's room here at Blithewood House, and that of her brother, and again found nothing. Either there was nothing to be found, or it was well hidden. It irritated Morrison's professional pride. Still, Blithewood House was never quite empty, never quite at rest. Give him an hour in an empty house, Morrison thought, and he'd have this assignment finished and be on a steamer back to London. But the constant buzz of activity kept him and the other domestics occupied, and usually someone or other was in his way; a mopping maid could shut off an entire hallway to him. But he waited patiently, knowing that he would have his chance to finish this thing properly.

And he found he was at least mildly curious about the séance business, if only in a detached way. With so many people carrying on, there must be something in it all. Perhaps he would see a séance before he was finished here; it certainly seemed that it would be entertaining, if nothing else. But, for now, Reverend Barrows claimed that his sister was still recovering from what he always called "that evil night at the hotel." The spiritualist herself seemed healthy enough, however, swirling about the house in those fetching French gowns.

Someone came up the steps at the far end of the corridor, and the sound of tuneless humming told Morrison it was Eileen, the maid, even before she rounded the corner. Eileen, nervous and freckle-faced, had emigrated from her native Dublin two years before. Irish maids were so common that she had become one of the familiar figures of the day, along with the English butler and the French cook, eventually taking her place among the stock characters in vaudeville and melodrama. Eileen was only one of thousands of young girls who made the trip and entered service in America. She startled when she saw the tall Morrison there in the hall.

"Good Lord, Mr. Morrison, you nearly scared me half to death! You're always so quiet."

"A quality to be encouraged in an underbutler," he replied.

"I was just comin' up to give The Room a good dustin'," she said. Morrison could hear the emphasis she placed on those two words, The Room. She meant Mrs. Hornbeck's bedroom and boudoir, which Colonel Hornbeck had occupied for the last week, since she herself had seen the ghost.

"It's so strange to have a man in here, it's such a woman's room, so," Eileen said, moving past Morrison and into The Room. "But it's a strange house to be in just now, isn't it?"

"I couldn't really say, I'm still only just getting settled."

"Ah, politeness is another thing to be encouraged in an underbutler, now, isn't it?" Eileen asked, attacking the pale woodwork of The Room with a huge feather-duster. "But I'm glad you're here with me—don't quite feel comfortable here alone, so if you'd just stay here with me till I'm done, that'd be kind."

"Of course. Might I ask what you saw in here?"

Eileen paused and slowly sat down on the edge of the bed, knuckles going white as she clutched the handle of the feather duster. The white curtains fluttered in the breeze from the open window, and the scent of roses was carried in from the garden.

"I come in here late one afternoon, to light a lamp for the picture there; the sun was going down," she motioned toward the large portrait of Mrs. Hornbeck that the Colonel had ordered moved into The Room probably some days before. It was a large gilt-framed portrait of Blithewood House's mistress, hung in heavy black crepe. Amelia Hornbeck stared out from the canvas with a stern, unblinking stare; her eyes had that disconcerting trick of following the viewer around the room.

"My mother always said to leave a lamp burnin' next to a dead picture. So I lights the lamp and then I nearly dropped it—there she was, just for a moment, just a flicker, right there behind the picture, lookin' right at me." She stared at the empty corner and then turned away and crossed herself. "I went right to Henry and told him what I saw, but I don't think he believed me."

"He evidently believed you enough to tell the Colonel, who has moved into the room to catch a similar glimpse, correct?"

"Even so."

"You saw what you saw, and I wouldn't worry too much about Henry."

"You're a nice man, aren't you, Mr. Morrison? Well." Eileen rose from the corner of the bed and smoothed down the covers. "I suppose I need to finish the dustin' here—if you wouldn't mind waitin' just a few more minutes for me?"

"Not at all."

"Sure, you're a nice man for certain, Mr. Morrison."

Four o'clock found Morrison back downstairs. Madame Priestley would be finished with her sitters for the afternoon, and Colonel Hornbeck would be back from his afternoon walk. Morrison moved quietly through the room, to see if there was anything to do, and, more importantly, to overhear; he found them comfortably sipping lemonade in the drawing room. He stood just outside the open door.

"I was at the Casino earlier," the Colonel was saying. "Manning, an old broker friend of mine, has an option on some railroad stock and he's offered me the chance to go in with him."

"Is there money to be made?"

"Possibly quite a bit—possibly. Railroad speculation can be either profitable or costly. Another old friend lost quite a bundle that way. Daniel Drew used to print up worthless stock certificates, of course, so I suppose you never do know."

"So are you going to invest?"

"I don't know. I was thinking that perhaps—perhaps you could... see something? I'm sure you know nothing about stocks, women simply don't have the head for it, but I thought you might have other ways of knowing."

"I see."

"I've been reading quite a bit lately," he continued clumsily, almost embarrassed, "and it seems that there are a few mediums who give uncannily accurate business advice. Take those two women Vanderbilt had working for him—what were their names?"

"Victoria Woodhull and her sister, Tennessee Claflin," Madame replied softly.

"The Bewitching Brokers," Hornbeck said.

The aging Commodore Cornelius Vanderbilt had fallen under the spell of these two sisters some twenty years before, setting them up in a Wall Street brokerage house while attending séances and magnetic healing sessions with Tennessee, and later bankrolling Victoria's unsuccessful Presidential bid. There was some controversy as to whether the brokerage's success came from the sisters' professed clairvoyance, or the Commodore's insider's advice. They lived in England now, having left the country after a fierce legal battle with the Commodore's children, who insisted that the unfavorable (to them) terms of their father's will had been unduly influenced by the two Bewitching Brokers.

Madame hushed the Colonel and settled back into her chair, closing her eyes and breathing deeply. After a moment's meditation, she shook her head.

"As you say, women have no head for stocks, but I should be inclined to advise against it. It does not feel safe to me, somehow. You could invest a small sum, if you feel you could absorb such a risk. But without meaning to cast aspersions on your friend Mr. Manning, I think it does not feel safe, for now."

"Thank you, Madame."

"I'm beginning to worry about the effect that woman is having on your father," Sarah Newland was telling young James and Rachel when Morrison found them an hour later on the wide verandah. "I do not like having her in this house—in Amelia's house—and I do not like her whispering in his ear."

"He mentioned to me that he declined to buy some stock based on her advice just now," Rachel said. "Father's never kept any counsel but his own, especially in his business."

"I think it would be far worse if she urged him to accept a disastrous proposition," young James replied. "Women don't have a head for business, but I trust Father's judgment."

"It isn't Father's judgment, it's hers. I agree with Aunt Sarah, he listens to her a little too much. And have you seen the books he's been reading since she came to stay here?"

In the past two weeks, the Colonel's desk had been piled high with thick books with ponderous titles. Things like Alfred Russell Wallace's *On Miracles and Modern Spiritualism*, and *The Scientific Aspect of the Supernatural*, written by the man who collaborated with Charles Darwin on the evolution theory and now wrote that spiritualistic phenomena "are proved quite as well as any facts are proved in other sciences." The Colonel was halfway through *Lights and Shadows of Spiritualism* by the famous medium Daniel Dunglas Home, who not only levitated but had an accordion which was played upon by unseen spirit fingers. Also on the desk were Mrs. Home's books about her now-deceased husband, *D. D. Home: His Life and Mission* and *The Gift of D. D. Home*. Next on the reading list were books by Blavatsky and another by A. Leah Fox

Fish Brown Underhill, the eldest Fox Sister, entitled *The Missing Link in Modern Spiritualism.*

"She's poisoning his mind," Sarah Newland said.

"She is helping Father through a very difficult time," Rachel replied. "I may not quite approve of her methods, but I positively shudder to think what Father would be going through without her."

"Do you really think she's in touch with Mother?" young James asked, trying his best to make the question nonchalant.

"I don't know."

"We are warned not to seek out those with a familiar spirit— such things are not to be trifled with," Sarah said with a quiet vehemence. "I think if she is in touch with Amelia, she shouldn't be. It's too dangerous."

"I don't know if I believe in half of what these spiritualists say," young James said, almost to himself. "But I suppose I don't have to, now do I?"

"It's Father's decision."

"And if Madame Priestley can keep him from suffering, then she has my sincerest thanks," Rachel said.

"But he must be careful," Sarah said.

Morrison went back inside.

Chapter XI

NEWPORT WAS PLASTERED with von Hellmann's posters seemingly overnight. He employed a small army of otherwise-unemployed bootblacks, newsies, and shackers from the Casino to cover every available surface with his advertising. Anywhere a summer colonist turned there was a huge four-color portrait of the magician staring back from under the bold announcement, *Von Hellmann Returns!*

This caused quite a bit of talk, excitement, and speculation. It was observed—in the Reading Room and at the Casino, along the bar at the White Horse Tavern and even in the cool parlors of the marble cottages of Bellevue Avenue—that nothing had been heard of von Hellmann for quite a few years. After a lengthy world tour, in which he had garnered much publicity by challenging and exposing fraudulent spirit mediums at each stop on his itinerary, he had settled into a quiet retirement. And now, after years of silence, he had suddenly reappeared at the same time that Madame Priestley had chosen to summer at Newport.

The posters proclaimed:

> *Von Hellmann's Wonders!*
> *Marvelous Prestidigitation!*
> *Baffling Illusions!*
> *Von Hellmann's World-Famous Automata!*
> *With the Uncanny Esperanza Von Hellmann!"*

The last line, in a bold red, was *"Fake Mediums Exposed!"*

The box-office couldn't sell tickets fast enough.

The Casino theater was small and almost intimate, in a time and place that most millionaires had drawing rooms twice its size. The five hundred seats were removed for the twice-weekly balls or "hops." The high ceiling was painted sky-blue and scattered with gold stars, and the rest of the room was all ivory, trimmed with gold that glinted under the lights. The Opera House, Newport's other grand theater, while much larger and catering to a broader audience, couldn't compete with the draw of von Hellmann's return.

The Professor began his show with his usual flair, swaggering boldly from the wings in immaculate evening clothes, white hair tied back by a long silken ribbon. He tossed his white gloves into the air and they became doves, which flew to the corners of the theater, only to return to their beckoning master and be placed in a large gilded cage. Throwing a velvet cloth over them, birds and cage vanished to the delighted applause of the audience.

He conjured with cards, coins, and borrowed handkerchiefs. A beautifully made but bare orange tree, delicately made from copper and tin, blossomed and bore real fruit on his stage. Plucking a fat orange from among its filigreed branches and paper leaves, von Hellmann carefully peeled it to discover a playing card which had been selected and signed by a gentleman a moment before. He performed a miser's dream, reaching out into thin air to find silver dollars at his fingertips. These were tossed into a champagne bucket, which, by the time he concluded the piece, was filled to overflowing.

The beautiful Esperanza, garbed in a turban and curly-toed slippers like a dreamy princess from the *Arabian Nights*, reclined on an opium bed in the center of the stage. Her uncle stood over her, making sweeping mesmeric passes. When she seemed to have fallen deep into trance, she began to slowly lift from the couch, floating higher and higher until she levitated over her uncle's head. He allowed her to remain there for a few moments before she descended and rested once again on the low bed. A few more mesmeric passes and she blinked awake, with the half-bewildered expression of the dreamer waking to moonlight.

Von Hellmann's three famous automata were brought forth. Mechanical men had held the public's fascination since Baron Wolfgang von Kempelen introduced his famous chess-playing clockwork Turk in 1769. The Turk was eventually sold to Johann Nepomuk Maelzel, who was perhaps better known for patenting the metronome. Both Napoleon Bonaparte and Edgar Allan Poe saw the Turk and were mystified by it. That famous automaton's descendants were now being exhibited by von Hellmann's old friend, John Nevil Maskelyne, royal illusionist and anti-spiritualist, onstage at Egyptian Hall, England's home of mystery.

Von Hellmann's automata were all female, with porcelain china-doll faces and delicate golden curls of spun silk. Psyche sat cross-legged upon a pillar of glass, tapping her rigid finger on one of the playing cards ribbon-spread before her. When it was turned over and discovered to be the card named by a volunteer a moment before, Psyche winked mischievously. Euterpe, Psyche's sister, stood behind a toy xylophone and played any tune the audience called for. And Mnemosyne, in a tall pointed cap and wizard's cape, opened a heavy book, gestured for von Hellmann to turn a few pages, and located the line of poetry previously selected.

To close the first half of his show, von Hellmann went down to his audience and borrowed a tall top hat from a portly, elderly gentleman seated on the aisle. In the dark of the theater, he almost didn't notice the mourning band blending into the flawless black of the man's evening clothes.

Bringing the topper back to the stage, the magician showed it to be empty and set it down on his bare little table, smiling. He shot back his cuffs and reached into the hat, withdrawing a huge bouquet of roses, and then another, and then another. Again, the hat was shown to be empty before yards of paper streamers, red, white and blue, were produced, along with dozens of India rubber balls (which were briefly juggled) and a long string of lighted Japanese paper lanterns.

The hat was upended and shaken once, twice, thrice, when a very solid cannon ball tumbled from it and hit the stage with a resounding *thud*.

And finally the hat was shown empty one last time before von Hellmann pulled a fat white rabbit from it.

Grinning like Satan himself, von Hellmann returned the borrowed hat to its owner. Colonel Hornbeck, inspecting his silk topper, was impressed but not amused. He had bought the hat not a month before, for Amelia's funeral.

The applause was deafening.

The curtain went up on the second half of the show, revealing von Hellmann standing center stage, hands modestly folded.

"It has been said that the belief in materialization of spirits, and the visits of spiritual inhabitants of another world, back to the scene of their mortal sojourn for the sole purpose of leaving specimens of their calligraphy on slates and ceilings, rapping and playing upon tambourines, accordions, guitars, and so forth, affords yet another proof that there are no bounds to human credulity.

"And who am I to argue with such wisdom?"

"In the spring of 1850, when I was still a young man," he continued with a smile, "I went to a fashionable hotel in New York City to sit with Katherine and Margaretta Fox, who had arrived from their village upstate, near Rochester, a short time previously. The Misses Fox had been brought to New York by none other than Horace Greeley to give séances for the public. I went every day for two weeks, hearing the famous spirit raps sound from nowhere, answering questions asked by the sitters. They even replied to queries that I myself posed—and they answered them incorrectly, I must add. I was finally forcibly ejected as being a disruptive influence.

"The next time I saw the Fox sisters was only five years ago— in October of 1888. I went to the New York Academy of Music in Brooklyn to hear Margaretta Fox's confession. Again I heard the famous Rochester Raps respond to questions, but this time a more mundane explanation was on offer. A packed house was told that these mysterious communiqués from the spirit realm, these unearthly raps which had brought so many to the séance chamber and founded a new religion, were produced by Katie and Maggie cracking the joints of their toes.

"That night, five years ago, Margaretta Fox said, 'I am going to expose Spiritualism from its very foundation. I have had the idea in my head for many a year now but I have never come to a determination before. I have thought of it day and night. I loathe the thing that I have been. I used to say to those who wanted me to give a séance—you are driving me into Hell.'"

"And who am I to argue with the mother of modern Spiritualism?

"From that day in the spring of 1850 to this very day in the summer of 1893 I have seen nothing—nothing!—that would convince me Spiritualism is anything other than what Margaretta Fox declared it to be that night five years ago: fraud of the worst description!"

A voice sounded in the darkened theater. *"And what about Madame Priestley?"*

That was Jack Westlock, seated in the back row, right on cue. With a smile, von Hellmann thought briefly that perhaps he had been wrong about his dear niece's choice of husband. Perhaps.

"I have not had the honor and pleasure of making the lady's acquaintance," von Hellmann replied suavely. "And while I do look forward to that day, I do not expect to revise my opinion after that occasion. I trust that she and her miracles are as false as any of her dubious brethren and their tricks. And let me say here tonight that I invite that good lady to prove me wrong. And I do hope she will not be so discourteous as to decline such an excellent invitation, extended as it is with such sincerity."

So began the second act—*Spiritualistic Mysteries Exposed!*

While he had been speaking, a number of von Hellmann's assistants—"floorwalkers," in the parlance—had passed writing tablets and envelopes among the audience. Each person dutifully wrote down a question to be answered, a thought to be divined, or an item of trivia no one else knew. This was a familiar routine, as famous as it was mysterious and inexplicable. The sealed envelopes were collected in big wicker baskets by the floorwalkers and then carried onstage.

The Uncanny Esperanza sat center stage, small hands folded neatly and calmly in her lap, and with the spotlight focused tightly upon her. She wore a long, flowing white gown, gathered at the waist, with her long dark hair loose. She was blindfolded by a sash of black velvet. Dipping her hand into the basket placed in her lap, she selected an envelope, and with a slight smile held it at her fingertips, high above her head.

"This is a question, which has been written by a woman with the initials J. B.," she began slowly, voice not much above a whisper. The audience was perfectly silent. "She has on her mind some question concerning both herself and another—her daughter. The query is regarding her daughter's future happiness. I feel that this is a good woman, with the best of intentions and the greatest of affection for her daughter. The question is about her daughter's marriage to a doctor. I feel that they will be married soon, and I wish them all the happiness in the world."

This was the classic question-and-answer act, popularized by vaudeville mind-reader Anna Eva Fay. "There is no living person who has created such a furor in the Spiritualistic world," magician and author H. J. Burlingame had written just two years before. While working at the astonishing rate of answering three questions every minute, Fay made no claims and issued no denials. She left it to her audience to puzzle out for themselves whether they were witnessing a clever deception or a demonstration of some genuine occult power.

Standing in the shadowy wings, von Hellmann nodded approvingly. He had taught Hope this routine years ago—long before her marriage—and the Uncanny Esperanza had picked it up quickly. Within a couple of months she was as smooth and skillful an operator as Fay herself.

"This question has been signed with the initials M. M. The writer has on his mind a question regarding certain property he is desirous of finding or obtaining. I feel that the discovery of this property is at hand, sir, and you need not wait much longer. I may add, however, that it may not be quite where you think it is, which is perhaps why its discovery has not been made heretofore.

"This next query is from a lady, asking if her husband *knows*. She does not supply any more information than that. She simply asks '*Does my husband know?*' And I can only reply to her: no, he does not... but he certainly *suspects*."

Yes, von Hellmann thought in the shadows, Hope was good—twice as good as that Priestley virago could ever hope to be.

"My friends," Professor von Hellmann said, taking the stage once again, "my niece and I have come to offer a few demonstrations which seem to be mystifying or even supernatural, but we both wish you to remember this—that we are not Spiritualists, mediums, sorcerers, or necromancers; we are not soothsayers, witches, warlocks, clairvoyants, or diabolists. We hope to show that what many have claimed to be the work of otherworldly agencies can be achieved by dint of hard work and long practice; no recourse to spirits is required."

From a side-table, he picked up a large papier-mâché skull, all brown and discolored with extreme age. He placed the skull on a sheet of glass resting on the backs of two chairs.

"My friends, I give you the Skull of Kalustro."

There was a heavy, expectant silence.

"The Skull of Kalustro acts as what might be termed a spirit telegraph, allowing those who have shuffled off this mortal coil an opportunity to reach out to those they have left behind."

After a moment's silence, von Hellmann turned to the skull and asked, "Are there spirits here, tonight?"

Kalustro's jaws clicked together loudly. Von Hellmann heard the sound echo back to him onstage.

"Many spirits?"

The skull chattered its teeth, made of inlaid glass.

The audience chuckled nervously.

"The spirits will, perhaps, prove their existence tonight?"

The jaws clicked almost peevishly.

"The spirits will be so good as to favor us with a message?"

The Skull of Kalustro skittered a few inches across the glass with the force of its madly chattering jaws.

The curtains went up behind him, revealing a small drawing-room set, and von Hellmann placed the Skull of Kalustro on a shelf of the bookcase there, where it joined such unusual items as a stuffed owl and a wavy-bladed dagger. A small round table and a pair of chairs completed the modest set.

A lady in a Worth gown and diamonds was invited up onstage and von Hellmann seated her at the table, taking his place opposite.

"Welcome to my parlor," the magician said with an evil smile. "Here you will experience the unknown… I am sure. I would like you to satisfy yourself that these are nothing more than children's school slates."

As a body, the audience shifted excitedly, sitting up a little straighter in their seats. By now, all of Newport had heard of, and many had seen, Madame Priestley's mysterious spirit slate writing. It seemed beyond all explanation—but that was before von Hellmann's arrival.

She examined the slates carefully, even dusting them with a cloth, before they were put together and placed on the table with the usual chalk between. Von Hellmann took a small school bell from the bookcase and placed it on the floor, under the table.

"Now dear lady, there are a few things I must ask you to do. The first is to control my feet by placing your own upon them. Do not let me remove my feet from under yours at any time. The rest of the audience is depending upon you. Your second task is to similarly control my hands." He placed his hands on the tabletop, motioning her to place hers firmly atop his. "Now, as we cannot plunge the entire theater into darkness, we must at least plunge you into darkness... and so I will ask the Uncanny Esperanza to blindfold you. Esperanza ?"

The Uncanny Esperanza appeared from the wings, bringing with her a long scarf of velvet. She gently tied this around the woman's head, who accepted her plight with good humor. Esperanza withdrew once this was complete.

"Now my dear lady, you have no doubt heard of the many wonderful manifestations of spirit power which are to be witnessed in the séance chamber, have you not? Ah, good. I am told that that often, the first manifestations are... of an auditory nature."

The blindfolded lady startled in her chair when she heard the bell beneath the table begin to ring.

Unseen by the sitter, von Hellmann had slipped his right foot from its shoe. The shoes were specially constructed for him, with elastic sides and a reinforced toe; the woman with her foot atop von Hellmann's never felt a thing. A small titter of laughter ran through the audience as they saw the toe of his sock had been cut away, allowing him to take the wooden handle of the school bell between his toes and give it a vigorous shake. The little bell rang loudly in the theater.

"And then, once the spirits have announced their presence, manifestations of a much more physical nature begin to take place."

Bringing his knee to the underside of the table, he lifted the table a few inches before letting it fall again. He paused for a moment before lifting it higher and higher.

"Spirits, begone!' he cried in his sonorous voice. "I bid thee leave this place, and trouble this company no more!"

The table slammed to the floor, wobbled on its legs, and finally settled. The lady was breathless. Von Hellmann slipped his foot back into its shoe.

"Good lady, I thank you for taking part in this small séance. If what you have experienced here seems real, think that perhaps you have simply slumbered here a while, and now wake from a strange dream. My thanks to you. But before you go...." He gestured toward the slates.

The lady reached gingerly for them, slowly lifting the top slate. Written boldly across the black surfaces was "*Beware Those with Familiar Spirits.*"

"My dear friends," von Hellmann said, walking his charming volunteer back to her seat, "it has been my distinct pleasure to amuse you with a few trifles which are so often presented as miracles of an almost religious nature. I have demonstrated how a few of these are accomplished, and I have brought about by trickery and strategy still other effects. When next you find yourself confronted with someone insisting that their occult abilities are real, I pray you remember our little excursions tonight, where you saw so much accomplished by thoroughly natural means. The dead do not return, it pains me to say; but it pains me more—it outrages me!—that so many purloin the methods of my profession to convince the foolish otherwise.

"The twentieth century is fast approaching us. Shall we walk proudly in the light of knowledge and truth, or stumble blindly, shackled by ignorance and superstition? I hope you will all join me in the fight against those who would deceive us all, solely to achieve their own avaricious ends."

Chapter XII

"I WENT TO SEE VON HELLMANN'S SHOW last night,"
Colonel Hornbeck said to Professor Townsend the next day in the
Clubroom of the Casino. "Didn't you say he was a friend of yours?"

"Yes," Townsend smiled a little guiltily. "I was there last night
myself, but I missed you. What did you think?"

"The man's an ass! Coming to my club and insulting my
guests," Hornbeck sputtered. "He stands there on his damn stage
in a white tie and tails and declares every spirit medium in history
to be a fraud and a charlatan. And what does *he* know? Has he
ever sat with a good medium? And why should pulling a rabbit
out of a hat make him an expert on communicating with the
spirits? It's absurd."

"He has always maintained that his familiarity with all
manner of trickery and deception make him uniquely qualified
to detect a fraud's methods—set a thief to catch a thief, so to
speak. But of course he assumes at the outset that any medium
is a fraud…."

"Which is ludicrous—five minutes with a reputable medium
would make him a believer."

"He has had much more than five minutes with some very
reputable ones—several of whom convinced *me* of their powers."

"And?"

"And he remains unmoved. He has certainly done some good
work; he has a long string of worthy exposures to his credit. I must
admit, Colonel, that if it were not for his efforts there would be a

good many frauds still in operation. I know that there are good mediums out there, and the sooner we purge the ranks of the fakes the better for all of us."

"You can't say you approve of what this man does?" Hornbeck asked sharply.

"He and I are very different people; he once told me that every exposure sells tickets, and that's what he wants."

"But he must have damaged the reputations of countless honest men in the process; and he's every bit as avaricious as those he claims to combat, if that's his motive. You must have seen him brand as fraudulent mediums you knew to be genuinely gifted. Well, Professor?"

Townsend let out a long breath and glanced quickly around him. He leaned in a little closer to the Colonel and spoke in a low voice.

"Once, years ago, when we were both serving on the Wraeburn Committee for the Investigation of Psychical and Spiritualistic Claims, we had a series of sittings with a medium named Mrs. Greene. She was as gifted a medium as I have ever met. Mrs. Greene was the first to... to put me in touch with my boy." The Professor's voice caught slightly. "And I still believe her.

"During her séances, she would be bound to her chair—she insisted upon this—and then she would go into a trance. While in this trance, and with the lights extinguished, heavy objects a full six feet away from her were heard to move. Vases fell off the mantelpiece and shattered on the floor. Unlit candles on the table were tipped over. On one occasion, a gilt-framed oil painting dropped right off the wall.

"When the lights were turned back up, she was bound as securely as she had been at the beginning. We were all impressed— there seemed to be no evidence of wrongdoing on her part at all. The Committee was to give a one thousand dollars reward to any medium or psychic who could produce genuine phenomena under test conditions, and it looked as though she was going to be the one. Even von Hellmann was impressed, but he wouldn't talk to me about it—he wouldn't talk to anyone, really. He almost seemed angry that we finally had what the Committee had spent nearly three years looking for.

"He demanded one more séance—to double-check our findings and assure ourselves, he said. Reluctantly, the lady agreed. He insisted on searching her thoroughly himself, even though we had a pair of matrons on the Committee specifically to search female mediums and guarantee that they were sneaking nothing into the séance chamber. Von Hellmann said that it was not good enough for him, and he searched Mrs. Greene thoroughly. Need I say we were all scandalized and insulted, including the two matrons who had already searched Mrs. Greene and found nothing suspicious.

"He insisted upon extending his search to the séance room itself, and we allowed him to continue. Of course we were all shocked when, attached to the bottom of the medium's chair, von Hellmann produced a reaching rod."

"A reaching rod?" Hornbeck startled.

"It had a hook on one end and could be telescoped out to about six feet or so. Von Hellmann spent the next half hour lecturing us all on how we had always overlooked the chair and, if Mrs. Greene could get one hand free she could use the reaching-rod to manipulate almost anything within its reach. He demonstrated that, by leaning and stretching, she could reach an object nearly ten feet away."

"He planted that reaching-rod didn't he? She was going to get the award and he wouldn't allow it."

"I never saw anything—he reached under that chair and said, 'Oh, my—what's this?' and there it was in his hand. Of course nobody thought we would have to search him first. So when the Committee drew up its report, he would not sign it, and filed his own denouncement of Mrs. Greene. The money went unawarded."

"Damn the man. So he can't be trusted?"

"He can be," Townsend said a little uncertainly. "He behaved shamefully, disgracefully—I've never quite forgiven him for it. He went on to claim it as another of his brilliant exposures and ticket sales jumped again. But... I still believe very strongly that he's an honest man, fighting the good fight in his own peculiar way."

"Flapdoodle," said Colonel Hornbeck.

That evening around the long supper table at Blithewood House, the subject of von Hellmann's challenge was finally acknowledged after hanging heavily in the air throughout the meal.

"How was the theater last night, Father?" Rachel asked. In full mourning, she would not attend the theater for a year at the least.

"It was... entertaining," Hornbeck said, choosing his words with care. "That von Hellmann's a clever devil."

"A most apposite term," Reverend Barrows said. "Or perhaps chief inquisitor. I have been aware of him for years, of course, and a more foul-mouthed slanderer I have never seen. How many lives has he destroyed? There on that stage," he went on, pointing with his fork for emphasis, "is just the sort of narrow-minded atheist who ransacked our rooms at the hotel."

Ignoring her brother's outburst, Madame Priestley asked quietly, "What did Professor von Hellmann do last night? His advertising was so... striking."

"Oh, the usual stuff," Hornbeck replied with a dismissive wave of his hand. "Card tricks, Chinese rings and so forth. Nothing very interesting."

"And what about the 'Fake Mediums Exposed' act?" Reverend Barrows asked suspiciously.

"Oh, that—nothing, really," Hornbeck said a bit nervously. This was getting uncomfortable. "I certainly wasn't impressed. What he did was... clever, but not at all realistic. Any truly gifted medium," with a flattering nod to his guests, "would surely put his paltry little demonstrations to shame. Think about it; this fellow probably has a dozen hidden assistants backstage and a couple tons of mechanical equipment to aid him—to say nothing of confederates in the audience! No, the fellow's a clever trickster, nothing more. No one's likely to mistake him for a great medium."

"But he doesn't claim to be mediumistic. He's playing the usual trickster's game."

"Oh, who knows what game he's playing," Reverend Barrows said peevishly. Still…" he gave his sister a little sidelong glance. "He'd be an interesting sitter, wouldn't he, my dear? You've made so many other conquests in your career; how'd you like to be known as the medium who convinced von Hellmann?"

Her only answer was a polite smile.

"If I remember correctly, von Hellmann used to issue public challenges to mediums in whatever city he was in at the time. You have said you've felt your strength returning. If only we could get him to challenge you, my dear…."

"He already has," his sister replied softly.

"He *what*? Why didn't you say something sooner?" He was almost choking, and took a moment to compose himself. "I am very sorry, but my sister has quite taken me by surprise with this abrupt announcement. Helene, do you mean to say that he has actually challenged you?"

"From the stage last night," she nodded.

"But how did you know?"

"I knew," was the tart rejoinder.

"Well, this is something—quite an opportunity for you, my dear."

Again, Hornbeck noticed what troubled him most about Reverend Barrows. In his role as his sister's manager, he often came across too much like von Hellmann himself; too concerned with publicity, with the next opportunity, and with how she should be known. In his quiet way, he almost seemed like a showman exhibiting a curiosity. And Hornbeck found himself once again thinking that he had never before seen siblings so dissimilar.

"I should gladly invite von Hellmann into my house a skeptic, secure in the knowledge that he would leave a believer," Hornbeck said. "However, he does not seem, to me, to be completely trustworthy." As Mr. Morrison poured coffee, the Colonel quickly outlined what Professor Townsend had told him that afternoon.

"A worthy opponent," Reverend Barrows declared. "But I think the Colonel and I could keep him out of mischief while you changed his mind, my dear. I am sure your powers are sufficiently strong to overwhelm his more skeptical vibrations."

"Doubtless."

"Ha!" Hornbeck slapped the table. "It's settled, then. I'll have my new man make up the invitations. You can do that by tomorrow, can't you, Martin? Excellent. I think you'll agree. Madame, that there should be a few reliable witnesses on hand to see von Hellmann get his comeuppance? With your blessing, of course, Madame?"

The blessing was given and the invitations went out the next day.

Von Hellmann's cackle could be heard halfway down the hall at the Ocean House.

"Hope!" he cried. "Come look at this! Professor Erasmus von Hellmann is most cordially invited to attend a séance with Madame Helene Priestley acting as medium."

"That is too wonderful!" Hope grinned. "Oh, Uncle—I'm so happy!"

And so was he—this is what he had come to Newport for, after all. He could feel his heart pound, his pulse quicken. He rubbed his hands together and chuckled deeply.

I never should have given this up, he thought. There was no good reason to have. What have I done in the last seven years? he wondered. Nothing. I sat in my brownstone, writing my memoirs and getting fat. And my public almost forgot my name. More than almost. Living death.

But now! Standing in front of an audience once more, and now stalking a spirit medium to her lair. He felt young. Was he really nearly seventy? His voice had filled the theater and echoed back to him from the darkness. Seventy-year-old men do not sound like that, he assured himself. He never realized how he loved to bask in the applause, to command the stage, to revel in the stunned silence. Never realized it until he gave it up and then reclaimed it.

And now he had a spirit medium to expose, the kind of challenge he hadn't risen to in years. He came to show her up for the fraud she was, and by God he would do it.

In a strange way, he thought to himself, feeling young and alive again—I owe all this to her. He loved nothing so much as a good chase. Perhaps these spirit mediums really could bring back the dead.

His cackle echoed down the long hallway.

Chapter XIII

THE CLIFF WALK was a footpath beginning at Easton's Beach and winding its precipitous five-mile way down Newport's coast to Bailey's Beach. It had been popular with summer colonists for years, with some of the most fashionable and palatial cottages arranged along one side, with the Atlantic waves breaking against the jagged rocks on the other. This was where Colonel Hornbeck strolled arm-in-arm with Amelia on warm summer evenings, tipping his straw hat to other couples out for their own constitutionals.

During his first week on the Hornbeck staff, Morrison found the servants from the surrounding houses held dances along the Cliff Walk a couple of times a week. The usual place was the top of the Forty Steps, a flight of stairs reaching from the Cliff Walk down to the rocky shoreline. On Maids' Night Out, a half-dozen butlers, gardeners, and valets would turn up with fiddles, guitars, concertinas, and perhaps a bodhrán and a set of uilleann pipes; the dancing would go on long after sunset.

As Henry had mentioned during the interview, most of Newport's millionaires preferred European servants, and so most of the dancers were either Irish or English, with a few Italians, Germans, and Swedes thrown in for good measure. And of course there were some Americans whose families had been in service for years—since some ancestor's arrival at the turn of the century. Others, such as Henry himself, were the younger sons of well-off families, victims of primogeniture who were forced to earn their wages. Henry's elder brother was building a cottage along Bellevue, while the younger waited on the table at Blithewood.

Miss Broughton of Schenectady, a maid at Alva Vanderbilt's fabulous Marble House, limped with an advanced case of "housemaid's knee," which, she declared, would not prevent her from dancing with Mr. Morrison. Mr. Morrison always gently declined her hints, insisting that he did not wish to aggravate her condition. She would pat him affectionately on the arm and flutter, "Oh, that haccent, Mr. Morrison! That haccent!"

"We were just talkin' about your employer there, Morrison," Florence McMurphy said. McMurphy was a big redheaded Irishman who worked as a groom at a neighboring estate. Trying to look his best tonight and always hoping to turn a parlor maid's head, he was wearing the nicest of his employer's castoff suits, which were routinely handed down to favorite servants. It didn't quite fit, but nobody said anything to big Florence.

"And what were you saying?" Morrison asked, momentarily shrugging off Miss Broughton's attentions.

"Heard there's going to be a big séance in a few days. Heard he's inviting that magician."

"There will be a show," someone said.

"So Morrison—does your old man actually believe all that about spirits and messages from the dead?" McMurphy asked. "Sounds like nonsense if you ask me."

"And nobody did!" someone called.

"I heard he's gone half-crazy since his wife pegged out like that. I probably would too, come to think of it."

"Pegged out like what?" Morrison asked.

"Nobody's told you? Nah, I don't suppose they would. Out of respect, like," McMurphy said. "Seems she and the Colonel had an argument—a huge big fight, screamin' in each other's faces when *bang*! Down she goes. Apoplexy. Dead at his feet."

"And may I ask how you come to know all this?"

"Me friend Arty Lake saw the whole thing—him and his girl, Sadie. They was right there when it happened, and he sent them both packin' the next day. Didn't even give 'em a reason, but said he'd give 'em nothin' but the best reference."

"I'd sure as hell get rid of anyone who saw me shout my wife into her grave," said a footman.

"What was the fight over?'

"Ah, well, it seems that Mrs. Hornbeck had found out about a few of the Colonel's... indiscretions."

"You're joking!" cried Miss Broughton, perhaps a bit irked that Florence was occupying more of Mr. Morrison's attention than was she.

"No joke. Way I heard it, the Colonel was no stranger to the Peacock Room over at Blanche's." Blanche's was an extravagant house of ill-fame, known to all men of society. "And he didn't stop there, either—apparently he'd had it off a couple times with Sadie herself. It's a rare millionaire who doesn't help himself to a bit of parlor maid now and then around here, eh? This was a bit ago, before Arty, but I guess Mrs. Hornbeck was none too pleased. So when she goes on him, Hornbeck gets rid of Arty and Sadie both."

Affairs were an accepted, although hushed, fact of Newport summer life, but Amelia Hornbeck was well-known to be a strict moralist, even in the fact of such rapidly-changing mores.

"Anyways, you didn't answer me question—what do you think of the old man and his medium?"

"He seems very sincere in his beliefs, and of course he doesn't discuss it with me at all."

"And what do you make of her?" someone called. "Nice to look at, from what I've seen."

"I haven't made up my mind about her quite yet—I've had too much to do. Too much on my mind. But she certainly does seem mysterious."

"What was Eileen saying about finding a rose?"

Morrison nodded glumly and briefly related the story. Eileen had been saying that she found a rose on the big bed in Amelia Hornbeck's room shortly after the séance with von Hellmann was decided upon. Several in the house took this as a sign from Beyond, that the séance should go ahead. A few others, including Mr. Morrison, thought Eileen might be letting her imagination run riot. Again.

"I heard that her relationship with Hornbeck isn't entirely... *spiritual*," said Gaskell, a Cockney coachman.

"And I heard that her brother's not really her brother," said Riddell, a cook's assistant. "And am I the only one who heard she was an artist's model? In *Paris*?"

"Yeah, and I heard that the two of you were engaged to Consuelo Vanderbilt," big Florence McMurphy snapped. He'd never liked either Gaskell or Riddell. "So what do you think, Morrison? You think the conjuror's going to get the old girl?"

"I really can't say. It remains to be seen."

"Any vacancies on the staff there at Blithewood House?" Gaskell asked. "I'd give me right arm to see something like this."

"I'll be happy to oblige you anytime, you worthless English bastard, you," McMurphy said out of the corner of his mouth. "No offense to you, Mr. Morrison."

"Papist bogtrotter!" Gaskell retorted.

"Ah, go run some poor innocents off their farms like the rest of yer black-hearted race. Anyway, I still think this whole séance business is rubbish."

"Come on there, Florence—what about in the Bible? The Witch of Endor and all that," said Riddell. "She summoned up yer man there. What was his name?"

"The Witch of Endor summoned up the spirit of the prophet Samuel," an elderly and unfamiliar manservant said quietly. "It is recorded in the second book of Samuel in the Old Testament."

"Thank you, sir. So what about it, Florence? It's right there in your Bible."

"Well that's different—it's the Bible."

"And you know that plenty of strange things go on around here—the Casino's haunted, the Old Stone Villa's haunted, and God himself only knows how many other houses around here are. And just last year, remember, they dug up that vampire girl. What was her name?"

"Mercy Brown," the unfamiliar man said. "But that was in Exeter. Not Newport."

"Yeah, well… still."

"You can't be from around here with that accent, lad," Florence McMurphy said to the new man.

"No. My employer lives in New York. I am originally from London. myself."

"And who do ya work for, then?"

"Professor Erasmus von Hellmann," Edward replied.

"The man himself! We were just talkin' about the séance at Blithewood House in a few nights' time."

"The Professor is very much looking forward to it."

"I'll just bet he is. You think he's going to get her?"

"The Professor has never failed to expose a fraud."

"He's not going to get her," someone called. "She's the real thing."

"As has already been said, gentlemen, that remains to be seen."

Up at the top of the Forty Steps, the musicians were playing a slow waltz as another bunch of servants arrived. One of the newcomers had a couple of big picnic hampers packed with leftovers from the dinner his employer had thrown the night before. There was ham and cold beef, bread and cheese and pickles. A gleeful shout went up as the food was shared around, and the waltz's tempo jumped.

"So how did you know about that vampire girl?" Morrison asked some time later. The debate had died down and the two men were standing together halfway down the Forty Steps. Morrison could see Edgar, Blithewood House's poetic footman, perched down on Ellison's Rocks with a notebook balanced on one knee, mesmerized by the crashing surf.

"The Professor has a taste for anything which savors of the strange," Edward replied. "He heard about the case in a vague way, and had me collect anything I could find on it."

The previous March, George Brown panicked when his young son Edwin began exhibiting symptoms of the same strange wasting sickness that had already claimed his wife and two of their daughters. Several of his neighbors in the little rural village of Exeter convinced George that this pestilence worrying the family emanated from the deceased family members. After much deliberation, George Brown and a few burly neighbors, along with a doctor, went to the graveyard to exhume the bodies of his wife and daughters, and to search for anything unnatural about the corpses.

Upon exhuming nineteen-year-old Mercy, her body was found to be uncorrupted and her cheeks rosy. The group concluded that this girl was the cause of the family's woe. In accordance with certain uncomfortable superstitions still practiced in rural Rhode Island, Mercy's heart was removed from her chest. It dripped seemingly-fresh blood. The heart was set aflame on a nearby rock, and the ailing Edwin was brought over to inhale the smoke of his sister's burning heart; afterwards the ashes were mixed with water and given to him to drink. It was believed that this would protect him from further decline, but he perished two months later. Strangely, no other member of the Brown family was troubled after Edwin's death.

"So does von Hellmann believe in vampires, then?" Morrison asked, only half-joking.

"No more than he believes in spiritualists," Edward smiled.

"So how long have you been in his employ?"

"Almost thirty years—ever since I first arrived in this country. And how long have you worked in Colonel Hornbeck's household?"

"Also since I arrived in this country—but in my case that's not quite a month."

"Where are you from originally?"

"London. Paddington, actually. My first employer was a bachelor physician in Kensington."

"Mine was a banker and his wife in St. John's Wood," Edward smiled. "They used to hold séances, as well. Their daughter was a convert. So what brought you over here?"

"I suppose you could say I was looking for something."

After an awkward silence Morrison said, "So it would seem that our present employers are on opposite sides of the question."

"It would seem so. But surely that should not affect our friendship, Mr. Morrison? I understand that you are quite a chess player?"

"I enjoy a game. I have a friend back in London and we telegraph moves to one another."

"Splendid. Please do remember your board on the night of the séance—we'll both need something to pass the time."

Chapter XIV

COLONEL HORNBECK BEGAN to marshal his forces that afternoon, hours before the séance was to begin.

"Now remember, all of you, that von Hellmann must not be let out of your sight for an instant," he charged his corps of servants. "The man's a troublemaker and he mustn't be allowed the slightest chance to cause any mischief. Henry, you have moved the large table into the library as I asked?"

"Yes, sir."

"Good. And I think we will need a dozen chairs, and you'll need to be able to lay hands on more as it proves necessary. You've sent someone for candles?"

"I sent Martin not fifteen minutes ago."

"And you specified white candles? They must be white, Henry, Madame Priestley insists on white candles."

"Martin was given instructions to procure four dozen white candles, sir, and white candles only."

"Good, Henry. You have had the drawing room and the smoking room put in order?"

"I believe Eileen and Brigit are just finishing up now, sir."

"Good. Now, Edgar—you have the guest list and it is as much as your life is worth to let anyone not named on that list into this house. There's been too damned much gossip about this evening already and I won't have curiosity-seekers or riffraff or, God forbid, *journalists* in my house. Am I clear, Edgar?"

"Perfectly clear, sir," the liveried footman bowed deeply.

"Back to you, Henry. Tell cook I'd like him to put something together, something light. Some ham, cheese, fish, whatever he likes. Put it on the sideboard in the drawing room. And bring up a couple of bottles from the cellar, Henry. Whatever you think is suitable."

"Of course."

"I think that's everything," Colonel Hornbeck said, looking at his pocketwatch. "The guests will start to arrive at eight. And remember—don't let von Hellmann out of your sight."

Mr. Rathbone came by later in the afternoon, to keep his three o'clock appointment with the Colonel. Hornbeck kept two sets of lawyers: one set in New York and the other in Newport; Rathbone and his firm comprised the Newport set. He had worked for Hornbeck for many years—since shortly before Blithewood House was built. He had helped Amelia draw up her will. He was the family's trusted old legal retainer.

"Of course you've heard about what's going on here tonight," Hornbeck said, and offered the elderly lawyer a cigar.

"If you don't mind me saying so, James, I think the whole town has," Rathbone said politely.

"Well I don't care about the whole town just now. This séance tonight is very important to me."

"I understand."

"I don't trust von Hellmann."

"Then why on Earth did you invite him?" Rathbone asked, puffing on his Havana.

"Because… I want to show him up for the conceited old fool that he is—to show him that he's wrong. To shut him the hell up," he laughed gruffly.

"All right. So why am I here?"

"I need someone I can rely on, someone I can trust."

The lawyer nodded.

"And… well here it is: I fully expect von Hellmann to pull some fool stunt and try to splash it all over tomorrow's front page."

"And you can't stop him from doing that."

"If he does try something tonight I want to be ready to take action when he does—legal action, if necessary."

"You can't haul the man into court because you and he disagree about séances, James," Rathbone said a little sharply. "The law doesn't work that way. You know that. Now there have been some pretty sensational trials in the past concerning spirit-mediums, but what in the world makes you think anything of that kind is going to happen here?"

"I just want you on hand to help me keep an eye on him and... advise me as needed."

"Fine, then. Mrs. Rathbone and I will be here at seven,"

"Good. Good, I can rely on you then?"

"Of course."

The two men shook hands and the lawyer departed.

Hornbeck spent a few meditative moments sitting in Amelia's room upstairs. Despite having lived in this room for the past few weeks, and passing countless nights in it before, he was uncomfortable here.

He sat in her favorite chair by the big window looking down into the garden. The scent of the roses wafting in from below mingled pleasantly with the fragrance of the rose in his hand, which Eileen claimed to have found on the bed a few days before. It almost didn't matter to him if it was true, or another one of Eileen's stories.

When he closed his eyes, he could feel Amelia all around him.

"I know you're still here, love," he whispered. "I know you are. Tonight we'll show von Hellmann how wrong he is... oh, God, Amelia. How I wish you were here with me. Still here with me. Do you know how much I miss you...?"

When he opened his eyes her portrait was staring right through him.

He found his sister Sarah in a wicker sun chair in the garden.

She had withdrawn to the relative safety of the garden early that morning, when he had begun marching excitedly around the mansion, giving the servants their orders. He was in high dudgeon, and it seemed best to simply keep out of his way, so she sought out the sun chair. In Newport, a sun chair resembled an oversize beehive, enclosed on three sides and with a tall domed top, to protect the occupant from the sun; the design suited Sarah's desire for seclusion that morning. But he had found her, as she knew he would, and he would ask what she hoped he would not.

For the past few weeks, things had been strained between them; she had come to Newport to help her brother through a difficult period, that of mourning, and now found herself in the midst of an altogether different—and much more difficult—situation. Still, she reminded herself, this was her brother and she had begun the season with a quiet resolution to help him; this sudden and weird change in circumstances should not, she felt, change that resolve.

"James," Sarah said, as he approached, "you know I can't come to this séance tonight."

Hornbeck shifted uneasily from foot to foot. "Actually, Sarah, I wanted to speak with you about that."

"It's blasphemy—it's consorting with necromancers, with sorcerers. I won't do it."

After a long and thoughtful pause, he said, "I don't think you quite realize what's going to happen here tonight, Sarah. It's a miracle—we will reach out to the departed, to souls who have moved on to a higher plane. Amelia is one of those souls, Sarah. We've been over this before—"

"We certainly have, and you know how wrong this is."

"This is not wrong—if it were wrong Amelia never would have made contact with Madame Priestley in the first place, she never would have contacted *me*. She's still here. Don't you feel her sometimes? I do. And I cannot turn my back on my wife."

Sarah folded her arms, shifting and shivering as though cold, despite the sun.

"You have changed," she said quietly.

"Yes… yes I have," her brother replied quietly, as though not entirely happy with that change. "But my life changed, too, and it's all I can do to keep up. Don't you feel that, too…?"

"This is not your answer, James."

"No, perhaps not—perhaps it's simply another series of questions for me."

Sarah would not meet his gaze. "Perhaps so."

"That's why I need you there tonight."

"I don't think I can be there in all conscience…."

"I need you there. I know it makes you uncomfortable, and believe me, it makes me uncomfortable, too, having von Hellmann about. But I need those I can count on tonight. Can I count on you, Sarah?"

"You're asking much of me."

"I know. But I am only asking this of you because you are my sister; there's no one else I trust as much, now that Amelia's gone."

"What do you… what do you want of me?"

"Only to come tonight, and tell me what you think afterwards. You've always been more devout than I, and I confess I'm at bit at sea on some of these matters. That's why I need you. And to help me keep an eye on von Hellmann; I'm sure he'll try some fool stunt tonight, and try to turn the whole thing into a mockery."

Sarah stood for a long silent moment before saying, "I will consider it."

Hornbeck nodded. He knew he was asking much of her, and appreciated even a moment's consideration of his request.

"Thank you, sister."

Chapter XV

THE FOOTMAN ANNOUNCED Professor von Hellmann and his party promptly at eight o'clock.

The guests had gathered in the drawing-room: a grand, high-ceilinged room paneled in black walnut and richly furnished with French antiques. Gilt candelabra, each holding a dozen long white candles, provided the only light, and sweet incense smoke drifted through the room. The room was dominated by the large portrait of the Hornbeck family at the far end.

The polite murmur of conversation and small talk died when the footman made his announcement.

Hornbeck, standing with Rachel and chatting pleasantly with the Rathbones, stiffened slightly and turned to meet the new arrival as though answering a challenge.

Von Hellmann entered, followed closely by Jack and Hope. He looked around slowly, silently demanding the room's attention and just as silently receiving it. He acknowledged the Townsends with a curt nod—he hadn't expected to see them here tonight but was pleased. He waited for Hornbeck to approach and was grinning slyly, as though at a private and devilish jest.

"I am Colonel James Hornbeck. May I present my daughter, Mrs. Charles Christie. This is Mr. Rathbone and his wife. And I believe you already know the Townsends...."

"Yes, thank you. And may I present the Jackson Westlocks?"

"Welcome to Blithewood House," Hornbeck said gravely. "May I offer you something to drink? Martin, sherry for our guests."

Greetings were made, sherry was served. After a long and heavy pause, Hornbeck excused himself and rejoined his daughter.

He seemed suddenly uncomfortable, as though the room had grown too warm for him.

He's sizing von Hellmann up, Townsend thought, observing from a few paces away. Hornbeck had been no more polite than good form demanded, and his abruptness almost bordered on rudeness. Von Hellmann, of course, couldn't have cared less. Why should he? He didn't come here tonight to see the Colonel. Look at them now, each man in his own corner, like prizefighters waiting for the bell.

Townsend sipped his sherry and wondered just how long this forced calm could last.

"I wasn't expecting to see you tonight," von Hellmann said to Townsend a few minutes later. He kissed Mrs. Townsend's hand and made a few quick introductions before adding, "I should have known, of course. You wouldn't miss a good séance for the world."

"Neither would you," Townsend replied. "I just hope you keep an open mind tonight."

"But not so open that my brains fall out—but hush, Professor. Let's not argue here. You know your wife doesn't want us rehashing old debates." He smiled charmingly. "So tell me, where's our medium?"

"Upstairs, I suppose. Resting, meditating."

"I see. Who's Rathbone?"

"Hornbeck's lawyer."

"His lawyer?" Jack startled. "Why would he bring his lawyer to a séance?"

"I brought you, didn't I?" von Hellmann smiled. "Do you think Hornbeck's expecting… trouble tonight?"

"Who can tell? So, what do you think of Hornbeck, now that you've finally met him?"

Von Hellmann shrugged. "Ask me again later."

Hornbeck kept stealing little glances at his adversary across the room.

Von Hellmann and the Westlocks had been talking quietly with the Townsends for a good quarter-hour now. The new underbutler, Martin, had made his rounds and refilled their delicate crystal sherry glasses. They seemed to be enjoying one another's company well enough, smiling and nodding to one another familiarly.

Excusing himself, Hornbeck crossed the room to the corner where his guests were, over by the fireplace. The men stood, and the women sat on a Louis XV divan. He pretended, even to himself, that he had simply come over to see if they wanted for anything—ever the gracious host. He felt his face redden with rising heat as he approached.

"Everything's just fine over here, Colonel, thank you," Townsend said. "I suppose we should be a little more sociable. But Professor von Hellmann and I were just debating Ashley Place. Again."

"D. D. Home," Hornbeck nodded.

"That's right," von Hellmann said.

Daniel Dunglas Home was usually referred to as "The Enigma," and the Ashley Place levitation only served to widen and deepen his already-sensational reputation. It was said that Home was never detected in outright fraud, but some of his sitters were convinced they had viewed nothing less at his séances. When spirit hands crowned Elizabeth Barrett Browning with a crown of laurels at one séance, her husband Robert scoffed, and scoffed loudly. "On the whole I think the whole performance most clumsy, and unworthy of anybody setting up for a 'medium,'" he wrote, adding, "There are probably fifty more ingenious methods at the service of every 'prestidigitateur.'"

"If I remember correctly, the medium left the séance chamber and went into an adjoining room. A moment later, he was seen floating back into the séance chamber through an open window—a window several stories off the ground," Hornbeck said. "The witnesses were all British noblemen of good character."

Von Hellmann smiled. Hornbeck had certainly done his reading, and was playing the spiritualist trump card; Ashley Place was often cited as the one unanswerable demonstration of spirit power.

"Well, the case has some very serious doubts against it," von Hellmann said. "Not the least of which is the differing accounts of the eyewitnesses. They do not entirely agree in the particulars. Having read the accounts of the evening shortly after they were published, I am not at all clear about what happened at Ashley Place—and I venture to say that neither were the gentlemen present."

"And yet the men were all of unimpeachable character—a captain, a viscount. Such men must be believed."

"I have performed for captains and viscounts," von Hellmann replied with ice in his voice, "and they are no more difficult to fool than anyone else."

"Well then, how do you account for it?" Hornbeck demanded hotly.

"I don't think we'll ever know what happened at Ashley Place. It was twenty-five years ago, and Home is dead. I am afraid it ends in a stalemate, Colonel. We may debate and debate—Professor Townsend and I have been wrangling over it for years—but I think we will never really *know*."

"And while we may never know about Home, am I correct in assuming you believe all mediums are, as you so often say, clever charlatans?"

"Oh, no—not at all," von Hellmann gave another chilly smile. "Some of them are not in the least clever."

"But they are all fakes," Hornbeck pursued.

"Every medium I have ever encountered has been, yes."

"Then we shall have to see what you have to say after tonight."

"I shall be only too happy to render an expert opinion," von Hellmann said, and then changed the subject with a gesture. "What a charming portrait!"

"John Singer Sargent painted that," Hornbeck said proudly, wondering why von Hellmann had brought it up. "Some years ago when we were in England. My wife was especially fond of it."

"She's quite striking there."

"My Amelia was quite a beauty," Hornbeck said softly. "Came of an old Newport family; I'm from New York, myself. Sixth Avenue."

"I live off Seventh. We're neighbors and don't even know it. My family's been in the city since it was New Amsterdam; in the old days they were patroons. But that's all changed, of course. Now it's swarming with filth. So much has changed, especially since the War."

"Yes," Hornbeck replied quietly. "Newport has changed, as well. Now it's swarming with gawkers and rubber-neckers and social climbers and vulgar rich wastrels. It's changed since the War, too. Utterly changed after that. It changed everything. We lost so many good boys—damn fine men."

"They should have hanged Lee," von Hellmann said with a touch of bitterness.

"Yes, they should have," Hornbeck replied, surprised. "You were there? In the War?"

"Everyone was in the War, in one way or another… but yes, I was there. Carried a Springfield. I remember the night before Gettysburg, staying up all night doing card tricks for my regiment; even did one for Mead that night, trying to keep everyone's mind off what was about to happen. But that's a long time ago, now."

The two men regarded one another for a long moment. Born into the same time in the same place, their faces were lined with the same cares, their hair whitened by the same worries; they were cut from the same crystal. Although their brownstones may have been only a few streets away their lives had gone in such very different directions, one to society, the other to the stage. It was not at all surprising that the two would not so much as meet in the street, they moved in such disparate circles. And yet despite that they were both drawn together tonight by Madame Helene Priestley. Apparently, Madame truly could bridge worlds.

Sarah came into the room with a slow, dignified step, arrayed in her best lavender-and-white gown, the half-mourning widow's weeds she had worn for over twenty years. In her hair she wore a wide Spanish comb her brother had once given her upon his return from a trip to Spain. She nodded to her family and crossed the room to stand by her brother's side.

"Professor von Hellmann, may I present my sister, Mrs. Jonathan P. Newland?"

"Very charmed to make your acquaintance, Madame. I am Erasmus von Hellmann."

"And pleased to make yours, as well. I hope my brother has been a good host?"

"He has been a very excellent host, indeed, here in his very beautiful home."

Sarah returned the magician's smile; von Hellmann was at his most charming.

"If you will excuse me for a moment, I need to speak to Henry," Hornbeck said, withdrawing. Sarah came with him, on his arm, as he whispered, "Thank you, thank you, thank you."

"I'm here more to keep an eye on you than on him," she whispered in reply.

"Your uncle is a most interesting gentleman," Rachel said to Hope, fanning herself with a big fan of embroidered silk.

"He certainly is," Hope replied with a proud smile. "And I might say the same of your father."

"Papa's a good man. He's very strong, very determined."

"And he has a lovely house."

"Blithewood House is my mother's, really. Naturally Papa owns it, but he built it for her and she arranged everything—the furniture, the tapestries, everything."

"She's very beautiful in that picture."

"My father says that Mr. Sargent captured her beauty there better than any photograph. Papa used to summer here and Mama was a debutante. They were introduced at a cotillion."

"How very wonderful."

"If I may be so bold as to ask," Rachel began carefully, "what is it like? Being the Uncanny Esperanza ? Being onstage every night? Of course I can't go to the theater, but Papa described it all to me and what you do sounds so mysterious."

"I do my best to make it so. And I like nothing better than being in front of an audience, working with my uncle," Hope replied. "My husband, of course, does not approve, but Uncle Erasmus usually bullies and hectors poor Jack and intimidates him until he gives in. But, of course, I was doing the show long before I ever met Jack."

"They're two of a kind, aren't they?" Professor Townsend asked, coming over to join the ladies. He gestured over to Hornbeck and von Hellmann, who had retired to separate corners.

"I wouldn't say that to Uncle Erasmus," Hope replied. "I've been listening to him call Colonel Hornbeck a fool ever since we arrived in Newport."

"And now?"

"I'm not sure. But it doesn't really matter, of course."

"Why not?" Townsend asked.

"It's the medium we're after," Hope replied more than a little coldly.

Chapter XVI

TOWARD MIDNIGHT, when the moon rode above the stars and the wind swept through the trees, Reverend Barrows appeared, coming into the room with his innocent grin. Introductions were made. He seemed especially happy to make Professor Von Hellmann's acquaintance at last.

"A very great pleasure, indeed sir," he said, with a polite little bow. "I am sure that you will find the evening most… edifying."

"That remains to be seen," was the coolly skeptical rejoinder.

"Well, my sister has been resting and readying herself all evening long and now informs me that she is ready. She awaits us in the library."

The guests drained their glasses and quietly filed into the big, high-ceilinged library with the air of a procession entering a church. Framed antique maps hung on the dark walls and somber busts of Milton, Shakespeare, and Plato stared down from atop the tall bookcases. Amelia had bought and arranged them—the Colonel couldn't tell one from the other. An oval mirror hung over the great Carrara marble fireplace. Like all of the fireplaces in Blithewood House, this one was false; it was a summer cottage, only tenanted in July and August, and there was no need of real fireplaces.

At the round table in the center of the room, the medium waited.

Madame Helene Priestley stood in the shadowy light of the table's large candelabrum, all white candles again. She wore a simple décolleté gown, all black brocade and silver thread. Her dark hair was piled high on her head with little old-fashioned finger-curls falling behind, brushing her bare shoulders. The candles lit her beautiful, ageless face strangely as she stood there, regarding her sitters.

If she recognized Hope, she showed no sign of it. And while von Hellmann stared at her, as though drawing a bead on a target, she seemed perfectly unruffled by his presence.

"My friends," she said quietly, "the air is thick with spirits tonight."

The sitters arranged themselves around her table, lady and gentleman alternating as Spiritualist tradition decreed, with Reverend Barrows overseeing the arrangement. On the medium's left was Mr. Rathbone, with Jack Westlock to her right. Von Hellmann found himself placed across the table from her, with Rachel Hornbeck to his right and Mrs. Townsend to his left. Reverend Barrows was very particular about the order; he insisted that is would be very important to achieve the proper balance and "spiritual harmony."

At a word from the medium, each sitter took the wrist of the person sitting to their right, this also according to Spiritualist tradition.

"The séance circle must not be broken by anyone, for any reason. The results could be extremely dangerous for myself."

They certainly can be, thought von Hellmann.

"I know of more than one medium who has been killed where he sat because some sitter broke the circle," Reverend Barrows said breathlessly. "For my sister's sake, I ask you to maintain the circle no matter what may happen. So, please keep your feet flat upon the floor, relax yourselves; you have nothing to fear here tonight. We are all friends…"

Hornbeck gave a nod to the underbutler, who had followed the guests in from the sitting room. Martin silently did as he had been instructed by the Colonel and the Reverend that afternoon.

First, he removed the heavy gilt candelabrum from the table and placed it over on the desk near the door. The desktop was littered with papers and notebooks and the stack of Spiritualist volumes the Colonel had been slowly working his way through.

Next, from a long leather case, the underbutler removed a tin trumpet, something like a megaphone or a long ear-trumpet. It was about three feet long, and at intervals along its length were painted a half-dozen bright blue bands an inch or more wide. Martin stood this in the center of the table, where the candelabrum had been, wide mouth down, narrow end pointed toward the ceiling.

"Thank you Martin," Hornbeck said. "That will be all."

Martin nodded and blew out the candles before leaving the room. He closed the door behind him, leaving the library in complete darkness. He and Reverend Barrows had spent the entire afternoon going over the room, making certain no light penetrated the heavily curtained windows or anywhere else. A light in the séance chamber, much like breaking the circle, could be fatal to the medium.

The bands painted around the trumpet glowed a pale blue in the darkness.

The spirit trumpet had been a fixture at séances for at least forty years. The luminous paint helped sitters keep track of it in the blackness. Von Hellmann bought his luminous paint from Devoe and Company in New York, who sold six six-ounce jelly jars of the stuff for five dollars.

He wondered where the medium got hers.

Martin returned to the sitting room, where the others servants were sequestered. By previous arrangement, all the household staff, from Henry on down to the stable boy, was to remain in this room together until the séance was concluded. Neither von Hellmann nor Hornbeck, it seemed, wanted there to be any chance of mischief or collusion this evening.

"So what's happening?" Eileen demanded.

"Nothing so far," Morrison replied. "They're only just beginning."

"Oh, this is just awful, isn't it?" Eileen tittered. "To think what must be goin' on in that room!"

"Eileen, calm down," Henry said sternly. "This will all be over soon enough, and you can get back to your duties—which, I might say, you have been neglecting. Mrs. Hornbeck's room needs a very thorough dusting, and has for at least a day."

"You know I don't like goin' in The Room!"

"Your position here at Blithewood House—and, I might add, your *continued* position here at Blithewood House—requires that you do so."

"Everyone is here, Henry?" Edward asked from his corner. Von Hellmann had charged him with keeping an eye in the servants.

Henry glanced at the faces gathered in the room and nodded. "All here, yes."

"Splendid. Martin, you have remembered the chessboard?"

"Oh, blast—no, I've forgotten the thing."

"Ah. That's unfortunate."

"It won't take me a moment to fetch it—it's just up in my room. I'll be back in a jiff—"

"Martin," Henry interrupted. "Stay here. We have our instructions."

"But this will only take a minute—what harm can there possibly be?"

"That would be for Colonel Hornbeck to decide. And it would give von Hellmann room to object, and we can't allow that—with all apologies to Edward."

"I'll be gone for two minutes—" he insisted, reaching for the doorknob.

Henry grasped his wrist.

"Martin—what has gotten into you? We are all to stay in this room until the séance is concluded. You know that. Now sit down."

"I quite agree with Henry," Edward said. "We have all agreed to these conditions, and we must keep our word. It is improper for any of us to leave."

Morrison stood still for a moment, clearly reining in his annoyance.

"Well then, Edward, what about our game?" he asked after a tense pause.

"We will have to entertain ourselves in some other fashion, Martin."

A sullen Martin took his seat on the couch, between Eileen and Brigit.

Reverend Barrows had led the assembled company in a few hymns, and then they settled into a long silence in the dark. The sitters looked around, blinking and squinting, but the blackness was absolute and uncomfortable. All that was visible were the glowing bands painted upon the trumpet.

"There are spirits all around us tonight," Madame Priestley intoned. Her voice sounded odd—faraway, as though speaking across a great distance. She was said to become entranced during her séances....

"Teddie...?" Reverend Barrows asked.

"*Yes*?" Madame replied in a husky whisper.

"Teddie, we have many here tonight reaching out... please bring us some of the departed that the scales of doubt may fall from their eyes."

"Spirits all around us here tonight...." Madame's voice came out of the dark. "Spirits all around."

The very solid table jarred, vibrated.

The sitters startled—the men sat straighter and the women gasped.

The table jarred again, then shifted—moved a few inches across the floor; von Hellmann felt it coming toward him, sliding under his hands resting on the tabletop. The trumpet wobbled with the movement. And then... *rap*!

Rap!

Von Hellmann couldn't place the sound. It could have come from anywhere in the room: the far corner, the ceiling, or even under his chair. Long experience had taught him how difficult it was to place sounds in the dark.

Rap!

On his right, he thought. Definitely on his right. He even felt Rachel start at the sound.

And then another *Rap!*

This one was off to his left—it sounded only a few feet off. Damn.

Nearby, Colonel Hornbeck was clasping Mrs. Townsend's wrist so tightly she felt he would cut off her circulation. Hope, on the other side of him, could feel his pulse racing excitedly through his veins. Mr. Rathbone sat between Hope and the medium, holding her arm rigidly.

Very faintly, Hope thought she could just smell roses.

There was a final rap and a final jarring of the table, and the trumpet clattered over noisily. It rolled for a moment, then came to a stop. It lay still for a long, breathless moment before moving very slightly... rolling across the tabletop and then slowly, gently, rising up and floating.

It floated up about a foot, then further. It hovered there before moving a little toward Mrs. Townsend.

"Teddie?" Reverend Barrows asked.

"No," Madame replied in a voice that was not her own.

"*Mmmmmother—*" a small voice whispered from the trumpet. "*Mmmother—*"

Von Hellmann felt Mrs. Townsend's trembling hand tighten its grip upon his.

"*Mother, it has been too long--*" the whisper continued, weirdly distorted by the tin trumpet. "*But know that I am here, as always. I am never far from you or from Father.*"

Mrs. Townsend was heard sobbing in the dark.

"*Always here... never far...*" there was more, but the voice died away.

Mrs. Townsend was trying to compose herself, and her husband earnestly said from across the table, "It's all right, Anne, it's all right."

The trumpet swung gently back and forth, and came to point at Hornbeck. It was still for a moment, and then actually fell into his lap.

"*James—?*" said a female voice. "*James? You are here, James?*"

"I'm here, Amelia. I'm here."

"*James and Rachel and our dear Jim. Oh, my family, I have prepared a place for you here, and wait for the day we will all be reunited…*"

Hornbeck swallowed thickly, and either forgetting or blotting out for one moment that he was in a roomful of people, he blurted, "I love you, Amelia. I love you and I'm so sorry."

He wanted to say more; to tell her how he missed her, how lonely and dead Blithewood House was without her, how the only sounds he could now hear were his own footsteps echoing down the empty halls. He could smell the fragrance of roses and felt hot tears streaming down his face. There were so many things he wished to tell her, things he should have told her before.

The trumpet rose, swung again, and pointed at von Hellmann.

"He must put his hands in the wounds before he believes," Reverend Barrows called out.

Von Hellmann leaped out of his seat, throwing himself across the table and grabbing madly at the trumpet that floated no more than a foot away. He caught it, held it tight. It was cold to his touch and he struggled as it was pulled violently back and slipped from his grasp and clattered loudly to the table.

"God damn it!" he shouted. "Lights, someone! The lights!"

"He's broken the circle!" Rachel cried. "Father! He's broken the circle!"

The circle was broken and the séance spun out of control.

Jack Westlock pulled away from the medium and Mrs. Rathbone and took two steps toward the electric light on the Colonel's desk. Someone slammed into him in the dark and Jack saw stars as he was sent crashing to the floor. He tried to get up but the wind had been knocked sharply out of him.

Hornbeck shrieked, "Von Hellmann you bastard!"

"Is everyone all right?" Reverend Barrows shouted. "Is everyone all right?"

A babble of voices was heard—accusations, concerns, confusion. As the sitters calmed down, Reverend Barrows struck a match.

"My God, Mr. Westlock!" he cried. "Are you all right? Let me help you up."

Jack struggled to his feet and collapsed into a chair as Reverend Barrows switched on the electric light. The sitters blinked in the sudden and harsh light. Hope went to her husband's side quickly, but as she did so the others turned to the medium.

Madame Preistley's head was thrown back over the chair. She stared blindly at the ceiling and her thick dark hair had come loose. She was pale. Her mouth hung open and her lips were flecked with a bloody froth. Rathbone still grasped her left wrist and she was not breathing.

Her brother bolted over to her. "Helene," he said, cradling her head in his arms. "Helene—answer me. Helene?"

She was deathly still for a half a minute, and then a sharp gasp for breath convulsed her entire body. She fell forward, hands slapping the tabletop, her face a few inches from the dark wood. Deep coughs wracked her slender frame for a long minute before she slowly straightened up and dabbed the bloody foam from her lips. Weakly, she asked, "What happened?"

"Von Hellmann nearly killed you," Hornbeck snapped. "Are you all right?"

"I'll be fine."

"Why the hell did you break the circle?" Hornbeck turned furiously on the magician.

"Don't you realize what just went on here?" von Hellmann was every bit as angry.

"Yes, I do. You nearly killed her, and my wife—"

"The woman was in no danger."

Hornbeck grabbed the iron poker from the fireplace and brandished it at von Hellmann.

"I want you out of my house."

"Don't you know a blasted fraud when you see one?" von Hellmann asked, pointing at the medium.

"Get out of my house!"

Von Hellmann stalked over to where his niece and her husband stood.

"We're leaving," he said. "I've certainly seen enough."

The uncomfortable moment of silence which followed was broken by Mr. Rathbone saying, "Look at the trumpet."

Hornbeck turned and picked it up; its middle was dented from the struggle. He looked inside and could not believe what he saw. He tilted it....

A full two dozen red rosebuds, perfectly fresh and spattered in dew, tumbled out onto the tabletop.

Chapter XVII

WHILE THE UNDERBUTLER was showing Professor von Hellmann and his party out, Hornbeck took his butler aside and spoke sharply.

"Henry," he said, "That man is not even to be allowed on the property from now on. Is that clear? You must tell Martin and the others. I never want that scoundrel near my house again."

"I understand perfectly, sir. I will spread the word."

"Good." He dismissed the man with a curt nod and went to rejoin his guests.

Madame Priestley lay half-reclined on the sofa, fanning herself weakly as she sipped a glass of water. Her color was just beginning to come back and she stared out the window at nothing. Her concerned brother stood over her with a grave face.

My God, Hornbeck thought, he nearly killed her.

Townsend approached him cautiously.

"How is she?" Hornbeck asked.

"I think she'll recover. She seems to have had quite a shock, but I think she'll be fine tomorrow. She's strong for a woman."

Strong like Amelia was strong, Hornbeck thought.

"So, what did you think of the séance?" Townsend asked.

"I think von Hellmann's a dangerous man."

"You're not the first."

"Aside from him… tonight was incredible," Hornbeck shook his head wonderingly. "Absolutely incredible. That trumpet—it landed right in my lap and I heard her voice. *Amelia's voice.* Damn it, I could feel the thing vibrate when she spoke. It was her. She was here. I could feel her—I thought I could almost smell her. And the roses. My God, those roses!"

He shook his head again and took a deep breath, composing himself. After a moment he asked, "Was that your son, then?"

"Yes," Townsend replied. "Michael. He's been gone over fifteen years now. He drowned when he was ten. There have been a few mediums who have tried to put us in touch with him, but not many have succeeded."

"She certainly did tonight."

"I think she did, yes. I must admit that in all my years as an investigator, even back in the days when von Hellmann and I were on the Wraeburn Committee, I've never seen anything like this. I've seen mediums use trumpets before, of course, but they were always so clumsy and the voices were so pathetic that they were obvious. One fellow didn't even try to disguise his voice. Just awful. But tonight was different."

"What do you think von Hellmann's next move will be?"

"I'm not sure. But I'll warn you, this is only beginning. I know von Hellmann and I've seen him like this before. He will not stop until he gets her. Somehow."

Hornbeck nodded his agreement. The séance had been the kind of reconnaissance he had conducted during the War, or a brief skirmish to test the strength of the opponent. But he knew Townsend was right. The real fight was still ahead.

"Well, Colonel, we must be going," Rathbone said. "I'm afraid Mrs. Rathbone has been upset by all this excitement, though not so upset, I think, as Madame Priestley."

"A night's rest and a few of Beecham's pills and my sister will be fully recovered, I assure you, Mr. Rathbone," Reverend Barrows said from across the room. She had arisen from the sofa and was leaning heavily on his arm, smiling weakly. She didn't speak as her brother guided her upstairs.

The clock showed a quarter to two when von Hellmann and Hope and Jack arrived back at the Ocean House.

Hope had asked the night clerk to send some ice up to their suite. Jack's eye was swollen half-shut. He sat there in his shirtsleeves, without collar or tie, while his wife wrapped the ice in one of her lacy cambric handkerchiefs. Jack winced when she applied it, but thanked her anyway.

Von Hellmann sat brooding in a deep armchair. He had not spoken since they left Blithewood House, and this caused Hope some concern. Something was bothering him.

"All right," Jack Westlock said finally, banging the table, "Court is now in session. Tonight's séance—real or fake?"

"Fake," von Hellmann said defiantly.

"Fake," Hope seconded.

"Very good. You may make your opening remarks."

"The usual catalogue of medium's tricks. Nothing startling, nothing convincing."

"We shall start at the beginning," Jack said. "The table moved. Twice."

"Of course it did," von Hellmann snapped. "Either she moved it, or her brother did, or they did it together, with a knee or a foot. Nothing to it."

"It was a very heavy table."

"Then it took them both to do it."

"All right. Then there were the raps."

"Any number of ways to produce raps in a dark room. The Fox sisters cracked their toes and changed the world with it, and countless other mediums have done the same. Perhaps Madame used a rapping-device."

Rappers had been available for years from not only reputable dealers in magicians' apparatus, but also from dubious businesses which catered to mediums as well. Under the heading *"Raps Here! There!! Everywhere!!!"* one catalogue had this to say about its eighteen-dollar rapper: "With this you can produce raps anytime while standing or sitting, in light or dark, and in any room or circle, as often as you like. It is the only perfect means of its kind for this effect. No inconvenience in using it. You know what you can achieve with it."

"So much for the raps," Jack conceded. "Now for the matter of the trumpet."

"No matter at all," von Hellmann snorted from deep in his armchair. "I will admit that she handles a trumpet as well as any medium I have ever seen, but it was certainly she who was handling it and not some disembodied spirit guide or what have you."

"And how could she have handled it with me holding her left wrist, and she herself holding the wrist of Professor Townsend?" Jack asked, more in the role of devil's advocate than spiritualistic convert.

"Simplicity itself," Hope smiled. "She got one hand free."

"But I was very careful," Jack insisted, and he had been. That afternoon, which now seemed like weeks ago at two in the morning, von Hellmann had lectured him and taught him what to watch out for, and what to do.

With Hope's help, he had shown a blindfolded Jack just how easily one hand could be freed in the dark, and how the other hand could be made to do double duty, with one sitter holding the wrist while the same hand gripped the next sitter in turn. Later, the men on either side would swear that each of the medium's hands had been controlled. It was a very old dodge.

"It was probably her right hand, the one that was supposed to be holding onto your wrist, Jack. She was actually using her left hand to do that, while she made mischief with her free right," von Hellmann said. "It would be easy to momentarily let go with the right hand under some innocent pretext, such as sneezing or moving something on the table, and then immediately grasping your wrist with her other hand. She would have done this as soon as the lights were extinguished. Do you remember if she coughed or some such? If she did anything under the cover of which she could make the exchange?"

"Yesss…" Jack said thoughtfully, then, "No… I'm sorry, I'm not really sure."

"You're a poor witness."

"I don't quite remember," he said sheepishly. "But she did seem to get quite restless for a few minutes, with much shifting about and so on."

"Probably getting into position for the switch. Pray proceed with your questioning."

"So she gets one hand free and uses it to manipulate the trumpet. How, exactly?"

"She slides that free hand inside the wide mouth of the trumpet. With her hand inside she does not obscure the bands of luminous paint."

"And the voices?"

"She whispers into the wide end, doing her best impersonation of a dead person, and her eerily distorted voice comes out the narrow end, focused on one particular sitter," Hope smiled.

"And of course she didn't say anything particularly meaningful or insightful," von Hellmann added. "Just the usual Spiritualistic twaddle about the departed always being near and so on. Neither of those voices said anything that would positively identify them as belonging to the supposed speakers. Too vague and non-specific to be considered a very palpable hit."

"Objection Your Honor," Jack boomed, waving his icepack. "There is, equally, nothing to show that those voices were not who they were supposed to be."

"Objection sustained," von Hellmann grumbled. "Although how anybody but a medium's deluded dupe or a lawyer could think so is beyond me."

"All right. By the way—if she was doing all this business of getting a hand free and playing around with the trumpet, wouldn't we have heard her moving?"

"Not if she moved very slowly and deliberately, and only as much as she needed to and when she needed to. She's been doing this for years and she's no amateur," Hope pointed out.

"And her gown is silk, and silk is the best material for a medium because it is very quiet and lightweight and does not rustle as other fabrics do."

"Fine. Now, we all saw the trumpet fall into Colonel Hornbeck's lap. I saw his hand grab onto it—I could see the silhouette of his fingers against the luminous paint," Jack said. "And then we heard what was supposed to be the voice of his departed wife. It then floated up out of his lap and higher than a seated person could reach. It behooves us to ask for an explanation."

"The floating could be done with a reaching-rod," Hope said with an expectant glance at her Uncle. "And there's no telling where those voices were actually coming from, as it's almost impossible to place sounds in the dark."

"She was too far away from Hornbeck to be whispering into one end of the trumpet," von Hellmann said gloomily. "And as far as the reaching-rod, I'm not sure even I could deposit a trumpet in a sitter's lap, get out a reaching-rod, extend it, pick up the trumpet and then drop it again, collapse the rod and slide it back into its hiding-place before the lights came on. Not deceptively, anyway. It all happened too quickly."

"We've both done things which are much more complicated, and in less time—you know that, Uncle," Hope said.

"Can you explain the voice we heard when the trumpet was in Hornbeck's lap? I believe he said something about feeling it vibrate."

Von Hellmann nodded silently and thoughtfully and stayed still for a few long moments. He took a deep breath and admitted, "I can't explain that.

"I know she made those voices," he went on. "She probably would have worked her way around the circle making voices for all of us if I hadn't started that melee." He chuckled humorlessly. "But I don't know how she did it... *yet*."

"And then there are the roses to be accounted for," Jack said carefully.

With another humorless chuckle, von Hellmann said dismissively, "Well, either she apported them from the spirit world, or she found a way of sneaking them into the room with her. Probably the latter."

Apports were gifts from the spirits which appeared mysteriously and dramatically at séances; some mediums apported candy or jewelry, some others apported seashells and flowers and occasionally lost articles. The most dramatic apport on record took place at a London séance when the spirits produced the obese English medium Mrs. Guppy. When one sitter struck a match, she was found to be standing on the table, in a trance and clutching her ledger-book. She later claimed she had been settling up her household accounts in her study at home when she was whisked away. A friend who had been in the room with her at the same time said the rotund Mrs. Guppy had just suddenly vanished, "leaving only a slight haze near the ceiling."

"Without meaning to shock either of you two gentlemen, may I say that a lady is capable of holding quite a bit in her skirts," Hope smiled modestly. "And of course she met us in the library—she was there first."

"And she could have smuggled in almost anything and hidden it before we arrived," her uncle nodded. "But the roses were a distinct touch. Very cleverly done."

"And I suppose when that pandemonium broke out she could have gotten away with almost anything," Jack said, pressing his icepack to his eye painfully. "Barrows really clobbered me in the dark."

"He knew someone was making for that lamp on Hornbeck's desk. He couldn't let you reach it."

"He said light could be fatal."

"The only true words spoken in that room tonight. It would have been pretty fatal for her if the light went on and there she was holding that trumpet, or folding up a reaching-rod. He had to stop you."

"And he did just that. And when the light came on the circle was already broken. How do you explain the bloody froth on her lips, by the way?"

"A sliver of soap stained red with confectioner's food coloring. Pop it in your mouth and chew. It's an old, old trick that goes back to the carnival. Tastes awful but it's very dramatic. I've done it a couple of times myself."

"And it elicits sympathy from your sitters," Hope added. "It makes then think you were really in some danger, and the skeptics nearly killed you with their disruption. Well, that's everything, then."

"Not quite," Jack objected. "Your case is still far from complete. There's still reasonable doubt about those voices which were produced while Colonel Hornbeck held the trumpet in his lap and Madame Priestley was a good four or five feet away. And the roses, too."

"I need time," von Hellmann said bitterly. "Time and sleep. I did not come here to lose. I'll get her, but I need time."

Chapter XVIII

AFTER THE SÉANCE, Colonel Hornbeck gave his servants strict orders that the next couple of days were to pass quietly and uneventfully. He did not, he insisted, want anything to disturb or discomfit Madame Priestley's recuperation. Henry and Martin and the others did all they could to ensure this, but the quiet days abruptly ended when Edgar came into the sitting room one morning with Miss Brooke's card on a silver tray.

Hornbeck stared at the card for a full minute. A journalist? In his house? Absurd—insulting. No one of that class should even be allowed past the gate, never mind through the door. Still, he knew that the séance had been the talk among the townies and—damn them!—they would make up whatever they pleased in the absence of facts. Newport had always been a gossipy, rumor-mongering place, and Hornbeck heard what the other summer colonists said about people like the Astors and the Vanderbilts and the Lorillards. He could only imagine what was now being said about him and his unusual guests. And of course von Hellmann would waste no time in letting his version of the story be known.

With a deep and exasperated sigh, Hornbeck shrugged. "All right, Edgar," he said, "show her in."

The lady reporter proved to be more than he had expected. She wore a very crisp bicycling outfit and broad straw hat. She shook his hand, admired the décor, smiled prettily, and opened her small notebook. Hornbeck did not ask her to sit down.

"Colonel Hornbeck," Miss Brooke said, "I am sure you are aware that Madame Priestley's summering in Newport has caused some excitement and even more comment."

Hornbeck nodded gravely.

"And you are further aware that there are a large number of very fanciful rumors being heard just now concerning the séance held here a few nights ago?"

He nodded again.

"So you've come for a statement? Something for the society column? If you've come to collect gossip, Miss Brooke, I must disappoint you."

"Not at all, sir," the lady reporter replied, choosing her words with care. "I simply thought you should be given the opportunity to dispel any falsehoods which may be circulating just now. I myself attended one of Madame Priestley's séances when she first arrived here, and I must say I was quite astonished."

"She is an astonishing medium," Hornbeck said. "No doubt, in fifty or a hundred years, people will still be speaking her name with reverence."

"And yet, if you will forgive me for saying so, there are some today who would not quite agree."

"They have not sat with Madame Priestley."

"But certain of them have. So you have no doubts about the genuineness of her powers?"

"There is no explanation for what I have seen and what I have heard. I must accept the evidence of my own experience, Miss Brooke. I have always done so in the past and shall continue to do so in the future. May I ask what you thought of your sitting with Madame?"

"I was very impressed," she slowly replied. "I cannot account for any of what I saw, and am sure that the other sitters that night were no less impressed."

"So you are inclined to accept the evidence of your experience as well?" Hornbeck asked smilingly.

"I have not been able to make up my mind," Miss Brooke replied firmly. "There are those who would say that there are many possible explanations for what occurs in the séance room."

"There is at least one explanation, Miss Brooke—contact is made with departed spirits."

"But of course not everyone is agreed on that point, Colonel. There are some even here in Newport who doubt any such claim—"

"Like von Hellmann," Hornbeck snorted.

"Yes, like Professor von Hellmann. He was one of your guests a few nights ago, wasn't he?"

"Yes, he was, and he will never be a guest of mine again. I invited him into my home and he behaved abominably. The man should be horsewhipped—and you may quote me on that, Miss Brooke."

"So he was not convinced."

"Nothing could convince him! His mind is closed. His mind was made up before he even came to Newport. He only came here to fan the embers of a dying career—of a dead career. He does not care one whit for the truth, only himself. And he could have done Madame Priestley irreparable harm. Fortunately, he was stopped before that could happen. He came here to ruin her—only to ruin her, nothing else—and I will do all that I can do prevent him from doing that."

"I see. So are there ghosts here at Blithewood House?"

"There most certainly are, Miss Brooke."

"Is Madame Priestley receiving visitors this morning?" she asked.

"No," was the firm reply.

The lady reporter closed her notebook and was making ready to depart when she said, "We were all saddened by Mrs. Hornbeck's loss. She was a good woman; we all remember her for the wonderful charity work she did."

"I hope she will be long remembered for it," Hornbeck said. Amelia had done much work through Trinity Church, and in various temperance societies, and on behalf of the poor and the insane. "She was a wonderful woman."

As she made her way back down Blithewood House's main hall, Miss Brooke reflected on just how appropriate the mansion was to its occupant, with the suits of armor and portraits of

Colonel Hornbeck with one hand upon his saber. It seemed very much the home of a knight defending a lady's honor.

When her interview with Colonel Hornbeck was concluded, Miss Brooke pedaled her Hawthorne Ladies' Safety Bicycle down Bellevue to the Ocean House. It was a dry day, and carriages rattling down the unpaved Avenue threw up great yellow clouds of dust.

She sent up her card and Professor von Hellmann received her graciously. She found him charming; he was always charming with reporters. He couldn't remember how many interviews he had given over the course of his long career, he said, and the only interviewer he didn't like was a journalist in San Francisco who consistently left an 'n' off his name.

The first half of the interview was familiar enough—von Hellmann rattled off his answers almost by rote. There were obligatory questions about his upbringing, his family, his early career, and his exposures of notable spirit mediums. He had spent years polishing and smoothing his replies. But at last Miss Brooke came to her point.

"So may I ask what brings you to Newport this season, Professor?"

"The water, the air...." von Hellmann smiled wickedly. "Madame Priestley."

"So you have come to investigate her?"

"Oh, yes. Any medium of her supposed powers and reputation is certainly worth looking into."

"And you were looking into her claims a couple of nights ago at Blithewood House?"

"Yes, I was," von Hellmann replied. He was already enjoying this interview. The lady reporter had a keen straightforwardness that he liked; he remembered her being in the audience on the opening night of his show at the Casino theater. He never forgot a face, and certainly not a young, pretty one. "Have wild stories already been told?"

"One person told me you were all chasing the table around the séance room; I heard elsewhere that Madame Priestley put you in touch with the spirits of your deceased parents," Miss Brooke said. "Still another told me that you were quite unable to account for any of Madame Priestley's manifestations."

"Tricks, my dear, not manifestations. I never once met a medium who was capable of producing what one would call genuine manifestations. They all showed tricks—and tricks of the grossest, most simplistic sort."

"Are all mediums tricksters, then?"

"Every one that I have ever met, my dear. From the Fox sisters right on down to today. Frauds, every last one."

"What about Madame Priestley?"

"She is of course a fraud," von Hellmann said easily. "And you may quote me—but please do spell my name correctly."

"So nothing you witnessed a few nights ago seemed genuine?"

"In my career I have traveled to every major city in the United States and Europe, I have sat with mediums at every opportunity. I have been to well over one thousand séances, Miss Brooke, and in all of those séances I have never seen anything—anything, mind you!—which savors of the genuine. This Priestley woman is no better than the rest of her pathetic tribe."

"You feel very strongly about this."

"I certainly do, Miss Brooke. I feel very strongly about human vultures that prey on the bereaved, holding out false hopes to them. They are villains, Miss Brooke. I could tell you stories that would curl your lovely hair. I know of people who have committed suicide to join departed loved ones in the Summerland, all because some medium told them the spirits were waiting for them. These are dangerous people, Miss Brooke," he said, leaning back into his chair, "Dangerous. And the sooner we can shrug off the clutches of superstition, the sooner we can rid ourselves of that particular cancer of ignorance, the sooner we can all walk together into the new century we are approaching—a century of hope and progress, free from vile and pernicious nonsense which insults our dignity as thinking men."

"Do you think Madame Priestley is dangerous?"

"I do."

"A dangerous fraud?"

"Yes. There are no ghosts at Blithewood House, Miss Brooke. No ghosts at all."

Chapter XIX

ON THE DAY that Miss Brooke's article appeared. Colonel Hornbeck went for a long stroll along the Cliff Walk, as he had so often done with Amelia.

He had read the article over and over again, at least a dozen times. He turned the freshly-ironed and still warm pages and tried to focus his attention on other things, other stories, but always found himself returning to that particular article before too long. By the time he left the house for his walk, he knew the article almost word-for-word.

"It seems that each season in Newport brings some new and fresh sensation, and this season is certainly no exception," the article read, "save that this year's sensation threatens to eclipse those of past years. For this is the year that Madame Helene Priestley has chosen to summer in our old town, and her name has been on everyone's lips since even before her arrival.

"Having made her name in Europe as a powerful and remarkable spirit medium, she and her brother elected to return to the land of their birth and pass a few pleasant months in relaxed seclusion. They have, however, found themselves embroiled in a controversy the likes of which has not been seen for many years past. The argument rages between two very vocal camps: the believers and the skeptics.

"One of the believers is Colonel James Hornbeck of Blithewood House, a summer-colonist of many years standing as well as Madame Priestley's patron. The medium, he says, has allowed him communication with the spirit of Mrs. Hornbeck, whose sad and recent passing all of Newport still deeply mourns.

"'I have heard things from Madame Priestley which could only be known to my wife and me,' Colonel Hornbeck states with grave certainty. 'The only explanation is the obvious one—that she is a very gifted spirit medium.'

"Not so, say the doubters, represented here by Professor Erasmus von Hellmann, known far and wide as a magician of exceptional skill and a crusader against what he calls 'The bogus and inflated claims of frauds like that Priestley woman.'

"'I have sat with Madame, and I have seen nothing— nothing!—that would make me think that she is any different from the rank and file of devious mediums I have seen and exposed in my career. Madame Priestley is of course a fraud,' he says, adding, "There are no ghosts at Blithewood House.'

"And so the battle will go on, quite probably through the remaining weeks of this season and on into the next, until there is some resolution. All of Newport will no doubt be keenly watching these two men, the Colonel and the Professor, the believer and the skeptic, the champion and the crusader."

There on the Cliff Walk, with the waves crashing against the rocks below and the memory of taking this stroll with Amelia on one arm countless times, her presence was almost palpable. He could almost feel her next to him, almost glimpse her out of the corner of his eye.

Hornbeck was furious. No ghosts at Blithewood! What did von Hellmann know, anyway? He was simply a washed-up publicity monger trying to resurrect his pathetic career. Sooner or later, Hornbeck thought, something would have to be done. He couldn't simply stand idly by while von Hellmann slandered a good woman like Madame Priestley. He wasn't going to let it go on. Something would have to be done.

To think that after what von Hellmann had seen, he still stubbornly refused to believe. That séance was a miracle—it was a miracle that Madame had been able to produce manifestations at all, with the skeptical vibrations emanating from von Hellmann so strongly that Hornbeck had felt it himself.

He walked along the path like a somnambulist, neither recognizing nor acknowledging the acquaintances and strangers he passed. They glided by him like ghosts. He glanced at one or two of the cottages as he stalked by them, old memories of balls and parties vaguely stirring. He and Amelia had been honored guests at many of the estates arranged up and down Bellevue and along the cliffs, part of Society. But now he moved past the houses without seeing them.

Hornbeck stood in the long shadow of Cornelius Vanderbilt II's half-completed mansion, the Breakers, blinking up at it in amazement and with a little fear.

The house had been under construction for a year, and would not be completed for another two. Cornelius's wife, Alice, was locked in fierce feud with her sister-in-law, Alva. The Breakers was to be greater and more sumptuous than Alva's Marble House. Richard Morris Hunt, the architect in charge of the project, was using imported marble and alabaster, towers and terraces, Flemish tapestries and double loggias, crystal and gilt, all in attempt to rear the grandest house Newport had ever seen.

Hornbeck and Amelia had been guests at the original Breakers, a rambling wooden house Cornelius Vanderbilt had bought from Peter Lorillard, another wealthy summer colonist. It had been the Vanderbilt summer haunt for several seasons until it burned to the ground last year. So the new structure was to be entirely of stone.

"I don't care much for the house—that can be rebuilt; but I hate to lose my pictures," Vanderbilt had confided to Hornbeck one evening shortly after the fire.

Hornbeck looked up at this massive hulk and thought, Oh, my God—it's all changing as I stand here on the Cliff Walk in the shadow of this house; everything is changing around me.

In Newport, everything was changing too fast to keep up with. Impossible and absurd buildings like this one were mushrooming up all along Bellevue and Ochre Point. It had been such a quiet place, once, when he and Amelia were first married. But now… all changed utterly. Marble houses with whole rooms done in gold leaf, the yearly invasion by ever-increasing numbers of self-important parvenus and social-climbers. Some of the younger set—perhaps most of the younger set, even—would have thought him outdated, old-fashioned, a relic.

And out in the world, the twentieth century was fast approaching. He and Amelia had already made their reservations at Delmonico's for December 31st, 1899, to welcome 1900 in style. America was flexing her muscles abroad, annexing Hawaii even as financial panic spread across the nation like a pestilence. Things were changing too fast.

And at Blithewood House, Ameila was suddenly gone.

Gone, and then just as suddenly returned by Madame Helene Priestley's gifted mediumship. Was she really gone, then…? He couldn't be sure of his footing on such a rocky question. Dead but not gone?

Spiritualism held out hope for those bereft, for those left behind; hope for all those who needed hope. It had given him hope when he needed it so badly.

But… *séances?* If someone had told him ten years ago, five years, a year even, that he would be holding séances at Blithewood House, Hornbeck would have kicked the fool down the stairs. But now here he was, sitting in the dark circle with a medium. But it was a great leap forward, like the telegraph, like electricity, and certainly no stranger a discovery than those had been. Still, he sometimes felt as though he had awakened one day to find himself in the middle of one of Jules Verne's wildest fictions.

Nothing is what it used to be, he thought. Everything is changing, and nothing will ever be the same. This is the last summer like this one. I'm not the only one standing on the edge of a cliff, in the unwelcome shadow of the future; all of Newport is here with me, all the country, all the world.

When Hornbeck returned to Blithewood House a few hours later, he was greeted by the somber-faced underbutler, who informed him that several journalists had been turned harshly away whilst he was out.

"I don't want another journalist in this house any more than I want von Hellmann here," Hornbeck snapped. "Thrash any one of them who comes near."

He wasn't quite sure which annoyed him more—the reporters, or his new underbutler. He didn't like Martin, couldn't quite warm to him. He seldom took much notice of the servants at all; those who were good in their jobs were invisible, and only the problem servants ever got noticed, and such was the case with Martin. He was too quiet, for one thing, and had this way of seeming as though he was watching and waiting for something only he knew of. Henry had already been informed that Martin was to be discharged in a few weeks' time, when the season was over and the Colonel would return to New York.

Hornbeck locked himself in the ballroom—the big high-ceilinged ballroom that looked out across the back lawn and offered a splendid view of the Atlantic. The door creaked like the door of a haunted house. It was quiet here. He had not set foot in it since arriving in Newport. No one had.

Every season the Hornbecks threw two or three lavish balls, inviting half of Newport—the old half, not the newcomers. Indeed, Amelia regularly set aside upwards of two hundred thousand dollars for these balls, and the old guard awaited their engraved invitations eagerly. But there would be no ball this year. The piano and the harp were still shrouded in their pale dustcovers, mute, the huge gas and electric chandelier similarly draped. The usual orchestra had been cancelled, along with the phalanx of caterers and the need for a small corps of footmen, waiters, and general help. This was a house in deep mourning. Hornbeck wondered if he should be here in Newport at all this season.

He sat at the piano bench, staring blankly across the room. When he closed his eyes tight shut, he could see it all plainly: the women in their gowns from Doucet and Pingat, glittering with jewels. The men, their squires in white ties, offering their arms and begging to be saved a dance.

He remembered the carriages lined up outside his house, and the arguments in the smoking room—not always so good-natured—about the relative merits of this lady versus that, and some of the flirtations being carried out like military campaigns or business deals. He remembered some men having the foresight to have their valets bring fresh collars, and sometimes even extra shirts with them. A ballroom in August could be almost intolerably hot, with the swirling of a couple hundred dancers.

Rachel and young James had been taught to dance in this very room by some of Newport's finest dancing masters; they had been taught well. Rachel's coming-out cotillion and young James's wedding celebration had both been held here, and were highlights of their respective seasons.

And of course he remembered Amelia, elegantly beautiful in a gown he had bought her in Paris, with her hair swept up high on her head and looking as lovely at sixty as she had at twenty…

When he opened his eyes it was gone, vanished.

Furious, he closed his eyes again. He clapped his hands over them so hard he saw stars. But they were gone—the dancers, the music, Amelia…

Goddammit, he thought, there *were* ghosts at Blithewood House. He knew there were. No matter what that fool von Hellmann said, no matter how blackly he slandered Madame Priestley. No matter how hard he tried to wrest from him the hope she held out—there were ghosts at Blithewood House.

After a long while, he struggled to his feet, thinking, Something must be done about that man, I won't just stand by. Something will have to be done.

And after a moment's thought, he knew what.

Chapter XX

A VOICE SOUNDED in the darkened theater, echoing over the footlights and onto the stage.

"*What about Madame Priestley?*"

Von Hellmann feigned surprise for a moment, and then smiled wickedly.

"I thought I had made my position quite clear, but apparently not. Very well, then—what about Madame Priestley? She is a fraud of the worst description. The tricks which I witnessed a few nights ago were the sort of pale and clumsy manipulations I would expect from a sickly and not overly bright child with a toy magic set! She is not to be taken seriously. I have said it before and I shall say it again here tonight—I have never seen a mediumistic stunt for which I could not offer at least ten explanations, and I have never seen a spiritualist whom I thought to be anything more than a charlatan!

"And I assure you that I feel no differently about Madame Priestley!"

The audience was divided nearly in half; one half applauded and cheered while the other stamped its feet and hissed. But whether seen as a hero or a villain, he filled every seat in the house twice nightly and that was what mattered. Who cared what they said as long as they said something?

But still, he had spent the week analyzing and experimenting, lying awake at night and ruminating, and he could not explain Madame's spirit trumpet. He worked at it with Hope, and with two afternoons' practice they added their own trumpet routine to the act, to the delight and delectation of the audience. When Madame was using slates, von Hellmann had to demonstrate proficiency at producing the mysterious writings; now that she had seemingly expanded her repertoire—or perhaps her spirits had expanded theirs—von Hellmann rose to the challenge.

During those late nights, however, he knew that his trumpet routine bore nothing but the most superficial resemblance to Madame's. Try as he might, he simply could not replicate what he had seen in the library at Blithewood House a week before, and it infuriated him. A trumpet could not sit in a person's lap and produce voices so far away from the medium. The thing was damningly inexplicable.

But the cheering audience didn't need to know that.

After the show, Jack and Hope went out for a late supper, leaving von Hellmann to close up the act for the night. He preferred to do this work himself, alone, and said he would see them back at the hotel later. They had been so busy since their arrival that Jack and Hope had but little quiet time to themselves. A light supper and a nighttime ride along Bellevue would be perfect, and Jack had mentioned that Spouting Rock by moonlight would make for a dramatic stop.

Von Hellmann always found dark and empty theaters soothing, and altogether different from the feeling of a packed and crowded one. A theater after a show had a profound silence which von Hellmann needed as much as he needed loud applause. With its ceiling of stars, rows of seats and raised stage, the little Casino theater was almost like a church or chapel, and this was as close as von Hellmann had come to a church or chapel in decades.

The last thing he did before leaving was to turn on the ghost light. The ghost light was a superstitious old theater tradition, such as calling *Macbeth* "The Scottish Play," or not whistling backstage, either of which were supposed to bring bad luck. One light was always left on in the house to keep ghosts off the stage because, according to another old tradition, all theaters are haunted.

All theaters are haunted, von Hellmann thought, by at least one blockhead who was just the sort to fall off the apron in the dark and break his fool neck in the orchestra pit. A more prosaic explanation, he thought, and a good precaution to prevent clumsy stagehands from prematurely becoming ghosts themselves.

Despite all this, von Hellmann still tipped his hat as he was leaving and said "Good night" to the silent and empty theater.

He sauntered through the Casino grounds, past the lawn tennis courts, the long breezy porches, the gazebo and the horseshoe piazza and out the big archway and onto Bellevue Avenue.

It was a beautiful August night with a full moon and no clouds. Although just past midnight, Bellevue was bustling and crowded with people coming and going, carriages rattling past, couples strolling arm in arm, sailors and strumpets and late-night diners and drunks. The street was as alive at midnight as it was at noon, and von Hellmann, who loved the night, drank it all in eagerly. Across the Avenue, the eyes of the owls atop the Old Stone Villa's estate posts flickered with eerie gaslight; the birds seemed to regard him curiously. The old magician smiled at them and took a deep breath of the warm night air, feeling wonderful.

"Von Hellmann!" someone called from behind. "Von Hellmann!"

He turned to see three big men approaching. At first he smiled pleasantly, thinking they wanted nothing more than a moment of his time, some witty banter and perhaps an autograph. That sort of thing happened to him all the time.

But not tonight.

He realized, as the burly men came closer, that the last thing any of them wanted was his autograph. One glared at him, another shuffled along with heavy feet as the third asked gruffly, "You von Hellmann?"

"Yesss…" he replied uneasily. In the moonlight he could see the glint of the man's gold tooth.

"Come with us," he said.

"No," von Hellmann said firmly. "I will not."

"Yeah, you will."

"I don't think—"

The other two had circled around behind him.

"And who the hell cares what you think?" the man growled. One of his companions gave von Hellmann a rough shove from behind as the other clamped his hand over von Hellmann's mouth. They pushed him a few yards up the block.

On the crowded midnight street, with the great full moon riding high up in the sky, no one saw a thing.

Some twenty years before, in the '70s, William H. Travers, the famous financier, bon vivant, and member of some twenty-seven clubs, was a frequent visitor to Newport. One evening, gambling at Canfield House at the corner of Bellevue and Bath Road, he broke the bank during an incredible winning streak. Colonel Hornbeck, sitting just to Travers's right, had long ago quit the game and sat in something like awe as the winnings accumulated. No one could withstand the formidable Travers that night.

Desperate to cover his debt, the proprietor put up part of his property—the part fronting the increasingly-exclusive Bellevue Avenue—on the condition that an entrance from that Avenue to his establishment be maintained. Travers accepted those terms and built Travers Block on the property in 1875; when the Casino was constructed five years later, the promised entrance became a mean narrow alleyway running between the two grand buildings.

This was the alleyway into which von Hellmann was now dragged while one of the men stood lookout.

"I'm only gonna tell you this once," the man with the gold tooth said, swinging his broad face in close. Von Hellmann could smell whisky and stale sweat. "Just once, so you listen good—you lay off the medium, you get me? Lay off the medium, an' if you don't—"

He slammed his big fist hard into von Hellmann's stomach. Von Hellmann dropped and steadied himself with one hand against the damp brick wall. He thought he was going to be sick.

The second blow was a strong left which knocked him over sideways. He lay there crumpled at the man's feet and couldn't believe this was happening to him.

The other ruffian crushed his silk topper with one square-toed boot, and snapped his ebony walking stick over one knee. The man threw the broken stick and the ruined hat down next to von Hellmann's head.

"Get me, old man?" the first said again. "You lay off the medium or the only way you leave Newport is in a fuckin' box."

Von Hellmann sat up painfully and glared as the three men stalked out of the alley and went separate ways. Then he fell over again and lay unconscious for a long time. Eventually, he slowly hauled himself up onto his feet and made his unsteady way out onto Bellevue where he collapsed again; the crowd parted suddenly and he hit the sidewalk pavement hard. A moment later he found himself blinking blearily up into the face of a police officer, and he smiled.

The officer, who recognized the bloodied old man lying on the sidewalk, did not return the smile. All he could think about was how angry the chief would be about this.

Chapter XXI

COLONEL HORNBECK INVITED Mr. Rathbone to breakfast at Blithewood House a week after Miss Brooke's article appeared. There, over coffee and in the presence of Madame Priestley and her brother, he laid out his plans for von Hellmann. At certain points he appealed to the brother and sister to confirm certain statements, and pointed to the newspapers to back up others.

"This man has been nothing but trouble since his arrival here, and he has singled out Madame Priestley—*my guest*—for especially awful attacks. He is quoted here in the newspaper as saying that she is a dangerous fraud. It's actionable, Rathbone—it must be actionable. It's slander. He has spent the past week telling the whole town that Madame Priestley is a fraud, when anyone who has sat with her knows otherwise," he said excitedly. "He has to be muzzled, and shown up for the fraud and the liar that he is."

Mr. Rathbone sat in silence for a long moment, sipping abstractedly on his coffee, thinking it over. He didn't like where this was undoubtedly leading. James was a firm man, his sense of honor had been outraged, and Rathbone knew better than to try and dissuade him from an endeavor he had already chosen to undertake. But the thing would have to be handled carefully, if not delicately. This was a very uncertain accusation, and Madame's unusual profession certainly didn't make it any easier. At last he turned to her.

"You realize, don't you, that you are the one who must bring this suit? I understand that it may be the Colonel's idea, but he cannot file as the plaintiff in this case."

"I understand that, of course. Colonel Hornbeck and I have discussed this fully before putting it to you," she replied. "Professor von Hellmann's attacks on me have been vicious and defamatory, and are designed to damage my reputation and my mission here in Newport. I cannot leave these accusations unanswered."

"Very well, then. You do understand, don't you, that should this go to trial, it will subject you to the most intense public scrutiny? Greater scrutiny than you have already been under heretofore?"

"My sister has been under intense public scrutiny all of her life, Mr. Rathbone," Reverend Barrows said. "It is the price she must pay for sharing her gifts with others."

"It hasn't been easy watching von Hellmann run amok, blackening my guest's name," Hornbeck grumbled. "The man has no decency, no honor. We have been very patient with his nonsense, but now we must put an end to his abuse. And by God, I *will*."

In all the many years of their acquaintance, all the breakfasts and lunches like this one, discussing minor legal matters and options, Rathbone had never seen Hornbeck so vehement about anything. Hornbeck could barely contain his contempt for von Hellmann. The man was usually stoic, a rock, immoveable, but this was clearly important to him. Possibly more important than anything else before.

"Von Hellmann's no stranger to the courts, you know," Rathbone said. "I did some reading when you invited me to the séance. He has hauled spirit mediums into court no fewer than eleven times, on as many charges of fraud, fortune telling, taking money under false pretenses, conspiracy to defraud, even grand larceny… He's only lost one case, and that was because of a technicality in the wording of the charge. To give the devil his due, he's put together some brilliant cases."

"But those cases were all brought against frauds and criminals, Rathbone—and we both know that Madame Priestley is neither."

"It is not our decision, it is the jury's, James,"

"And any jury of men with eyes and ears and brains would see that von Hellmann is a liar and a fanatic and should be prevented from carrying this insane war any further. You'll take the case, won't you?"

"Of course. I'm your lawyer. And your friend. But this is very uncertain territory you're straying into here, James, and I can't guarantee you anything at all, you understand."

"I knew we could rely on you."

As the four of them sat at the long breakfast-table, planning the campaign against the enemy, Martin slipped unobtrusively into the room. He cleared his throat politely and said, "Sir?"

"What is it, Martin?"

"Callers, sir," the underbutler replied, offering a card. "Detective Richards, sir."

"Deal with him," Hornbeck replied. He wouldn't have policemen barging into his house again.

"Henry and I have tried, sir, but he is most insistent upon seeing you."

Hornbeck stared at the detective's card much as he had done with Miss Brooke's and weighed his options. At last he said, "All right, Martin, show him in."

Mr. Richards entered the room with his short sergeant behind him, and nodded a curt greeting to those gathered around the table.

"Good morning, Colonel Hornbeck. I am sorry to have disturbed you. Ah, Mr. Rathbone, a pleasant surprise."

"To what do we owe this visit, Richards?" Hornbeck asked suspiciously.

"Last night, Professor von Hellmann was attacked and viciously beaten," Richards began with his usual brusque and businesslike manner. "He will recover. He claims not to know the ruffians, but stated that one of them told him, and I quote, to lay off the medium."

Hornbeck sat up straighter in his chair at this announcement, his lips pursed in a tight strange smile. He glanced over to Madame Priestley; the medium herself seemed to be taking this with a smoldering resignation. Her brother's mouth hung open in dumb surprise.

"But you said he's all right?" Hornbeck asked finally.

"Yes," Richards said with a nod. Behind him, his sergeant was jotting down notes. Richards looked squarely at Madame Priestley and said, "Professor von Hellmann seemed to think that the men who attacked him were not acting on their own—"

"And what are you implying, detective?" Rathbone asked sharply.

"I am implying that these men were hired to accost Professor von Hellmann and give him that stern warning. Now, purely as a matter of procedure I must ask Madame Priestley if she has any comment."

"None," said the lawyer. "We know of no one who could do such a beastly thing."

"I hope, detective, you don't think that suspicion falls on some member of my household?" Hornbeck asked.

"I will have to take statements from each of you, purely as a matter of procedure," Richards replied, with a nod to Mr. Rathbone. "I trust everyone was indoors last night, Colonel Hornbeck?"

"You were out for a while, weren't you, Reverend?" Hornbeck asked. "I apologize for putting you in that position, but honesty is the quickest way to get this matter cleared up. And certainly Detective Richards will find out anyway."

"Of course," Reverend Barrows nodded, a little startled. "Of course. I went out for a couple of hours around nine o'clock. I stopped in at the Casino for a lemonade—I believe I saw von Hellmann's show letting out—there were quite a few people in evening dress filing by. I'm sure the shacker who brought me my lemonade would remember me. We chatted about tennis for a few moments."

"So you were at the Casino," Richards remarked.

"Yes. Is that significant?"

"Von Hellmann was attacked in the alleyway between the Casino and Travers's block—the one that leads to Canfield House."

Reverend Barrows caught his breath and said, "Detective Richards, I give you my word as a man of God that I have nothing to do with this."

"And if he hired some thugs to attack von Hellmann in that alley, would he really be so close by when it happened?" Rathbone asked. "And would he admit that? Of course not."

Inwardly, Hornbeck admitted to himself that there had always been something strange about this spiritualist reverend, something which had made him uneasy. It wasn't the simple earnestness the man exuded. It was, perhaps, that he seemed so eager to be earnest, as though one needed to be convinced. But whatever slight misgivings he might have had, Hornbeck would be damned if he mentioned them to Richards. He wouldn't have the police suspecting him of harboring a suspicious character.

"I am only trying to establish certain facts, sir—believe me when I say that I am confident that no one in this house has any connection to what happened last night. Unfortunately, Newport attracts undesirables every year, and Professor von Hellmann seems to have had the bad fortune to encounter a few of those."

"But you did come to question my guests," Hornbeck said peevishly.

"I only came to ask of she could throw any light upon our investigation," Richards said with a knowing glance at his sergeant. "And, as she cannot, I will make other inquiries elsewhere, and wish you all a good morning."

It seemed to be a morning of crises, Hornbeck thought; for no sooner had Richards and his sergeant withdrawn then Henry and Martin came into the breakfast room, followed by a slow-stepping Eileen. Henry was carrying a large and unfamiliar jewelry box, and looking troubled. But not half as troubled as Martin.

"Sir, I do beg your pardon. But I thought this could not wait."

"What is it, Henry?"

"Eileen was dusting in Mrs. Hornbeck's bedroom earlier. One of them had cause to look under the bed—something about retrieving a dropped duster. When she did, she found this. I have never seen it before, and thought it should be brought to you attention immediately."

He put the box down on the table. It was a large silver jewel-casket, with a domed lid, standing on four dainty Queen Anne legs and done all over in sterling filigree. The plate around the tiny keyhole was badly scratched and slightly twisted at one corner, as though the lock had been forced open. On the lid was engraved the name "*Belminster*" in deep curlicue lettering.

Hornbeck opened the casket and examined its contents.

There were a few loose stones, mainly diamonds, although there was also a pair of emeralds and a few small rubies. A number of rich cameos, bracelets, necklaces and semiprecious brooches, along with gold rings and ropes of pearls were also here, each in its own little velvet pouch. This was old jewelry, the kind of heirlooms passed down from mother to daughter, and it was all quietly beautiful.

He leaned back in his chair and ran a hand over his perspiring, tired face. The day had already proven too much for him.

None of this—neither the jewelry nor the box—was Amelia's. He had never seen any of this strange jewelry before, yet here it was in his house. In his wife's bedroom. Under her bed, where he himself had been sleeping for over a month.

Mr. Morrison stood behind the butler, silently watching.

Hornbeck glanced from the puzzled Madame Priestley to her stony brother.

He was sitting perfectly still, staring at the box. As Hornbeck watched, he saw a look of perfectly earnest bewilderment come over the Reverend's face. Barrows looked up from the casket to meet his gaze and say, "What is it?"

"What do you know about this?"

Hornbeck had spent enough time at the tables of Canfield House to know a good poker face when he saw one. He also recognized when one was being put on, and when he looked at the round little reverend, he saw that mask being slipped on, the innocent role being assumed. Barrows was at the bottom of this business, whatever it was.

"I know nothing of this, I assure you. Nothing at all. Is it yours?"

Hornbeck had had enough.

"You know damn well that it isn't, Barrows. Now what the hell are you playing at in my house?"

The two men glared at one another for half a minute, teetering on the brink, before Madame broke the silence.

"Colonel Hornbeck, please calm yourself. If my brother says he knows nothing of this box then you have my word that he is telling you the truth and knows nothing whatsoever about it."

"Very well, Madame," Hornbeck said reluctantly. "I suppose I must accept *your* word. Henry, lock this up. I'll decide what to do with it later. I have too much on my mind just now."

"Yes, sir."

The trio of servants were dismissed and quietly retreated. Henry sent Eileen back upstairs to continue cleaning The Room while he and Martin went down the hall to the Colonel's study. Henry locked the casket up in the Colonel's big Chinese cabinet, lacquered shiny black with gold cranes. He nodded to Martin, saying, "This has, undoubtedly, been the strangest season yet."

"Quite," Martin replied.

Finally, he thought happily. He would be able to recover it tonight, when the rest of the household was asleep, and be on his way back to England the next day, as fast as steam could carry him.

Chapter XXII

TWO O'CLOCK THAT MORNING found Mr. Morrison sitting awake with a box of cigars, a yellowback novel, and a nearly-empty pot of coffee. As underbutler, he was given a small room to himself on the top floor of the house, the servants' floor, with a tiny window overlooking the front lawn and drive. Henry and his wife had the big corner room down the corridor, the one with the bathroom, and the women were housed in the opposite wing.

Morrison rose from his armchair and stretched tiredly. He closed his book, ground out his cigar, and drank down the last mouthful of coffee. He picked up the neat morocco case of Old Nichol burglars' tools, a stout candle, and a paper of matches. He would tiptoe down to Hornbeck's study, take the jewelry casket from the Chinese cabinet, and vanish from the house before sunrise, leaving the whole business of spiritualists and grieving millionaires and crusading magicians behind him.

It had been a very frustrating few weeks. The constant buzz of activity at Blithewood House—busy for a house supposedly in mourning—had prevented him from doing a proper search. What should have taken a week at most had taken much longer, and after all this time he had nothing to show for his efforts except an aching back, dry hands, and scraped knees. It was amazing, he thought, how one maid sweeping an upstairs floor could prove to be such an impediment. But it was all over now.

Still, he had to admit that he was intrigued by some aspects of this assignment, by some of what had transpired in the last few weeks. A small part of him even regretted that he would not be able to see how the court case progressed; he planned to be safely on his way back to England before the jury was even empanelled. He didn't know what to make of Madame Priestley—it would be interesting to see what a jury made of her.

His thoughts were interrupted by the sound of someone on the gravel walk outside, the smooth stones crunching under a cautious tread. He switched off his electric light and carefully leaned out his little open window.

In the moonlight, Reverend Barrows was creeping across the lawn with a knapsack on his back and stealing furtive glances over his shoulder at the house.

Morrison cursed and quickly shrugged into his jacket. He threw open the trunk at the foot of his bed and got out the Adams six-shot, dumping a handful of extra cartridges into his pocket. He glanced out the window again; Barrows had just slipped through the gate and out onto Bellevue Avenue.

Morrison raced downstairs with the big Adams in one hand.

On the ground floor he dashed into Hornbeck's study and found what he had expected: the Chinese cabinet was standing wide open with the moonlight reflecting brightly off its black lacquered surface. The jewelry casket was gone.

"What the hell is going on?" a voice behind him demanded.

Morrison whirled around to see Edgar standing in the doorway in a rumpled linen nightshirt.

"Barrows stole the jewelry casket," Morrison snapped, pushing past the dumbstruck footman. "Get out of my way."

As he ran out of the house and down the broad marble steps, he heard Edgar yelling, "*My God, where did you get that gun?*"

Morrison could just make out the fleeing figure a hundred yards or more ahead of him. Barrows had seen his pursuer come through Blithewood House's gate and broken into a run.

I could drop him from here, Morrison thought, the Adams heavy in his hand. The light's good enough; just stop, steady, and gently squeeze the trigger. He'd done it countless times before.

But no, not tonight. There was no need, and besides, every shot he'd fired had been in the service of crown and country. If he brought Barrows down tonight, in a foreign country, he would be a common murderer.

Barrows turned and ran down a street to his left, downhill and toward the water. He glanced over his shoulder a few times. Morrison was right behind him.

They were heading into a decaying neighborhood of Colonial houses and tangled, narrow streets. The older areas of town had been left to rot when other neighborhoods such as those along Bellevue and Kay Street became more popular and fashionable among the wealthy summer cottagers. Many of the servants and domestics employed at the mansions a few streets away lived here, amid crawling neglect, cracked Georgian fanlights, and peeling paint.

Where does he think he's going? Morrison wondered grimly. We're on a bloody island. The only way off was the Old Stone Bridge, twelve miles away at the north end of the island. On foot, Barrows wouldn't get there until tomorrow, and there were no steamers leaving until daybreak.

Morrison lost all sense of direction as they chased down the maze of streets and little lanes. He had no idea which way he had come from, but he was slowly gaining on Barrows. He could hear his hurried footsteps ahead.

A dog barked in a yard as he ran past—up ahead, Barrows stumbled and fell, sprawling facedown in the street; it was a damp night, and the unpaved streets were treacherous. Barrows scrabbled to his feet and snatched up the knapsack.

"Leave the box," Morrison called from behind. "You can go, but leave the box."

Barrows got to his feet and watched Morrison slowly close the distance between them.

"Drop it," Morrison said. "I don't care about you—leave the box."

"You won't shoot me," Barrows said.

"I will if I have to."

They stared at one another for a few long seconds. Barrows started to take little sideways steps toward an alleyway. The barrel of the Adams followed him every step. Closer and closer.

"Just give me the bloody box, will you?"

Barrows threw himself down the dark alley. Morrison swore and followed carefully.

The alley emptied out onto a cobblestoned street lined with more dark and forgotten houses. Morrison hesitated for a fraction of a second as he reached the end—something told him not to run right out into that street. He paused, back to the wall, before dropping to one knee and hazarding a quick glance around the corner.

Two loud shots rang out and the bullets whizzed a foot over Morrison's head, splintering the soft woodwork of the house. Barrows stood on the opposite side of the street, perhaps fifty yards off, with the .44 Winchester, the frontier bulldog, clutched in one white hand.

Six shots total, Morrison thought. Now down to four. Now the game was more dangerous.

Standing back up slowly and inhaling deeply, Morrison swung around the corner and squeezed off two shots. But Barrows had already vanished around the corner. A thin haze of gunsmoke clouded the street and the dog was howling.

Too dangerous, now that shots had been fired. If Barrows fired and missed and that errant shot went into a house…

Morrison wondered briefly how many residents of this neighborhood had guns of their own.

He ran across the street and moved up where Barrows had been standing a moment before. He looked around the corner and saw nothing but more old, silent houses. One of them looked abandoned, and a kerosene lamp burned in the window of another. Gunsmoke lingered, its acrid smell stinging in his nostrils. He felt the hairs on the back of his neck prickling, there was a faint flicker of movement at the corner of his eye—

And he threw himself around the corner just as Barrows opened fire from behind. He'd circled back around this little plot of houses, creeping up on his pursuer. He fired wildly, crazily, like a maniac. Two shots—then a third.

Catching his breath, Morrison heard Barrows spit out an obscenity before pelting back across the street and diving back into the little alley. Morrison dashed across the street, gun ready, to reach the spot where Barrows had fallen without using the alley to get there.

Barrows had one bullet left. Unless he was reloading right now.

The round little Spiritualist minister was certainly more dangerous than he had looked.

Morrison raced down the block. At the next corner, he stopped and listened. He could hear Barrows's retreating footsteps, boots scurrying across slick cobblestones in the otherwise quiet night. He set off after the sound.

It wasn't long before he caught up with him. Morrison's ears were still ringing from the gunplay, and he was panting and soaked through with sweat.

Barrows was just ahead, no more than fifty yards, with one bullet in his pistol.

Morrison jumped into an arched doorway, pushing himself deep into the Georgian frame, and fired once straight up into the air.

Barrows whirled and shot once at nothing, and then froze in the middle of the dark street.

Morrison stepped from his doorway.

Barrows raised the gun.

Click.

Click. Click. Click.

A long string of invective was the only sound as he slowly approached the minister standing pathetically in the street, with his ragged breath shaking his body in a series of hysterical little gasps.

"Just give me the box. This will all be over if you just give me the God-damned box."

Barrows gripped the sack with both hands and glared at the approaching Morrison. Then his eyes darted left, right, and back again. He grit his teeth and fled into a nearby weedy yard, leaving his empty gun where it lay.

This was the end of it, Morrison thought. Check and mate. The man had nowhere to go, no gun, and he was trapped in someone's backyard. Morrison had to collect the jewelry casket and get away from this place before the residents decided to come out in force to see what was going on.

He jogged tiredly into the yard, taking the corner wide.

And Barrows came out of the dark, swinging the knapsack and smashing it into Morrison's face. The force of it sent him over backwards, to land on the soft grass. He saw stars. He clutched the sack to him, ready to fight off Barrows if necessary.

But it wasn't. As soon as Morrison had hit the ground Barrows took to his heels and bolted past him, running for his strange little life.

Let him go—it's not your job.

Eventually, Mr. Morrison stood up dizzily. He could feel the sweat drying on his skin and the blood trickling down his face. A lump was rising on his forehead and he suspected his nose was broken. Not for the first time, either, he noted ruefully.

None of which mattered. He open the bag and found the jewelry casket—dented, battered, with one dainty Queen Anne leg twisted at an angle, but there nonetheless. After so long, the object he'd crossed an ocean to retrieve was in his hands. The case was closed, the assignment completed.

He spent a minute or two pondering his next move. He was in no condition to travel—he wasn't even dressed for it and must have looked awful. His few belongings were back at Blithewood House. He would have to go back.

On his way down the Avenue, with the knapsack tucked under one arm, he wondered not only how he was going to explain all this to Hornbeck, but he also wondered just how well the angle of the twisted leg matched the swelling lump on his forehead.

Blithewood House was awake and alight when Mr. Morrison came painfully up the gravel walk a little while later.

The entire staff had gathered in the front hall, the men pacing back and forth and the women huddled together, speaking with hushed concern. No one knew why they were all speaking in whispers, but it seemed like the right thing to do at a time like this, the responsible thing. All were still in nightshirts and nightgowns, sleeping caps, robes and slippers. It was three and they were all bleary-eyed despite the pot of coffee brought up from the kitchen.

Every one of them stared when Morrison opened the door. Edgar, who hadn't been sure if he'd ever see the underbutler again, stared as stupidly as anyone. It was Henry who finally broke the silence.

"Martin! What in blazes happened?" he asked gravely. "Good God man, look at you!"

He was a mess—bruised, bleeding, drenched in sweat and streaked with gunpowder-soot. He'd gone out in a jacket and a collarless shirt; no tie, no vest, no hat. His jacket was torn and filthy, his shirtfront black. The reek of gunpowder permeated the hall.

"Alice," Henry commanded the housemaid, "get some water and vinegar for Martin, and some ice, too. Whiskey is not out of order, either. Edgar, please inform Colonel Hornbeck that Mr. Morrison has returned. Is that the jewel casket? Ah, excellent. I'm sure the Colonel will be most pleased."

"Is Madame Priestley still here or has she also taken flight?" Morrison asked.

"When Edgar gave the alarm, the Colonel went to see her. He found her sitting awake and staring out the window in her nightdress and shawl. She said she knew something in the house was amiss, but the Colonel tells me she did not seem at all concerned for her brother. I myself have not seen her tonight."

"I see," Morrison said, as Alice arrived with a bowl of water and a bottle of vinegar. From a pocket she produced a small flask of whiskey.

Colonel Hornbeck swept down the staircase as Alice began to apply the stinging vinegar to Morrison's various cuts.

"What the hell happened?" he demanded.

"I must speak with you privately, Colonel Hornbeck."

"What?"

"I must speak with you. It is very important."

"All right, Martin," Hornbeck sighed. "Come into the study."

Hornbeck dropped wearily into the leather chair behind the desk, his back to the Chinese cabinet. He still wore his richly-embroidered nightshirt and a heavy robe trimmed in brocade that was too hot for a Newport summer. Exhaustion showed plainly in his old, creased face.

He grumbled something to himself before saying, "Handsomely done, Martin. I always thought that devil was up to something."

Morrison nodded.

"He got away, I suppose?"

"Yes."

"Damn. I would like to have known just what he had to do with this," Hornbeck said, tapping the lid of the jewelry casket, now sitting on his desk. It wobbled slightly on the twisted leg.

"He stole it," Morrison replied.

"Presumably, but from whom?" Hornbeck asked, certainly not expecting an answer from his underbutler.

"From the household of Arthur, Lord Belminster."

The two men stared at one another for a long minute before Hornbeck asked, "What do you know about this?"

"Last September, Lord Belminster died. It was a deeply unfortunate loss. He was one of the preeminent subjects of the crown—Member of Parliament, cabinet minister, some said our next Prime Minister. I myself met him a few times when I was attached to the Foreign Office."

"The Foreign Office?" Hornbeck startled. He took a deep breath and said, "I see. Please continue."

"Madame Priestley and her brother arrived in England at about the time of Lord Belimister's death. In March of this year Lady Belminster extended them an invitation to Shudderleigh Park—the Belminster estate in Surrey. They came down in the earlier part of April. Lady Belminster had never fully recovered from the shock of her loss, and her son, the new Lord Belminster, described her as being in a weakened condition when she began to hold séances with Madame Priestley. Her son would not attend, being himself a skeptic.

"The séances continued for several weeks, ending upon Lady Belminster's own death in early May."

"How did she die?"

"She took her own life—a huge dose of laudanum. She left behind a note saying she had gone to join her husband in the Summerland."

"My God…" Hornbeck murmured. He had heard of things like this before—there were always rumors, but he had never quite believed them. The very thought of it made his stomach tighten.

"After the inquest, Madame Priestley and Reverend Barrows vanished quietly from Surrey. We heard rumors that they had boarded a steamer bound for New York, while someone else remembered they had talked about summering at Newport.

"In her will, Lady Belminster made reference to certain jewels and papers which were to be found in her jewelry casket. The casket itself could not be found, and a few other small but valuable items seemed to have gone missing. Suspicion naturally fell upon the brother and sister, but as nothing was known for certain it was decided to employ a discreet agent rather than the official police. My name was recalled and, though I have long ago retired from the Foreign Office, I do have a small but busy practice as a private inquiry agent."

"An inquiry agent?"

"Yes. Americans would call me a detective."

"I see." Hornbeck's head was spinning as he listened to the man flatly relate his tale.

"So I was engaged to recover the casket, and the jewels and papers it contains."

"Well, obviously Barrows stole it—that Madame would have done such a thing is unthinkable."

"I must say that it does not matter to me which one of them actually committed the theft. If it was the brother, well and good; if the sister, she has nothing to fear from me. I was engaged to recover the box, not to apprehend the thief."

"And for this you masqueraded as my underbutler?"

"I could see no other way to watch them as closely as I needed to. After finding nothing at the Ocean House—"

"My God! That was you?"

"Yes. I had an assignment, you understand."

Hornbeck leaned back in his chair and thought.

"I did not see any papers in that box this morning," he said at last.

"If I may?" Morrison gestured toward the box. Hornbeck nodded. The detective opened the little casket and gingerly removed the jewels and placed to one side. "You will notice that the box is some seven inches deep. However, the compartment inside is only six, and so there is an extra inch to be accounted for. Now, there is a hidden catch just here—"

With a sharp *click*, the floor of the box sprang loose, revealing a half-dozen small packets and bundles of paper bound up in tape.

"The whole story's incredible," Hornbeck said. "But tell me, Martin—why should I believe any of this? What proof do I have that you're telling me the truth?"

"You have only my word, for now, and I see no reason that you should accept that alone. I suggest that you wire my employer tomorrow and confirm what I have told you."

"I intend to do just that," Hornbeck said sharply, but he knew it was pointless. The man was telling him the truth. He idly picked up one of the little drawstring bags the box had contained, and emptied its contents into his hand. Three diamonds tumbled out, along with a small card. On the card was written, in a firm womanly hand, "*Apported by Madame H. Priestley, April 9th, 1893.*"

"You know I can't give you the box until I've confirmed what you've told me?"

"Very prudent, sir. I would expect nothing less. And if I might make two further suggestions, sir?"

Warily, Hornbeck said, "Yes—?"

"First, I see no reason that the police need to know the full details of the night. Reverend Barrows will certainly not return here, and will have appeared to have fled because of his attack upon Professor von Hellmann. It would avoid any number of complications to let the police believe that is what has happened."

"Agreed. Your second suggestion?'

"You shall have to advertise for a new underbutler."

Chapter XXIII

LATE THE FOLLOWING AFTERNOON, Benjamin H. Richards called on Professor von Hellmann at the Ocean House. The magician was in a foul mood, pacing the big room and shaking his head with annoyance.

"Well, Detective Richards," he said peevishly, "and what news have you brought me?"

"Good news and bad news, sir. I have made certain inquiries regarding the attack upon you, and suspicion very naturally fell upon Reverend John Barrows. The stern threats made by your attackers, coupled with his own very insubstantial alibi made me certain that he was our man."

Von Hellmann nodded. "Go on, Detective."

"I had a few other facts to check into late last night, and planned to arrest him this morning on charges of assault and battery, and conspiracy to commit assault and battery. Unfortunately, when I arrived at Blithewood House this morning, I found that he had taken flight during the night—to my mind, sir, no surer proof of his guilt may be offered."

"I see. And he is still at large?"

"Yes."

"And what steps are being taken to find him?"

"We have men watching the docks and the outgoing passenger-steamers. We have sent officers up to Middletown and Portsmouth to aid in efforts there. But to be perfectly honest with you, sir, I do not expect to find him; he has too great a head start on us—some seven or eight hours from what they told me at Blithewood House. We shall spare no pains to find him, sir, but between ourselves, I am not confident."

And the department was handling the case with diligence and zeal. Early yesterday morning, when report of the von Hellmann attack first reached his desk, Captain Garnett's groan could be heard halfway down the corridor. He ordered Richards into his office and closed the door. Chief Read was there, sitting by the window, looking out into Market Square and smoking pensively.

"Detective," Garnett had said sternly, "you've seen the report. I want an arrest made on this by tomorrow—find the bastard behind this and keep it *quiet*! Things like this do not happen in Newport and I will be *damned* if I'm going to let it start now. If word of this gets out, you and I will both be out of a job. Do you understand?"

"Understood, sir."

"Discretion, Richards," Chief Read had said. "Not that you have ever failed to display it in the past, but the utmost discretion is called for here."

The only scandals that were tolerated in Newport were the tiffs and trysts of the summer cottagers—scandals that might be colorful or even titillating, but that was all. Any hint of something more, something darker or more dangerous, was dealt with harshly. Danger would scare the summer people away, and the three men in the room had sensed something wicked brewing since the season had opened. Steps would have to be taken, and taken quickly.

"So you are convinced it was Barrows, then?" von Hellmann asked.

"Yes, quite certain."

"You don't think that the sister could be involved?"

"The lady, Professor?" Richards was a little startled by the suggestion. "No—quite impossible. Her brother is the villain here."

"So she has bewitched you, too, Detective?"

"Really, sir!"

"Pay me no mind, Detective," von Hellmann laughed darkly. "I'm an acrimonious old man and I've had a rotten morning. But you still might consider her…"

"What happened this morning, if I may ask?"

"*This* happened this morning," von Hellmann snapped as he snatched up a sheet of paper from the side table. "I am being sued. It arrived just after breakfast. It's absurd."

"Sued?"

"For slander."

"But by whom?" Richards asked, already knowing the answer.

"Who else? By Madame Helene Priestley."

"I see. Well, some of the statements you have made about her have been rather—lively."

"Thank you, Detective," von Hellmann grumbled. "Now, I wish you a good afternoon. You have your man to find, and I have to find a lawyer."

But the lawyer found Professor von Hellmann the next day, when Mr. Malachi St. Anne sent in his card. St. Anne proved to be a striking figure in a pearl-gray frock coat, ruffled shirt and a flowing tie. His face was as dry and grizzled as an autumn leaf, and his pale eyes never settled anywhere for more than an instant. Von Hellmann had heard of him in a vague way—people said that his quirks and eccentricities went hand-in-hand with a quick and penetrating legal mind.

"I hear that you need a lawyer," he said simply.

"Word travels quickly."

"This is Newport—I knew you needed a lawyer before you did."

"I see."

"I would have come sooner, but I've spent the last couple of days reading up on every spiritualistic court case I could find— The Slade and Home cases in England, Ann O'Delia Diss Debar's trial in New York five years ago, contesting the Commodore

Vanderbilt's will in '77, and the spirit photography cases, too—I can't believe that charges against Mumler were dismissed. A blind man could see that the photographs were fakes, and a competent prosecution could have torn his witnesses to ribbons. Still, fascinating stuff, really."

"Yes," von Hellmann said, warming to the man; he'd obviously done his research, and his reputation was a good one.

"My fees are quite reasonable," St. Anne said.

"All right. You've handled slander cases before?"

"Several. Good name in man and woman, dear my Lord, is the immediate jewel of their souls. Who steals my purse steals trash, 'tis something, nothing; 'twas mine, 'tis his, and has been slave to thousands; But he that filches from me my good name robs me of that which enriches him not, and makes me poor indeed."

"If you can quote law as well as you quote Shakespeare, Mr. St. Anne, we can hardly lose."

"No client of mine is allowed to use that last word, Professor."

"I see. So your confidence is high?"

"Of course. Before my retirement I had an eighty-nine percent success rate."

"I am flattered to think you came out of retirement just to represent me."

"Well, I'm only semi-retired, really. I'll still argue a case which seems interesting enough or big enough. And this certainly seems big enough. I have no doubt that it'll make all the papers."

"I had thought of that myself."

"It'll be good to be in print again," the lawyer said with a smug grin. Something about that grin bothered von Hellmann, an uncomfortable feeling that he'd seen that same grin on a different face.

"So how do we go about building a defense?" he asked.

"We start with a simple question, and that simple question is: are you telling the truth about Madame Priestley? The truth as you understand it?"

"She is as gross a fraud as I have ever encountered," von Hellmann replied firmly.

"Can you prove it?"

"Certainly."

"Then there is no slander and she has no case," St. Anne said with another grin. "That libelous statements are true is a complete defense in a civil action—Perry v. Mann, 1849. Now the only sticky part is proving the truth to twelve blockheads sitting in a jury box."

"Surely it cannot be that difficult?"

"You are perhaps forgetting that Lizzie Borden was acquitted of the murder of her father and step-mother not two months ago?"

"But we have thee and me, Mr. St. Anne—two things which Miss Borden did not."

"Quite. But still, Newport is convinced that Madame Priestley is not only real, but brilliant and gifted as well. She has recently been abandoned by her no-good brother, which will undoubtedly garner sympathy among the public. And she has Colonel Hornbeck backing her—a pillar of Newport society, that one. But aside from all that, it will be most difficult to show her up as a fraud in court."

"Why? Why most difficult of all?"

"Because so many believe her to be legitimate. I must confess, Professor, that I account myself among that number."

"You're joking."

"Oh, no. She seems most remarkable, and her demonstrations defy explanation."

"If you believe her, then why are you offering to represent me?"

"I'm a lawyer. It's what I do, Professor."

They cautiously shook hands.

Chapter XXIV

PRIESTLEY V. VON HELLMANN began a week later.

Hornbeck exerted whatever influence he could muster to ensure that the trial would not begin until after the season had ended. Rathbone and he were confident enough of their case, but Hornbeck did not relish the thought of his name being paraded through the courts before a gallery of gawking curiosity-seekers. He had enough of that just living on Bellevue Avenue. Fortunately, it was decided early on to begin the trial after the first week of September; the summer colonists and hangers-on would have returned home by then and, it was hoped, litigation could proceed with a minimum of sensation. But the more dedicated sensationalists simply decided to stay on for another couple of weeks. This was going to be quite a show, after all.

For von Hellmann, two weeks of waiting and inactivity was a horror. He was anxious for the trial to begin; spiritualists were no strangers to the courts, and neither was he. He waited impatiently to show Newport what a fraud this harpy was, how she'd made fools of them.

Every one of Newport's half-dozen newspapers had reporters following the story; the story of the season was now the trial of the century, even eclipsing the Borden case in certain circles. Word spread far and quickly, and Edwin M. Lillibridge of the *Providence Telegram* had arrived, along with Hutchinson Hatch, a reporter from Boston. There was even a rumor about a number of New York journalists due to arrive on the next steamer. Miss Brooke had to contend with all of them, in addition to the hated Mr. Carson.

"Von Hellmann's got a tough row to hoe," one of the reporters observed.

"What do you mean?" asked Hutchinson Hatch.

"That woman has all of Newport wrapped around her little finger, and that judge is a believer—I interviewed him last year and he said he's always believed in all sorts of strange goings-on."

"And all Rathbone has to do is find one trick von Hellmann can't explain and it's finished, over like *that*," said Edwin M. Lillibridge, snapping his fingers with violence.

"But the woman's a fake," another said. "Anybody with eyes in his head can see that."

"I wouldn't be so sure of that."

"Of which? Of her being a fake? Or of everybody being able to see that?"

"Both," Lillibridge said. "She's got quite the reputation to defend."

"So does von Hellmann. He's caught plenty of sharpers like her in the past, and I'll lay you the price of a new hat that he'll do it again."

"I'll take that bet," called a journalist in a worn derby.

"Me, too—you're on."

"And I'll lay you both double that she makes a monkey out of him. I've seen this woman at work and she's for real."

"You're on!" someone called.

"I'm in," another said, holding up a wrinkled dollar bill.

Miss Brooke smiled to herself and placed no bets.

The Newport County Court met in the Colony House. Standing at the head of the Parade, the Colony House had been a Newport landmark for over a century and a half. Originally built to house the Colonial legislature, the Declaration of Independence was read from its front steps on July 20th, 1776. Soon thereafter, the building served as a barracks and was also the scene of a grand reception for General Washington, after the redcoats withdrew.

There were two courtrooms in the building: a small one downstairs and a larger chamber upstairs. With the lawyers and litigants having to shoulder their way through the crowds thronging the courthouse steps and packing the corridors every morning (McMurphy nearly got into a fistfight with Gaskell over the best seat), it was decided to convene in the upstairs room.

"Gentlemen of the jury," Mr. Rathbone intoned, "you are here to hear a case of slander—the slander spoken by a washed-up performer of tricks and a self-proclaimed anti-spiritualist against a visitor to our town, a guest, and a woman of upright character. He denounced her from the stage of a packed theater, declaring he has, and I quote—*'never seen a spirit medium who is anything less than a charlatan, and I assure you that I feel no differently about Madame Helene Priestley.'* He added to this, in the newspapers, that *'she is of course a fraud'*, and implying that Madame Priestley is perhaps taking money from her sitters and, in return, demonstrating, and again I quote, *'The sort of pale and clumsy manipulations I would expect from a sickly child with a toy magic set.'*

"Surely, such vituperative and blatantly slanderous statements cannot and should not go unchallenged.

"The defendant in this action was exercising no freedom of speech here—he can claim no protection guaranteed by our First Amendment. No, he has crossed that line with his slurs, attacking and maliciously seeking to defame an innocent woman. And for what? A publicity stunt, in hopes of reviving a career long gone.

"How many of you in this courtroom have attended one of my client's séances?" Rathbone asked, looking from jury box to gallery. A murmur ran through the courtroom as those assembled traded uneasy glances. "Many of you, I am sure. And many of you have benefited from the gift of her mediumship. And there is no doubt in your mind that her abilities are both startling and genuine, and that Professor von Hellmann's accusations are both scurrilous and false."

"I ask you to consider this," Rathbone said with a bow to the jury-box, "That when von Hellmann sought to defame her for no other reason than to clutch at a few headlines, he not only attempted to blacken her name but he also thumbed his nose at all of you who have seen for yourselves, with your own eyes, proof of Madame Priestley's extraordinary abilities. In accusing her of fraud, he has accused all of you of being defrauded by her, fooled by her, deluded by her. As if you were unable to know the difference between a gifted woman using those gifts for the enlightenment of others, and the cheapest and most obvious of swindlers and imposters.

"I will leave you with this, gentlemen of the jury—if Professor Erasmus von Hellmann thinks that Madame Helene is a fraud, then let us see him prove it."

Wild applause and cheers echoed in the courtroom, only to be answered by skeptical hissing and foot-stamping. The judge severely gaveled the unruly courtroom back to order as Mr. Rathbone took his seat next to Madame, sitting placidly with her small hands folded on the plaintiff's table.

"Gentlemen," Mr. St. Anne said, rising to address the court and hooking his thumbs in the pockets of his bright silk vest, "my own opening remarks will be brief. My client, Professor Erasmus von Hellmann, is a man more sinned against than sinning. I will not for a moment contest any of the lively quotes my learned friend has introduced—my client has uttered every one of them. I will, however, add this—that every one of those statements is absolutely and unconditionally true! We shall offer you more than satisfactory proofs of their accuracy. Madame Priestley is a mountebank, and Professor von Hellmann sits in this courtroom today for simply having the audacity to say that aloud. And I need not remind you gentlemen that where there is truth, there is no slander.

"Her case is without merit, and has been brought simply to muzzle her opponent. We cannot let her do that. We must hear what he has to say, whether it is to our liking or not.

"Has Professor von Hellmann insulted Newport? And has he also, as my learned friend Mr. Rathbone supposed, thumbed his nose at Newport's ability to detect a fraud in our midst?

Hardly. He has, in fact, done us all a great service by unmasking this marauding, defrauding she-wolf prowling our island. There are many here today who would thank him—who should thank him. He is, indeed, uniquely qualified for the task—he is trained and practiced in the art of deception, where many of us are not. If anyone is able to detect and expose a fraud, it is he—set a thief to catch a thief. It is our good fortune that Professor Erasmus von Hellmann is an honest thief, working for the public good rather than against it.

"Nellie Bly has exposed the abysmal conditions in the insane asylums. Was she chastised for writing *Ten Days In A Madhouse*? No. Was she excoriated for bringing to light these awful injustices? No. She is a heroine, and we regard her as nothing less. My client, Professor Erasmus von Hellmann, is entitled to no less for his actions. Thank you."

He swept into his seat beside von Hellmann. The courtroom was strangely quiet.

Rathbone called Detective Benjamin H. Richards as his first witness.

The whole court sat a little straighter as the big detective made his way onto the stand. There had been excited rumors whispered about his possible testimony—this was a man Newport would listen to, whose word carried weight. Hornbeck leaned forward expectantly, and Miss Brooke turned to a fresh page in her notebook.

"Detective Richards, will you please tell the court how you came to be acquainted with Madame Priestley?"

"I attended one of the séances at the Ocean House she held when she first arrived. Madame Priestley sent an invitation to Chief Read, who was unable to attend due to prior commitments. He asked me to go in his stead and I did. I was deeply intrigued by what I witnessed there that night."

"Intrigued enough that you sat with Madame Priestley

several more times, is that not correct?"

"That is quite correct, sir. I have attended a total of four séances with Madame, in addition to a small number of private consultations."

"And what was the nature of these private consultations, Detective?"

"This season, I have had to conduct an investigation of a particularly insoluble character, in addition to my normally heavy caseload. I must confess that I had exhausted every possible lead and had reached no conclusions. This was a very vexing situation, as you might well imagine, so I sought the advice of Madame Priestley. I have heard of cases in which a spirit medium has been able to assist the police. I laid the facts before her and she was able, after some meditation, to suggest a line of inquiry which, though requiring something in the way of interpretation, did finally bear fruit. We got our man."

"And this initial consultation led to further sittings?"

"Yes, sir. I have long heard about the powers of mediums to assist the police, and Madame has given me the opportunity to test that rumor first-hand. And the results have been impressive. I met with her several more times to ask advice on a pair of cases, and each time her thoughts on the matter were most beneficial to me. She was able, in one instance, to describe a suspect merely by handling an object we had reason to believe he used in the commission of his crime. Of course I can give you no details other than to say that an arrest was made and that man is now awaiting trial."

"Please bring my card to your suspect, Detective—he'll need a good lawyer," Mr. St. Anne said.

The court laughed nervously, and was silenced by a scowl from the judge.

"Do you believe that Madame Priestley could have practiced any trickery on you, either at the séances or at any of those private consultations?" Rathbone asked.

"No, sir. I am confident that there was no trickery whatever.

How could there be?"

"We are all waiting for Professor von Hellmann to enlighten us upon that point," Rathbone said with a sly grin. "Thank you, Detective. I have no further questions."

"I have followed your career with interest, Detective Richards," St. Anne said graciously, rising. "Certainly a capable police detective—with a thriving private practice as well—has no need to seek the advice of an amateur such as this?"

"She has been very helpful to me, sir."

"But surely you have never needed such assistance before? Your record has heretofore been a very impressive one—I was under the impression that you needed no such... *unorthodox* methods to bring a case home."

"If I have not consulted with Madame Priestley in the past it is only because she has not been here to consult," Richards said blandly.

"I see. And you are sure that her advice to you is the product of her occult powers?"

"I am, sir."

"They couldn't simply be lucky, educated, or informed guesses?"

"Damned lucky guesses if they are, sir."

"And you're sure that you've arrested the guilty parties?"

"I am, sir."

"No chance of having arrested the wrong man on this... opinion of Madame's?"

"That is for the court to decide when the case comes to trial."

"Professor Townsend, you have a wide and distinguished reputation as an investigator of these spiritualistic phenomena. Could you give the court a small sketch of your career?" Mr. Rathbone asked.

"As a Professor of Philosophy at St. Stephen's College, I naturally was interested in the claims being made by the Spiritualists—claims which clearly warranted careful study.

Accordingly, I began attending séances, even holding a series in my own home to better study and test the mediums and the phenomena first-hand. After a few years, I joined the newly-formed American Society for Psychical Research and began to publish some of my findings. Some time thereafter I was invited to sit on the Wraeburn Committee for the Investigation of Psychical and Spiritualistic Claims, an honor I gladly accepted."

"And what were these findings which you published?" Rathbone asked pointedly.

"That some seventy-five to eighty percent of all spirit mediums I sat with were frauds."

Pandemonium broke out in the courtroom. Townsend was both applauded and cursed, cheered and denounced. The banging of the judge's gavel could barely be heard over the din.

"And the remaining twenty or twenty-five percent?" Rathbone asked when order was restored.

"Seemed to me to be genuine."

"Unreservedly genuine?"

"In some cases, but not in others."

"I am afraid that I don't quite follow you, Professor."

"There are mediums of genuine powers who will still, occasionally, stoop to cheating in order to produce a desired result," Townsend explained. "The powers which some of these individuals have been blessed are, at times, unpredictable, and I have sat through a number of what we call blank séances—séances at which no phenomena whatever were observed. The spirits do not always answer when we call upon them. I have found that on such occasions certain mediums, even those possessed of genuine powers, may cheat, lest their sitters go away disappointed. But simply because a medium cheats on one occasion does not mean that the medium cheats on every occasion."

"But why should they cheat at all?"

"The vast majority of mediums I have sat with have as their chief motive a desire to help those in grief, to help them through the period of mourning, to help them understand that those they love are not lost, but gone before. So most would think of a little cheat in the séance room as no more than a white lie. If you were in pain, and I told such a white lie to ease your suffering, would you brand me an untrustworthy liar?"

"I most certainly would not, Professor. Nor, I'm quite sure, would others."

"I object, Your Honor," Mr. St. Anne rose to his feet. "Mr. Rathbone is in no position to speak for others."

"Sustained. Mr. Rathbone...."

"My apologies, Your Honor. Professor Townsend, you have attended a number of Madame Priestley's séances, have you not?"

"Yes, I have."

"And what is your opinion?"

Townsend hesitated, took a deep breath, and said quietly, "I think that she is a very gifted medium who... *sometimes* cheats."

The judge's hand was upon his gavel before the outrage erupted in the room. This was unwelcome news to Madame's supporters and her doubters alike.

"And so she is genuine?" Rathbone pursued, once the hubbub subsided.

"I have seen her produce phenomena which are as startling and inexplicable as any I have ever witnessed—phenomena which I feel could only be produced by occult means. But I have also seen her perform a number of feats which, I know for a fact to be fraudulent."

"And how do you *know* this, Professor?"

"Because of my longtime friendship with Professor von Hellmann; he has shown me a thing or two about trickery."

"But can you prove that these phenomena which you feel are fraudulent are in fact so?'

"No, but I strongly suspect."

"So she only practices trickery *some* of the time?"

"Yes," Townsend replied. "For example, I have observed her 'fishing' on several occasions."

"Fishing, sir?"

"Yes—making a number of vague statements and waiting for a sitter to respond to one or two in particular, and then concentrating along those lines in her next statements. A good medium can pump quite a bit of information out of an unwary sitter in this way, delivering the information as though from the Beyond. As I am under oath, I must admit that I have seen her practicing this technique a couple of times now, although why a woman would stoop to this when she has such very real and amazing abilities is quite beyond me."

"Abilities such as?"

"Such as her ability... to contact those who have died. It is absolutely authentic."

"You are quite sure of that, Professor Townsend?"

"Quite sure. Just... just at the beginning of the season—" Townsend's voice caught in his throat, and he obviously struggled for a moment. He swallowed hard and said, "At the beginning of the season in July, she contacted the spirit of our son, gone over fifteen years now. There was no doubt in my mind that it was my boy."

"You have referred to your long friendship with Professor von Hellmann. You know him quite well?"

"I believe so. We've know each other for quite some time now."

"And never a cross word between you?" Rathbone asked slyly.

"I wouldn't put it that way, Mr. Rathbone—we've had words, on occasion."

"When you didn't see eye-to-eye on a subject? Perhaps on a medium's genuineness?"

"On a few occasions, yes."

"But you have always been able to settle the dispute, like friends?"

"Not... always."

"Can you cite a specific example?"

Townsend glanced at von Hellmann with an expression of apology. The magician showed no emotion at all.

"Quite some years ago, he claimed to have found a reaching-rod in a séance chamber—a rod we were quite certain had not been there a few moments before. The room had been thoroughly searched, as was the medium, and yet it was suddenly there in his hand."

"You think he sneaked it into the room, to frame the medium?"

"I thought that at the time, but I cannot prove—"

"Why would he do such a thing?"

"I think because he could not catch her red-handed—and I always thought there was nothing to catch."

"Meaning that he planted evidence in order to accuse a genuine medium of fraud?" Rathbone pursued doggedly. "What of the pursuit of truth? What of the testing of spiritualistic claims?"

"Professor von Hellmann is a showman, and his first concern has always been his career—and its promotion. Failing to expose a medium could only damage to his reputation. He felt he had to do something."

"Even something dishonest?"

"In this case, yes," Townsend said slowly.

"Thank you, Professor Townsend."

Chapter XXV

WHEN COURT RECONVENED the following morning, an excited buzz ran among the crowds gathered on the steps, lining the halls, and packed into the courtroom. Several newspapers speculated that this was the day Madame Priestley herself would take the stand, while others insisted that von Hellmann would be testifying. Miss Brooke's paper wisely supposed that neither would be called.

Excitement buzzed again when Rathbone put Colonel Hornbeck on the stand.

"Will you please tell the court how you first became acquainted with Madame Priestley?"

"Yes. I received a note from her shortly... shortly after my wife's funeral," Hornbeck began nervously. "A week after, I think. She said she had been dreaming of my wife, though of course the two had never met."

"And what did your wife say in these dreams?"

"Things that only she—only Amelia, would have said. She referred to an inscription on the watch she gave me as a wedding present."

"I see. And you had your first séance with her shortly thereafter?"

"Only a few nights later. In my library."

"And what happened?"

"Amelia wrote her name, and mine, on a pair of slates. In her own handwriting. It was... incredible."

"In her own handwriting? Are you quite sure?"

"Mr. Rathbone, in my desk I have a stack of sixty-seven letters, each one of them from my wife, and they are tied in a bundle with a ribbon she wore in her hair the day we met. Some of those letters are over thirty years old, going back before our children were born, and some even before our marriage. Each night since her funeral, before going to bed, I have read and re-read a few of the letters in that bundle. So yes, Mr. Rathbone, I am quite sure that I recognize Amelia's handwriting."

"I see. So after that, Madame Priestley became your houseguest, and she conducted a number of séances with you."

"Yes."

"And at any of these séances, could she have practiced any trickery or sleight-of-hand such as what the defendant alleges?"

"Certainly not," Hornbeck growled, with an angry glance at the defense table. Von Hellmann started back coldly. "Von Hellmann is trying to save his pathetic career—he'd do anything to get his name in the newspapers again."

"I understand that you invited Professor von Hellmann to a séance in your home."

"Yes."

"And what happened?"

Everyone in the courtroom leaned forward expectantly.

"Madame Priestley made use of a spirit trumpet—an instrument that allows spirit voices to be heard."

"Allegedly," St. Anne said dismissively.

"At this particular séance, Professor Townsend heard the voice of his son," Hornbeck went on, ignoring him. "My wife… my Amelia spoke to me."

"And were there any messages for Professor von Hellmann?"

"The spirits mocked him for his ignorance and his skepticism."

"Then what?"

"Then he tried to grab the floating trumpet; the circle was broken and the spirits vanished. There was chaos. I thought I heard Madame let out a shriek, and someone turned on a light."

"And—?"

"And there was nothing. The trumpet was on the table and Madame was in a faint brought on by the shock she had suffered."

"According to many spiritualists, striking a light in a séance chamber can be disastrous for the medium, possibly even fatal, is that not correct?"

"Yes—turning on that light was a reckless thing to do—and it was one of von Hellmann's flunkies that did it."

"I see," Rathbone said thoughtfully. "And when that light went on, did you see anything suspicious? Any wires? Any pneumatic tubing? Any secret assistants scurrying back to their hiding places?"

"Nothing of the kind," Hornbeck said firmly.

"And shortly after this séance, Professor von Hellmann renewed his public attacks upon Madame Priestley?"

"The very next night."

"Can you think of any reason for this?"

"Aside from a damned publicity stunt, no—unless finally witnessing a genuine demonstration of occult powers had unbalanced the poor man's faculties."

"I see. Thank you, Colonel Hornbeck. Your witness."

"Thank you, Mr. Rathbone," St. Anne said, rising. "Now, Colonel Hornbeck, I shall not belabor the points which I have already made, except to remind you that the court has already heard a lengthy discussion about the relative inability of the layman to detect the kind of fraud practiced in the séance chamber. I stand by what I said yesterday.

"You have acted as Madame Priestley's patron since shortly after her arrival in Newport, is that not correct, sir?"

"That is."

"And as your guest she enjoys a certain amount of security. As your guest, she has your good name behind her, and as your guest she has an entree into Newport society. A good confidence artist might well lay elaborate, even Machiavellian plans to secure so much."

"Objection!" Rathbone shot to his feet, scowling indignantly. "It is far from established that my client has laid any plans at all, and even further from established that she is any kind of confidence artist."

"Oh, I was merely making an observation, Your Honor. I have not said anything about the plaintiff; I was merely thinking aloud. But if my colleague is ready to take any mention of confidence tricksters as a reference to his client, perhaps this shows that he is more inclined to agree with the defense."

The spectators chuckled; even the judge smiled.

"I would like to make it absolutely clear that I do not consider her to be any sort of confidence artist," Hornbeck said firmly.

"Thank you, Colonel, it will be noted. Now, sir, the plaintiff first impressed you by knowing the inscription on your watch—something you are convinced no one but you and your wife knew, correct?"

"Correct."

"I would like you to keep that in mind for a little while; I will come back to it later. Now, the plaintiff next impressed you by producing those mysterious signatures upon the slates written, as I understand, in your wife's own handwriting?"

"Also correct."

"You are quite sure it was her handwriting?"

"I believe I have already made that clear just a few moments ago, Mr. St. Anne, if you were listening."

"Well now—I only have to ask you this. Are you sure it was her handwriting, or did you *simply desperately wish it to be her handwriting?*"

Whatever answer Hornbeck gave was lost in the uproar that followed. Nearly half the room was on their feet in an instant, booing and shrieking for St. Anne to be disbarred and von Hellmann to be run out of town. For a dangerous moment, the courtroom teetered on the brink of a riot. The only voice that could be heard over the din was that of the old veteran lawyer shouting, "No further questions, Your Honor!"

After a brief recess, the court resumed and the plaintiff called their next witness, Professor Erasmus von Hellmann himself. The magician was eager to take the stand, almost strangely eager. Standing in his deep black suit, crisp white vest, with his hair tied back by a long silk ribbon, he smiled hungrily as he approached the witness stand. Hope, seated in the gallery, beamed at him proudly.

"So in addition to your regular magic act, which I am sure delights children, you have also gained considerable notoriety for your attacks upon so-called fraudulent spirit mediums, is that correct, professor?" Rathbone asked icily. "Ah, but pardon me for one moment—from which institution did you receive your doctorate?"

"From the School of Hard Knocks," von Hellmann laughed. "It is customary among showmen in my profession to adopt some sort of interesting or exotic title—Anderson, Hoffman, and Kellar all styled themselves 'professor' at some point—and I simply followed suit. I have traveled with doctors, swamis, princes and princesses, none of whom had real claim to those titles." He smiled broadly and stroked his goatee. "It's all in fun, part of the show."

"So you are not actually a professor, then?"

"My formal education is almost nothing—I left school to take to the stage at a very young age."

"I see. And for a time, you seemed to do pretty well for yourself, but your name has not been heard much in the last few years...."

Von Hellmann visibly bristled at that, but kept quiet. The nerve!

"And now after some years passed in obscurity, you have returned, determined to destroy my client. Why?"

"Because she is a fraud and should be exposed for what she is."

"A fraud like all other mediums?"

"A fraud like every medium I have ever seen—fakes, charlatans, and mountebanks, every last one. I have never seen one I believed in, and I've never seen one whose tricks I couldn't duplicate, or at least explain."

"And it seems that you never tire of pointing that out. But why now? Why Newport? Why Madame Priestley?"

"My friend Professor Townsend wrote to me in New York. He has already mentioned that we served together on the Wraeburn Committee; he attended a few of her séances and thought I might be interested."

"So you came at his invitation?"

"More or less, yes."

"Not to stage a dramatic comeback? Not to bolster a faded career?"

"No," von Hellmann said through clenched teeth, and stopped himself there. He knew if he tried to say anything more, it would only end in a seething flow of invective and then there really would be a riot.

"And what did you think when you sat with Madame Priestley that night at Blithewood House?"

"It was typical of this kind of thing, which is to say it was a pathetic show of second-rate conjuring tricks, poorly executed. If I performed that badly, I would be booed off my stage."

"Nothing impressed you as genuine?"

"Nothing."

"But others present that night described some very singular occurrences at that same séance you attended."

"As a magician, I see these things differently," von Hellmann said patiently. "Where my friend Townsend may see a feat performed by mysterious occult forces, I see a trick explained by black thread or some other such contrivance."

"But surely that marvelous trumpet is not explained away by black thread, Professor?" Rathbone all but licked his lips has he posed the question.

After a long hesitation, von Hellmann was uncomfortably forced to admit that it was not.

"And could you please enlighten the court with your exposure of this particular spiritualistic... trick?"

"Anyone who has seen my act will have seen my spirit

trumpet routine—"

"A spirit trumpet trick which bears no resemblance whatever to what was seen that night at Blithewood House. Now, Professor von Hellmann, can you explain to the court how Madame Priestley could have manipulated the trumpet and produced not only the voice of Professor Townsend's son, but also of Colonel Hornbeck's wife? Can you explain it, sir? Can you?"

In the forced hush of the courtroom, von Hellmann's answer was a harshly whispered, "No!"

Mr. Rathbone turned first to the crowd packing the spectators' gallery, and then to the jury. He was smiling like a matinee idol taking his bows.

"You lied to me, sir," he said, turning sharply back to his witness. "You lied to me and you lied to this court. Just moments ago, you alleged you had never seen a spiritualist manifestation you could not duplicate or explain. And now you have just told us—under oath!—that you cannot explain what you saw the plaintiff do! Perhaps you cannot explain the trickery because there simply is no trickery! Perhaps you have just witnessed your first demonstration of genuine spirit power, sir!

"And having seen what would make a believer out of the most hardened skeptic, you chose to publicly condemn a woman whose strange talents you cannot explain away with trap doors, mirrors, and black thread. No, rather than admit the truth, you have slandered her, and all for the sake of a publicity stunt—for that is what all this is, isn't it, *Professor*?"

"No!" von Hellmann shouted. "No, dammit, this woman is a fraud—"

A howl of outrage echoed in the courtroom and the judge gaveled the mob back into submission. When they were finally quieted, he sternly cautioned them that if there was another such outburst, all spectators, including the press, would be banned from the courtroom for the remainder of the trial. The spectators lapsed into a sullen silence.

"You may continue, Mr. Rathbone," he said.

"Oh, we have no further questions, Your Honor."

"Your witness, Mr. St. Anne."

With a smile to his client, St. Anne said confidently, "No questions, Your Honor. We shall answer all questions and lay to rest any doubts when we begin the defense."

This was unusual, certainly. But the whole court could see that the attorney and his client had something up their sleeves.

"We call to the stand Madame Helene Priestley," Mr. Rathbone boomed.

The elegant medium glided across to the witness stand, her beautiful face without expression. She wore a gray silk dress of a dramatic cut, with a cameo at her throat and a folded fan in one gloved hand. Her hair was plaited into a long braid. She stood before the silent, staring court like a queen before her subjects.

"Now, Madame, please accept my apologies," Rathbone began. "It seems that in bringing a wholly understandable action for slander before the court, you have had to subject yourself to still further slanders during these proceedings."

"Objection, Your Honor, we are here to determine if she has been subjected to any slander at all," St. Anne said petulantly.

"Sustained," the judge said gravely. "You will withdraw the statement, Mr. Rathbone."

"And it is withdrawn, Your Honor. Now Madame, I have a simple question for you, and it is this—are you a fraud?"

"No, I am most certainly not," was the cool reply.

"You don't practice any sort of trickery or deception on the people who invite you to hold séances for them?"

"No."

"Professor Townsend has opined that some mediums—and only some, mind you—cheat some of the time," Rathbone said with a facetious grin. "Now Madame, I must ask if you are one of those mediums."

"I am not."

"You never cheat?"

"No"

"Never?"

"Never."

"I see," Rathbone said, bowing with mock-seriousness. "May I ask your opinion of Professor von Hellmann's performances?"

"I am told that they are a show of exceedingly clever and well-performed conjuring tricks, and that, as entertainments go, they are not to be surpassed. But I have only read what others have written and heard what others have said." She smiled a little coldly. "I myself have not attended a performance, of course."

"Of course," Rathbone echoed. "You have already heard it said in this courtroom that some, including Professor von Hellmann of course, would say that the resemblance between certain conjuring tricks and certain séance room manifestations might suggest that those manifestations are in fact themselves *tricks*."

"I have heard it said a few times, both here and elsewhere," Madame nodded.

"And what is your response to this allegation?"

Clearly amused, Madame Priestley asked, "Might it not also suggest that Professor von Hellmann is also a very gifted spirit medium?"

Her supporters chuckled; her detractors sneered.

"Moving on—you have never charged a fee for your services?"

"No."

"Never?"

"Never. Since my arrival in Newport, I have been very busy, and some of my grateful sitters have been very liberal in making me gifts. This very cameo here was given to me a few weeks ago as a show of gratitude by one such sitter. I was able to place her in contact with a departed loved one and she was most appreciative. Apparently the cameo had been in her family for a number of years, but she was most insistent and naturally I accepted it as I did not wish to offend."

"Naturally. No further questions."

St. Anne shot to his feet and called across the room reprovingly, "Now Madame Priestley, we know that not all of these... gifts... have been trifles and trinkets. I know for a fact that you have received some very large sums of cash. You accepted these, of course, because you did not wish to offend?"

"Some of my sitters have been most insistent that I accept money for which I never asked," she replied evenly. "A sizeable portion of which I have donated to some of the many worthy charities here in Newport."

"How sizeable a portion?"

"Objection, Your Honor," Rathbone said. "My client's finances and how she chooses to handle them can have nothing to do with her occult talents."

"It has not been established that your client *has* any occult talents," St. Anne shot back.

"*Gentlemen*," the judge warned sharply. "Mr. Rathbone's objection is sustained. I'm not sure what you thought you were doing, Mr. St. Anne. Find another line of questioning."

"Very well, then," St. Anne waved an apologetic hand toward the judge's bench. He smiled his best predatory lawyer-smile, and asked, "One final question—are you quite sure you're not a fraud? Now would be the time to mention it, you know."

"How many times must I answer this question?" she asked. "No, I am not a fraud, no matter how desperately you may wish me to be."

"You may call your next witness, Mr. Rathbone."

"No further witnesses, Your Honor," Rathbone boomed proudly. "The plaintiff rests."

Court adjourned until the following day, when the defense would begin its case.

Chapter XXVI

A WEEK BEFORE THE TRIAL BEGAN, St. Anne had ferreted out the name of Arthur Lake, the servant so abruptly discharged from Hornbeck's employ. Mr. Jameson, a man who had worked for St. Anne in various capacities over the years, searched far and wide until he tracked Lake to a Providence boarding house. Coming back to Newport, he became the first witness for the defense.

"Mr. Lake, will you please tell the court about the man you met shortly after you left Blithewood House?" St. Anne asked.

"Right. A couple nights after I got sacked, I'm in the pub looking for a pint to drown me sorrows in. So there I am, just thinkin' about catchin' the next steamer back to Liverpool, when this bloke come over and starts chattin' me up. Just friendly sort of bar-talk, you know, at first, but then he starts askin' me about me situation an' all and I tell him I just got sacked.

"That's awful, 'e says. And who would sack such a fine man as yourself? An' I told him it was Colonel Hornbeck, and he says what, him as wife just died? And I says yes. He says he always heard Hornbeck was a good sort, a good boss and all, and I said yeah, he was good enough, and I'd miss the position but it was probably just as well I left when I did, you see. And he asks why.

"So I told him about the big fight Hornbeck had with the missus, an' about her just droppin' stone dead at his feet, like, and there I am in the next room, overhearing the whole thing. So I knew the 'appy days was over, and when I got the sack it weren't a real surprise, 'cos if I were in his shoes I would've done the same thing. I wouldn't want anybody who heard it and saw it all polishin' my shoes and pouring out my drinks every day. No, I would not. Too strange. So he gave me a couple old suits and a bit of cash and off I go, 'appy as I suppose I could be at losin' a position."

"You mentioned that this man asked if Hornbeck was at all sentimental," St. Anne said.

"Yes, he did."

"And what did you say?"

"I said he was sentimental enough. His son and daughter had given him a few keepsakes that were precious to him, like, and his wife, the missus, 'ad given him a watch when they was first married. I remember one day, a few years ago, when the watch stopped and the old man was in a blind panic. He said he'd be heartbroken is anything happen to that watch, with it being inscribed an' all, so I ran it down to the jeweler on Bellevue. Turned out there was just some grit in the mechanism, that was all, and it was workin' just fine when I brought it back to him."

"And then what if anything did the stranger ask?"

"Well, he got very keen on that watch. He wanted to know if I could remember the inscription."

"And could you?"

"Yes. It was pretty simple. All it said was 'To my Colonel, you may have this dance forever,' with her name and a date. Sweet, really. Wouldn't mind getting' something like that from someone myself."

"And after you told this stranger about this inscription, what did he do?"

"Well, we chatted on for a bit more, buyin' one another rounds for a bit, and he says he'd best be getting' on, so off he goes."

"And what did this man look like?"

"He was short, round-built, and weighed… I dunno, ten or eleven stone, maybe. Little spectacles. Just a bloke at a bar, you know."

Mr. St. Anne turned to the jury and said, "Gentlemen, I would like to point out that the description fits Reverend John Barrows, the plaintiff's half-brother. I believe that Reverend Barrows obtained the information from Mr. Lake so that his sister could then startle Colonel Hornbeck with, as the Colonel himself has said, things that only his wife could know. Please remember that the watch and its inscription was mentioned by Colonel Hornbeck during his testimony. Certainly Mr. Lake has suggested a more plausible explanation for Madame Priestley's knowledge than she herself has. No further questions for this witness, Your Honor."

Rathbone rose and slowly moved toward the witness stand, hands clasped behind his back, chuckling as though he could barely contain himself.

"With his inability to build a strong case against my client, Mr. St. Anne is now reduced to leveling vague accusations at a man who is neither here nor in any way connected with the case before the jury," he said. "This really is laughable, Your Honor. The description Mr. Lake offers could fit any number of men. In fact, I see two on the jury and several more in the gallery who answer that description quite nicely. No, this won't do, Your Honor."

"Do you have any questions for the witness, Mr. Rathbone?" the judge asked.

"No, Your Honor."

"Thank you, Mr. Rathbone. You may call your next witness, Mr. St. Anne."

St. Anne's next witness was Hope Westlock, the Uncanny Esperanza. With a yellow gown nearly the same shade as her hair, she sat in the witness box, hands folded neatly in her lap, and seemed as sunny and warm as the medium had been cool and distant.

"Now Mrs. Westlock, I have seen your performances at the Casino Theater several times—they are very entertaining and puzzling. I am particularly mystified by your ability to answer sealed questions from the audience."

"Thank you. My uncle and I have worked hard on that particular number," she said courteously. "It is a very old feat... we refer to it as older than the pyramids, and it may very well be older than that."

"And what do members of your audience have to say about this interesting and, if I may say, uncanny act?"

"Many have told me that I must possess supernatural powers, and many others have asked me to help them contact loved ones in the spirit world."

"And what is your response to these people?"

"I tell them that what they have seen me do is an entertainment achieved by subtlety and skill, and there is nothing supernatural about it whatsoever. I cannot summon spirits or see into the future any more than I can fly to the moon—no one can," she concluded, fixing her blue eyes on Madame Priestley.

"And do they believe you?"

"Some believe me, others do not. They insist that I am some sort of modern day Circe, blessed with mystical powers. Every day since our arrival in Newport I have had people ask me for séances or prophecies and I don't know what else. And no matter how many disclaimers I issue, no matter how many repudiations of such superstition I may make, there will always be some poor, deluded souls who will not listen. Once their minds are made up it is very hard to dissuade them."

She shook her head sadly.

Late afternoon sunlight slanted through the courtroom windows as von Hellmann took the stand. He swept into the witness box with all the haughty swagger of an aged player reviving his greatest role.

"Professor von Hellmann, you have made a career out of debunking and exposing spirit mediums. You say you have attended thousands of séances and exposed hundreds of spirit mediums. Does Madame Helene Priestley seem any different from any other medium you have investigated in your vast experience?"

"Not in the least. Her tricks are quite commonplace, her methods are unremarkable," von Hellmann answered. "Having observed her at first hand, I can say with confidence that I could produce any of her phenomena. Easily! "

"We would be most interested in a demonstration in support of that claim," St. Anne said with a smile.

"With the court's indulgence," von Hellamnn said, stepping from the witness box and standing ramrod straight before the gentlemen of the jury. "I have here a pair of school slates...."

Rathbone shot to his feet and cried, "Objection Your Honor!"

"Indeed," the judge intoned. "Professor von Hellmann, the point has been made at length—we know that you can seem to produce these results by employing trickery, but you have not demonstrated that Madame Priestley likewise employs trickery. Put your slates away, sir."

"Your Honor—" St. Anne said, "by this brief but compelling demonstration we wish to show that humbug—"

"Find another way of demonstrating it, Mr. St. Anne; we try to keep the humbug to a minimum in this court."

Many in the spectators' gallery chortled at the statement.

"No further questions," St. Anne said disappointedly, returning to the defense table.

"I will not take up much of your time, Professor von Hellmann," Rathbone said, rising. "Just one question—have you, since last we spoke, solved the riddle of the trumpet séance? You said you needed time to think about it, and you have had time, so has a solution suggested itself to you? You said earlier that you could reproduce *any* of my client's manifestations, so obviously you must have fathomed this particular feat? So, how is it done?"

"I am sure that if I had adequate time and did not have to waste my days fighting a ridiculous muzzling-suit, being harassed by lawyers and harangued by stupid questions, a clear and simple method would be forthcoming, Mr. Rathbone," von Hellmann said with obvious forced calm. "Spirit mediums, in my vast experience, are not very clever in their deceptions."

"But," Rathbone smiled and held up a warning finger, stalking toward the witness. "But, Professor von Hellmann, you must answer now: yes or no. It seems to me you have had more than enough time to puzzle out a method, and if you have been unable to, then it clearly suggests that you have found no trickery because there is no trickery to find—and that Madame Priestley is genuinely gifted with supernatural powers."

The only sound in the courtroom was the reporters' pencils scribbling across the pages of their notebooks.

"Most spirit trumpets use a reaching rod, or a rubber speaking tube, or—"

The exasperated Rathbone turned to the judge. "Your Honor?"

"Professor von Hellmann," the judge said sternly, "the court is not interested in hearing how other mediums may or may not do things. You are asked to explain, if you are able, the trickery, if trickery there be, behind Madame Priestley's trumpet séance. Can you?"

"I cannot say with any certainty just what she is doing," von Hellmann said in a small voice. "But I know she is doing *something*. And I have a few theories about it, but I cannot at this time supply an explanation."

"No further questions, Your Honor!"

Von Hellmann shambled back to his seat, looking like a man who knew his battle was lost.

"We call our last witness, Your Honor," St. Anne said. "We call Madame Helene Priestley."

All eyes followed the medium as she stepped into the witness stand once again.

"That is a lovely ring you have there, Madame," St. Anne said with a smile. "What kind of stone is that?"

"A sapphire," she replied coolly.

"Another gift from a grateful sitter?"

"Yes," she nodded, as though graciously indulging an impudent question.

"I see. Well, Madame, I have a simple request to make of you today."

"And that is?"

"We have *heard* much about your frankly unbelievable powers, but we have actually *seen* nothing. A great deal of talk, but talk means nothing—any lawyer knows that," he said with a smile. "I think it is not unreasonable to ask for a demonstration of your supposed abilities so that the jury may decide for themselves—"

"Objection, Your Honor!" Rathbone thundered, leaping to his feet. "The request is utterly ridiculous!"

"I am not sure that it is, Mr. Rathbone," the judge said thoughtfully. "Unusual, yes, irregular, certainly, but not ridiculous."

"My client refuses to comply with this most outrageous, outlandish request!"

"And I shall then move to find her in contempt of court!" St. Anne countered with a foxy grin.

"You may try, sir, but we will not comply with this request!"

"She will if I direct her to," the judge said quietly and firmly.

"Your Honor—"

"Mr. Rathbone," Madame Priestley cut her lawyer off sharply. Rathbone startled and froze.

In her notebook, Miss Brooke observed that "Rathbone seems to be afraid of his own client."

"Mr. Rathbone, I agree—I will comply with the request."

He nodded dumbly.

"This trial has been very tiring for me," she went on. "If the court will allow me a couple of days to rest, I will be only too glad to hold a séance, with the jury as my sitters."

"I do not object to the request for a couple of days," St. Anne said; "But I would like it noted that my client did not ask for a couple of days to rest when he was called upon to testify!"

"Duly noted," said the judge. "This court stands adjourned for two days, at the end of which Madame Helene Priestley will be called upon to offer satisfactory proofs of her spiritualistic claims, at a time and place to be decided by the court."

The gavel echoed in the courtroom.

Chapter XXVII

AND SO NEWPORT held its breath for two long days.

"And what's the latest?" people asked one other on the street corners, in the bars, and over supper. "What have you heard?"

The reporters were no better, and in fact were probably worse. In desperate attempt to scoop one another they would publish anything, no matter how harebrained, misconstrued, or outright actionable it might be. Papers sold and rumors circulated.

Along Bellevue Avenue, in the center of town, was Touro Park, a popular and fashionable place named for Judah Touro, rabbi of the first synagogue in America, located just a few streets away. Women in Newport suits came to carry on flirtations with young men, children played ball and rolled hoops, couples picnicked, and pundits mounted their soapboxes to praise, condemn, exhort, and beseech.

"Workers of the world, unite!" cried one man in a shabby coat and dusty hat. "You have nothing to lose but your chains! Why should we live on our knees while *they* live in marble mansions and gilded parlors?"

A few yards away a prim woman called, "Sisters! Any man of age is given his vote! And why is a woman of age not given hers? Why should our voices be silent?"

But the topic of the day, of course, was Madame Priestley.

At the west end of the park rose what the fanciful called the Mystery Tower, and what the more prosaic called the Old Stone

Mill. It was a round stone ruin some forty feet tall and supported by eight arches. No one knew who built it or for what purpose, and the debate raged. Some said it was the remains of a windmill built by early white settlers, while others insisted it was what was left of a Viking church, built a thousand years before those settlers arrived. Hornbeck had spent some time examining the tower, and was somewhat inclined to think it Egyptian in origin.

Newport's newest mystery was discussed in the shadow of its oldest.

"I heard she took ship for England last night," big Florence McMurphy said to one of his cronies. There was no doubt among them who *she* was. McMurphy's employers had left weeks ago, at the end of the season, promising to engage him again next July, when they returned. "Yeah—England for her, and who knows where from there."

"I heard she went to New York," put in Gaskell. "To get on a train for San Francisco."

"Shows what you know, your worthless English bastard."

"Do you think she really levitated?" Riddell asked. "I heard she used to float up to the ceiling and write her name there."

"I wouldn't mind looking up those skirts," McMurphy chortled.

"She's still here," someone said. "A friend of mind works in the kitchen at Blithewood House and says she's still there, not to be disturbed, resting up for the big test séance."

"Where's that supposed to be?"

"Dunno. No one seems to know."

"I heard the Casino," Riddell said.

"That's stupid," McMurphy spat. "The Casino."

"I heard it was supposed to be in the—the—what d'you call 'em?" Gaskell faltered. "The judge's chambers—that's it."

"Fair enough," McMurphy said.

"I hope she turns von Hellmann into a toad," someone said. "Him sayin' all those things about her."

"She's a bloody fake," someone else countered. "Deserves everything she gets from him."

"Well, we'll all see what's what soon enough," McMurphy said thoughtfully. "Anybody going dancing tonight?"

"Yeah, I'll go. Forty Steps as usual, then?"

"Yeah. See you at six?"

"Six it is, then."

"Are you still up?" Hope asked.

It was well past midnight and von Hellmann sat by an open window in their suite, with a tall pale candle on the table next to him. Hope was surprised at how old and small he looked in the flickering candlelight.

"I can't sleep," he murmured.

"What's wrong, uncle?" She sat down beside him and rested a hand on his arm.

"It's this trial. I haven't had a medium in court for years and this... this one feels different from all the others."

As he spoke, he reached over and pulled a silver dollar from the folds of her silken robe. Hope smiled—it had been the first trick he had ever shown her, and the first trick he'd taught her when she was old enough. She watched now as the coin vanished from one hand only to reappear in the other, or to be pulled from his mouth or behind her own ear. But she could tell, as he smoothly executed the moves he had spent a lifetime perfecting and polishing, that his mind was far away and he was hardly even aware of the coin.

"I don't know if I'm going to win this one, Hope," he said thickly.

"Nonsense. Of course you are," she said. "Ten minutes in the séance room with that harridan and the jury will see her for what she is."

"Fooling people is what she does best, and she's one of the best I've ever seen. I can't explain that trumpet trick and she'll crucify me with it and—*dammit!*"

The silver dollar slipped from his fingers and rang loudly as it hit the floor. It rolled away under the couch.

"I'm getting too old for this," he whispered.

"Don't talk like that," Hope said soothingly. "You're just tired. Let's get you to bed."

"All right, all right. We should be hearing about the séance arrangements sometime tomorrow."

"Good. Then we can put an end to her," Hope said firmly.

"I hope so. Dammit, I hope so."

Hornbeck had spent his two days tiptoeing around Blithewood House, trying not to disturb the medium. His reading had taught him that the mediumistic were usually of a singular and high-strung temperament, and he did not wish to trouble her while she rested. He gave the servants strict orders to see to it that she had everything she could possibly want, and any desire she expressed or even hinted at should be catered to immediately and without fuss. She must have time to ready herself for the night she would defeat von Hellmann.

The night before the séance, Hornbeck sent word to Martin Morrison, saying that he wished to see him. Morrison had left Blithewood House and returned to his boarding house on Thames Street to wait there while Hornbeck contacted his English clients to inquire about the jewelry casket. A telegram had arrived promptly and read:

MR. MARTIN MORRISON ACTING ON OUR BEHALF STOP
PLEASE RENDER HIM ALL ASSISTANCE AND COURTESY STOP
SENDING FULL PARTICULARS BY POST STOP

The letter, in a stiff gray envelope bearing the Belminster seal, had arrived just before the trial began, but Hornbeck had been too distracted to deal with it all. But now, with nothing to do but wait, he had sent for Morrison.

"I'm glad you could come, Mr. Morrison," Hornbeck said as they sat in his study. "Cigar? Something to drink?"

"No. thank you, sir," Morrison replied, inwardly amused. Only a few weeks ago, it had been "Martin! Where the hell is my morning paper, Martin? Make sure it's freshly ironed—freshly ironed, do you hear me? I want to nearly burn myself on the pages, Martin!" And now he was being offered whiskey and cigars and addressed as "Mr. Morrison," and likewise being treated as one of the honored guests he himself had recently waited upon.

"I have had a letter from your Lord Belminster," Hornbeck said.

"He telegrammed me a short while ago, inquiring about my return."

"Yes, well, he confirmed your story. I have the box here, of course," Hornbeck rose to open the Chinese cabinet. The box stood on a top shelf, next to a stack of letters bound together with a faded ribbon. He took the box down from the shelf and set it on his desk, saying quietly, "It's all yours, Mr. Morrison."

"Thank you. You will pardon me, but I must make certain," he said, opening the box. He sorted through the jewelry quickly, nodding as he did so and placing the pieces off to one side. He released the hidden catch and the floor of the box sprang loose. He riffled through the half dozen packets of papers there before straightening up and nodding his satisfaction.

"It all seems to be in order," he said.

"I should hope so. I've had it under lock and key since—since that night."

"Of course."

"There are some very fine pieces there," Hornbeck went on, admiring a few. Idly, he picked up one of the little drawstring bags containing the apported diamonds. His hand closed tightly around it.

"So, you're a detective, then?" he asked foolishly, feeling hot and uncomfortable.

"Yes, sir."

"A detective posing as one of my servants, and I didn't suspect a thing."

"That was rather the point, I'm afraid."

"Of course," Hornbeck flushed. "And if I may ask, how long have you been… been in the business, for want of a better phrase?"

"Six years now, sir. Ever since I retired from the Foreign Office."

"The Foreign Office?"

"Yes. I was in intelligence."

"My God—you were a spy?"

"Yes," Morrison replied matter-of-factly.

Hornbeck was dizzy. "What was that like?"

"Rather like a huge game of chess, at times."

"With the world for your board."

"Yes. I was in Egypt for a time. Then India, and China. I certainly never expected to end up in Rhode Island."

After a long, uneasy silence, Hornbeck asked, "So what are you going to do now that you've got the box back?"

"Return it to the new Lord Belminster, collect my fee, and go home to my wife and family."

"You're married?"

"Sixteen years now. She's a wonderful woman, Mrs. Morrison."

"I'm sure that she is…"

"I plan to wait until the end of the trial, however. I've watched things this far, it would seem foolish to leave before the endgame, as it were."

"As it were," Hornbeck echoed wearily. "Well, the final séance is tomorrow night in the judge's chambers."

"You've heard, then?"

"Just this afternoon."

"Well, we'll know then, won't we?"

"We certainly will," Hornbeck laughed hollowly. "What do you think of her, Mr. Morrison?"

"Honestly, Colonel, I have not given it a great deal of thought. Not my bailiwick, you understand."

After a few more moments of cramped small talk, Mr. Morrison extended a hand and said, "I really must be going, Colonel Hornbeck."

"Of course, Mr. Morrison," Hornbeck wrung his hand weakly.

"You gave me several suits while I was here. I have given them to Edgar, the footman. And here is a check refunding the wages you paid me; I cannot take payment from you as I was actually employed by another."

"No, no—you keep that, Mr. Morrison. And don't argue with me—I'm too damn tired."

Morrison silently gathered up the papers and jewelry and replaced them carefully in the box. After a minute, he smiled politely and said, "Sir?"

Hornbeck had forgotten the little drawstring bag still in his hand. He mumbled an apology as he handed it over.

He did not tell Morrison that he had taken the contents of the bag—the apported diamonds—to his Bellevue Avenue jeweler earlier that afternoon. With his lenses and instruments, the jeweler had minutely examined each stone in turn, several times. He kept shaking his head as he worked, and at the end of a long hour, he had handed them back to the Hornbeck, telling him the stones were just worthless glass.

Chapter XXVIII

JUDGE WARREN CAREFULLY ARRANGED the séance chamber according to Madame Priestley's instructions.

A stout round table was placed in the center of the room—a table big enough for twelve jurors and the medium to gather around. The judge placed his chair in a far corner, to observe events from outside the circle. Most of the fourteen chairs had to be brought in from other rooms. The windows were closed, locked, and shuttered; no light from the outside penetrated into the chamber. In another corner, opposite the judge's chair, stood the velvet-draped medium's cabinet.

The cabinet, in its various forms, had been a familiar sight at séances since the beginning. According to the spiritualists, many mediums needed to retire to the cabinet in order to produce some of their more startling demonstrations. Thus sequestered, and often securely bound by ropes or even chains to prevent any trickery, gifted mediums offered manifestations that changed minds and lives alike. At his home in London, Sir William Crookes had held a long series of séances with a rising young medium named Florence Cook, often called "The Queen of the Cabinet." After entering her cabinet, Miss Cook materialized her famous spirit guide, Katie King, clad in flowing white. Katie walked among her sitters, often arm-in-arm, while the entranced Florence remained in the cabinet. On one special occasion, Katie King allowed Sir William to check the cabinet, where he found the medium slumped to the floor, insensible, while the spirit remained with the dumbfounded sitters.

Not all such cabinet séances were so impressive, however. Ira and William Davenport, mediumistic brothers from Buffalo, New York, traveled with a large wooden cabinet like a wardrobe. Tied up within it, they still produced startling manifestations to standing-room-only audiences throughout Europe, the Americas, and Australia as instruments were played upon by spirit fingers, messages were written on blank pages placed in the cabinet, and spirit hands waved from a small, diamond-shaped window in the door. One night in Liverpool, some suspicious sailors tied the brothers as only sailors could, and when no mysterious manifestations were forthcoming, the audience rioted and smashed the cabinet to matchwood.

But there would be no such melee tonight. Judge Warren had taken precautions. He kept the location of the test séance secret, quietly revealing to the jurors only that afternoon that it was to be at his little home on East Bowery Street, not far from the Ocean House. He had done this to confound the inevitable crush of reporters and sensationalists. The last thing he needed was a mob on his doorstep, demanding to know what was going on inside.

But still, he wondered how complete the secrecy had been. A pretty girl in a blue bicycling-costume had been pedaling her Hawthorne Ladies' Safety Bicycle up and down East Bowery Street all day, stealing little glances at the house as she went by.

He had politely declined Hornbeck's kind offer to hold the séance at Blithewood House.

"Since Madame has been my guest and grown accustomed to my house," the Colonel had explained, "perhaps she would be more comfortable here in familiar surroundings, and therefore be more able to produce stronger manifestations…"

But that obviously could not be allowed. By choosing to hold the test séance in his home, the judge retained a certain control over the proceedings. He could ensure everything was fair, and, if tonight was to be a fair test at all, Madame Priestley must be given every chance to succeed, and no opportunity to cheat.

So all was prepared: a table, the cabinet, a darkened room smelling faintly of rose incense and lit by pale white candles…

The jurors arrived shortly before midnight, the hour named by Madame Priestley.

Guided by the judge and his wife, they silently filed upstairs to the room where the medium waited. They entered nervously; with the candles and incense and reverent silence broken only by the shuffling of feet and the creaking of floorboards, the room seemed to be a chapel devoted to an obscure and forgotten saint.

The medium, in a long dark gown, sat with her back to the door and her hands folded neatly in her lap. If she noticed the thirteen men clustered behind her and holding their breath, she did not acknowledge them.

After a long moment, the judge cleared his throat and spoke. "Madame—?"

"Yes," she replied coolly. "The spirits wait for us, as we wait for them."

Mr. Browne, the jury foreman, was a plump man who owned a dry goods store on Spring Street. His friend and fellow juryman, Mr. Talbot, a wiry trolley conductor, led the brief inspection of the room. Neither they nor any other member of the jury knew what he was looking for, but each needed to satisfy himself that nothing was amiss, whatever it was. None of them discovered any secret doors, or sliding panels, or hidden assistants. They cautiously took their seats around the séance table.

"So this is it," Mr. Browne whispered. "This is what everybody's been waiting for."

Mr. Talbot nodded his dumb agreement.

The medium looked around the table, from face to face. A few of the jurors flinched and looked away, unable to return her steady gaze. The flickering candlelight brought out the grave beauty of her young-old face, and some of the men could not take their eyes off of her.

She placed a small velvet bag in the table and withdrew her now-famous slates from it. Each slate was passed around the table for careful examination. Once again, no one knew what they were looking for, but the slates were certainly blank.

At Madame Priestley's direction, the judge stacked the slates, tied them with a silk cord, and dribbled candle wax on the knots, sealing them. He placed the slates on the tabletop, between the candle in its silver candlestick and a small brass bell with a rosewood handle; the jury had minutely examined both in their search moments before.

Madame smiled approvingly.

"I would like all the candles, save one, to be extinguished," she said, "and then we are ready."

When the room was lit by only a single white taper, she instructed the men to join hands, forming the séance circle.

No one knew how long they had sat in the room before the first rap was heard, but the candle had burned far down. The darkness and the silence were deeply disorienting, and single spirit rap echoed like a gunshot in the small room.

A moment later, another rap was heard and the table vibrated slightly. And then…

Silence.

As before, the table rose up a few inches off the floor and dropped down with a bang.

More silence. Different silence.

Madame's eyes were closed; some of the jurors thought she must be slipping into trance.

The candle flickered in the stillness of the room.

Her head fell forward onto her breast and she was still. For a moment, the judge could not even tell if she were breathing.

Someone whispered, "Oh, Jesus—"

Her head snapped up suddenly and she gasped for breath; her eyes were wide and wild and for a long moment she seemed almost unaware of where she was.

"Perhaps you would open the slates for us, Your Honor?" she asked with a dry throat.

Trying to keep his hands from shaking, the judge reached over and picked up the slates, only glancing at the wax seals. They were perfectly intact. Even by the light of the single failing candle, the room was still just bright enough, and the slates had been sitting on the tabletop, not out of anyone's sight for a moment. No one could have gotten to them unnoticed. He broke the seals and opened the slates.

When he saw the writing, he could no longer keep his hands from shaking

Across one slate, in a thin unsteady scrawl, was written, *we are here.*

And on the other, in the same spidery hand: *we will show.*

A few raps sounded in the room, almost a self-congratulatory fillip.

Those jurors who were not dumbstruck swore quietly, with their hands fumbling over their mouths. A few of them had seen von Hellmann do this onstage at the Casino, but that was just a magician's trick. But here in this room, with this woman, this was… something else entirely.

"I think the time has come to offer you gentlemen unanswerable proof," she said quietly.

"This seems unanswerable enough," someone said.

Madame Priestley rose from the table and went to the cabinet in the opposite corner. Unlike the Davenports and their legendary cabinet, hers was simply a curtain rod and some tasseled velvet drapes. The judge moved his chair into the cabinet, facing into the corner.

She sat and, folding her hands in her lap once again, said, "You may bind me, if you wish."

The jury had discussed this among themselves earlier, and Mr. Browne had brought several lengths of strong cotton rope with him.

"Tell me if I hurt you," he murmured quietly as he tied the medium's hands behind her back, looping the ropes through the rungs of the ladder-back chair. He pulled the knots tight and gave each a tug to satisfy himself that they were secure. Wax from the candle was again used to seal the bonds.

"That should do it," Browne said, straightening up.

"Tie my legs as well," Madame Priestley said quietly.

"I don't—I don't think that is really necessary or appropriate, Madame," Browne stammered. He had a wife and little daughter waiting for him at home, and he really shouldn't be out tying some other woman to a chair. It was unseemly. "Not at all."

"I insist," was the firm reply.

"Your Honor—?" Browne appealed.

"I will do it, Mr. Foreman. You may take your seat."

A minute later, Madame's shapely ankles were lashed to the chair legs, and those knots were also sealed with candle wax. The jury took their places around the séance table.

"Once the curtain is drawn, one of you will have to extinguish that candle," she said sternly. "If we are to be fortunate enough to witness any manifestations at all, complete darkness is required. And I must insist that no one—no one—so much as lights a match, should a spirit appear," she continued seriously. "And of course you should *touch nothing* unless the spirit or spirits give you permission. Please keep your seats and do not beak the circle."

They nodded again. Everyone in the room had heard stories about that near-fatal séance at Blithewood House.

"Then we are ready to begin," she smiled.

Judge Warren closed the curtains, and crossed to the large music box, which stood on a bookcase shelf. Madame had requested music for the séance earlier that afternoon, and the music box, a wedding gift from the judge's legal colleagues, was deemed suitable. He pressed the button and a slow air began to play as he took the medium's empty place at the table, and instructed everyone to join hands once again. After a moment's nervous hesitation, he blew out the candle in the center of the table, and a heavy blackness swallowed the room.

They could hear the medium taking deep, regular breaths in the cabinet, but on their side of the curtain, every man held his breath.

Mr. Talbot looked to his left and to his right. He couldn't see the judge, couldn't see Mr. Browne.

Long minutes ticked by and the music box played through its program of six slow airs and fell silent. Just when some of the jurors, Mr. Browne among them, had decided that perhaps there were to be no further manifestations, it happened.

The curtains of the cabinet were slowly, tremulously drawn back.

Browne felt Talbot's hand tighten and begin to tremble in his.

A voice gasped, "My God!"

A spirit form, hooded and swathed in something diaphanous and radiant, slipped from the cabinet and into the room. It was the figure of a tall slender woman, nude but for the luminous mantle loosely wrapped around her, outlining her slim figure. A bright veil was drawn across her face like an odalisque, and she wore a wise, weary smile beneath it.

The spirit did not speak, but noiselessly glided away from the cabinet, circling the table once, twice, with her eyes glinting in the unearthly light as she glanced from one man to the next. Her dark hair hung loosely around her stunning face and she seemed to flow rather than walk.

Talbot clutched Browne's hand so hard he thought it would cut off the circulation.

The spirit woman stopped and reached between two of the sitters, taking up the piece of chalk that still lay on the table. Still smiling that strange, wise smile, she wrote *we will show* in a flowing hand on a blank side of the slate.

She carelessly dropped the chalk to the floor and pirouetted away from the table, her sheer garment swirling around her. Reaching over to the music box, she wound the handle a few times, starting the series of plinking airs once again.

And then she *laughed*—a low musical laugh. Unearthly. Otherworldly. Unbelievable.

She turned back to the table and smiled at the judge. She bent low, taking his face in her hands.

Warren stared back at her with huge unblinking eyes.

Moving her face close to his, she kissed him through the veil, pressing his trembling lips to hers.

She stepped back a pace and looked over to Mr. Browne, who stared dumbly back at her, his eyebrows knitted together. She reached out and stroked his face with one hand and he gasped at her warm touch. He had not been at all prepared for this. He had heard about spirits appearing in the séance room, but this was different— she was right here in front of him, smiling, playfully caressing his face, and it was no illusion, no trick of the light, no hoax.

He looked the spirit hard in the face, through the radiant veil, and decided it was not Madame Priestley's face, not at all. It was someone else—someone beguiling, mesmerizing…

And when she glided away from him, he felt a pang like a rejected suitor, and then, just out of the corner of his eye, almost unnoticeable, he saw it.

The hem of the spirit's long mantle whispered along the floor like a bridal train.

And then…

And then it snagged.

The edge of the luminous wrap caught on the head of a nail not quite completely driven in, and the spell was broken.

Browne shot from his chair and threw his arms around the figure, gritting his teeth and slamming her against the wall with such force that a framed picture there crashed to the floor.

The others leaped to their feet, shouting and knocking over chairs. Two or three men tried to get to Browne or the spirit or both but in the dark all they could do was run blindly into one another, swearing.

Judge Warren pounded his fist on the table, calling "Order! Gentlemen of the jury, order!"

"A match!" Browne shouted over the judge. "God dammit, a match!"

Pinned between him and the wall, the woman did not struggle or even move. She had said nothing other than giving a sharp cry of surprise or pain when Browne lunged, followed by a long, angry *hiss*. Now she stood perfectly still, impassive, prepared.

"Who's got that damned match?" Browne demanded.

Talbot finally struck a match against his boot heel.

Browne released his captive, backing uncertainly away from her. What he saw—what they all saw—was not some spirit come from the Summerland and cloaked in a vapor, but a naked woman draped in a few yards of cheesecloth streaked with phosphorescent paint.

He angrily pulled the veil away, ripped back the sheer hood and started into the coolly beautiful face of Madame Helene Priestley.

Chapter XXIX

"**GENTLEMEN OF THE JURY,** have you reached a verdict?"
Judge Warren asked early the next afternoon.

"We have, Your Honor."

The jury had heard the closing arguments that morning,
and had taken less than an hour for deliberation. The evidence
was plain enough. The medium, after slipping her bonds, had
removed the painted cheesecloth from a secret pocket inside her
gown; no man, no matter how suspicious, would have demanded
a search thorough enough to find that pocket. Von Hellmann had
to tell them to look for it when the jury assembled that morning,
as word of what had happened the night before spread. Madame
Priestley had stripped, wrapped herself in the yards of luminous
gauze, and stepped from the cabinet to beguile her sitters; but
what should have been her crowning performance in Newport
was thwarted by a bent nail.

The medium stood shoulder-to-shoulder with Mr. Rathbone
now, head held high and proud. Hornbeck stood ashen-faced
behind her, looking sick. Von Hellmann smiled smugly and St.
Anne chortled and hooked his thumbs in his vest pockets.

No one needed a crystal ball to see what the verdict would
be. The *Observer* and the *Herald*, the only two papers published
every morning, had both run long, garbled, conflicting accounts of what had happened. Each had had reporters perched
on Judge Warren's fence or skulking through his rosebushes

the night before, straining to hear what was going on upstairs. As the sun rose and the papers hit the streets, all of Newport gasped.

"On the charge of slander, how do you find the defendant, Erasmus von Hellmann?" the judge asked.

"We find him not guilty, Your Honor," said Mr. Browne.

The applause and cheers that greeted the verdict were answered with hisses and catcalls.

"The jury is thanked for its service, and is dismissed."

Hope hugged her uncle hard.

"I knew common sense would win out," she said. "I'm only glad this jury wasn't as blind as some of the others you've faced."

"So am I," von Hellmann replied. "But look—here comes Hornbeck."

Hornbeck stalked across the courtroom, flanked by his children and followed by his lawyer. He wore no expression on his lined, dignified face, no flicker of emotion. He did not take his eyes from von Hellmann as he approached.

When he was close, he glared at the magician and said softly, "You must think I'm a fool."

Von Hellmann opened his mouth to reply but suddenly found he had nothing to say.

Hornbeck turned and marched off through the crowd.

Von Hellmann shook his head dismissively, straightened up, smiled, and waited for the reporters to flock to him, pencils and notebooks ready, seeking a juicy quote, a witty bon mot, a barbed comment.

No one came near him.

"Well that's that," Browne said tiredly. "Thank God it's over."

"Strangest week I've ever had," Talbot mumbled, shaking his head.

"Do you know what I'm thinking?"

"No. What are you thinking?"

"I'm thinking that I don't even like von Hellmann," Browne said. "Arrogant bastard."

"Innocent arrogant bastard," Talbot corrected absently. "Do you know what I'm thinking?"

"No. What?"

"I'm thinking if I'm ever called again for jury duty, I'll shoot myself."

"Don't look so glum, Rathbone," St. Anne chuckled, clapping the other lawyer on the back. "You did your best, and you certainly had me on a couple of points, there."

"He never should have allowed that séance," Rathbone retorted. "I can't believe you would even ask for something like that."

"Oh, you would have done it in my position. I've seen you ask for worse. And get it."

"Like the Jamesion case in '77," Rathbone smiled. "And Sumner in '86."

"Blew me out of the water."

"I did indeed," Rathbone smiled; he hadn't smiled at all during the trial. "C'mon, I'll buy you lunch."

"Well, it certainly has been a most interesting assignment," said Hutchinson Hatch, reporter.

"Sure was," another journalist put in. "I wonder what the editor's going to send me off on next."

"I'm heading back home," said Edwin M. Lillibridge, smiling. "There's an old abandoned church in Providence that wants looking into. Gentlemen, I have enjoyed meeting each and every one of you..."

"Ah, before you go, Lillibridge, there's the little matter of a few wagers placed earlier in the week that still needs clearing up..."

Miss Brooke looked on as one half the assembled journalists settled up their accounts with the other half. She turned away to scan the courtroom for Madame Priestley.

But she was gone.

In the shadow of the Old Stone Mill in Touro Park, between the preaching vegetarian and the exhorting anti-vivisectionist, an elderly spiritualist in smudged pince-nez took to his soapbox.

"Friends!" he cried. "Do not be dismiss the glorious wonders of spirit communication because of one single wolf in the fold! Ponder this—the existence of wigs does not mean that there is no real hair!"

But no one was listening. Instead, people moved on to the recitation man who recited any poem called for, from Shakespeare to Moore to Gilbert and Sullivan. A passer-by requested Wordsworth and tossed a dime into the man's hat. After a moment's consideration, the recitation man smiled and began:

> *I look for ghosts; but none will force*
> > *Their way to me; 'tis falsely said*
> *That ever there was intercourse*
> > *Between the living and the dead....*

Strolling through the park, enjoying the sunny afternoon with a hint of autumn, Morrison saw Edward sitting on a bench, feeding the pigeons breadcrumbs from a bag.

"Hullo," Morrison said, sliding onto the bench. "Haven't seen you since the trial began."

"We've been busy," Edward replied, smiling. "But now that it's all over and done with, we'll be taking a steamer back to New York."

"As am I."

"Really? And where to from there?"

"Home," Morrison said. "And I can't bloody wait. I've seen enough of America."

"What kept you here this long, then?"

"The trial. My curiosity got the better of me, I suppose. I had to stay and hear the verdict."

"I see. And now it's back home… to wait for your next case," Edward said nonchalantly.

Morrison took in a deep slow breath and said, "I'm not quite sure I know what you mean."

"My father was a Scotland Yarder, and his father was a Bow Street Runner. I grew up around constables and detectives and bobbies and everything else. I can spot 'em a mile off."

"I see," Morrison replied uneasily. After a moment of awkward silence, he rose to go. "I really must pack. I shall miss our chess games, Edward."

"So shall I, Martin. So shall I."

Hornbeck hadn't visited Amelia's grave since the beginning of the season. Shortly after the funeral, he had come here every day, heaping roses around the stone and sometimes staying until dusk. Henry often had to send the footman to bring him home. But then Madame Priestley had insisted that there was no death, and no dead, and Amelia still walked the halls of Blithewood, sending messages of comfort to her Colonel, as always. And he had stopped coming.

Now as he stood by the grave the morning after the verdict was read, he absently fingered the rusty black mourning band around his left arm and buttoned up against a sudden chill breeze.

My God, Amelia—I don't know what to believe anymore. Did you ever speak to me? Can you ever—?

The sepulcher was mute. Just her name, the dates, and *Resurgam*.

He was unsure of how long he had stood there, leaning heavily upon his walking stick, when he heard someone approaching from behind. He turned.

Madame Priestley.

"What do you want here?" he demanded. "I have nothing to say to you." He took a few steps toward her, half-raising his walking stick, determined that she should come no closer to where his beloved wife rested. "What do you want?"

"I came to say that I am leaving; I have packed my things and left your home. You have been very courteous to me, and I thank you for it."

"God damn you!" Hornbeck shouted back at her. "I never should have let you into my house in the first place. I took you in in good faith and you lied to me, you deceived me, you and your thieving brother!"

"I may have deceived you, but in every deception you were my willing accomplice," the medium said bitterly. "I would have been powerless had you not been so eager to believe. And if I had not taken advantage of you, someone else would have."

Hornbeck fell back a step or two, unable to believe what he had just heard.

"You admit it! You admit it and blame *me* for it?"

"It's the truth."

"I don't know what to believe anymore…" Hornbeck murmured. The reverend was a thief, his butler was a detective, the medium was a fake….

But Amelia was still dead.

He turned his back on Madame Priestley, shoulders stooped under invisible weight. He stared at his wife's grave. *Memento Mori.* There was nothing else to do.

"I don't know anymore…" he said in a small voice. "Was any of it real? Did she ever come back? Just answer me that—was any of it real?" he pleaded.

"No," the medium said flatly.

He began to weep, tears running hot down his old face. He clenched and unclenched his walking stick fitfully, knuckles turning red, then white. A tear splashed onto the back of his hand.

"None of it?"

"No, none of it."

In the very back of his mind, buried beneath the betrayal and the bereavement, he realized, dimly, that this was really where the mourning began. It was only at this moment that he understood Amelia was truly, irrevocably lost to him.

"Oh, God, Amelia—I am so, so sorry...." was all he could say.

Just as the medium turned to go, Hornbeck said bitterly, "I hate you."

"Go back to your mansion, and your children, old man," she replied, and left him standing there by the grave, leaving him with whatever there was left for him. Memento mori.

A cab waited for her at the cemetery gate. She had another appointment to keep.

Von Hellmann sat at a corner table set for two, expecting her. The Ocean House's dining room was empty; the season was long over. The seasonal help had been discharged, the cottages closed up until next year, and the summer colony had all boarded steamers for home weeks ago. Even those curious enough to stay for the trial were finally packing to go, now that the verdict was in. With the closed shops and quiet streets, Newport was a ghost town.

The ceiling fans overhead revolved lazily as Edward brought a stiff cream-colored visiting card over to von Hellmann's table. The magician looked up from the deck of cards he'd been toying with, pulling fans of cards from thin air or out of his mouth. He put the deck away and glanced the visiting card—Madame Priestley's, of course. On the back, in her firm yet flowing hand, was written "P. P. C."—*Pour Prendre Congé*. She'd come to say goodbye.

He rose and bowed without expression as she crossed the dining room to take the seat opposite him.

"I am so glad you could join me," he said courteously.

"And I thank you for the invitation," she replied icily. "And I congratulate you on a fight well fought."

"I assure you that you were no less formidable, Madame."

"I had heard of you in a vague way before, of course, but I

confess I was quite taken aback when you arrived in Newport for the express purpose of persecuting me."

"Had to be done, of course. And you, in turn, responded by prosecuting me. Pity your Mr. Rathbone wasn't more clever."

"It makes very little difference to me," she answered coolly.

Von Hellmann squinted and peered across the table at her. She was still a puzzle, and she returned his gaze unflinchingly.

"So what will you do now?" he asked after an awkward silence.

"I intend to go west, back to San Francisco and, like so many going to San Francisco, to start over."

"Again?" von Hellmann startled. "No thought of giving up the spook racket?"

"Of course not," she laughed. "And why would I?"

"May I remind you that you have suffered a rather unanswerable exposé?"

"My dear von Hellmann, you cannot for an instant imagine that what happened here is of the least consequence? I have been challenged before, and yet here I am. If you think you have really won a victory here you are an even bigger fool than Hornbeck. Do you remember the name of Miss Helen Keene?"

"The trance medium?" von Hellmann nodded. "*You?*"

"And Mrs. Cadogon-Smith of Ohio? Famous for her spirit forms?"

"Who was taken to court for fraud by a long-time sitter."

"And acquitted," she said pointedly.

"You again." He shook his head. "You must be older than you look."

"Thank you. I owe it all to an elixir given me by Cleopatra," she said mockingly. "And what will you do now that you are finished with me?"

"I will go back to new York and finish my memoirs—I have a whole new chapter to add now. And I shall alert my friend and colleagues in San Francisco of your impending arrival."

They sat quietly for a minute or so, von Hellmann still trying to decipher her. She seemed completely unconcerned. Just a couple of weeks ago, such a meeting would have been unthinkable—the very idea of the two of them sitting at the same table together would have been preposterous. But now...

"I have just come from seeing Colonel Hornbeck," she said at last, breaking the chilly silence.

"Your latest victim."

"You make me sound like a murderess, sir."

"You're not much better, are you?"

"How dare you?" she cried indignantly. "How dare you draw such a comparison? I have done nothing of the kind—"

"You have taken advantage of a bereft and grieving man, and all for money," he shot back.

"I took advantage of a fool who should have known better—I took advantage of a fool who desperately wanted to be taken advantage of! I have done it before and I shall certainly do it again—there are more than enough fools in the world and the next time, my dear professor, you will not be there to interfere."

"Perhaps I won't. But there will always be someone like me to challenge someone like you."

"But there will always be the believers and the fools, as well," she smiled rapaciously. "There will always be those who will believe because it is better than not believing... and I shall be waiting for them."

Von Hellmann shook his head, saying, "You are a *monster!*"

"Am I? Am I really? I was born into a family with no name, no money, and no prospects. By using the gifts I was born with, I now possess all three. If I were a man, you would clap me on the back and congratulate me for being a stout fellow and a self-made man. But you call me a monster instead. I am not, like so many of my sisters today, taking to my couch in a fit of nervous prostration—I have lived my life. I have traveled the world and been received by royalty, been the honored guest of the proud and the powerful. Mine is a story that Horatio Alger and George

MacDonald could not have dreamed up between them, and I do not seek to destroy people for the sake of another chapter of my memoirs. But *you* call *me* a monster."

"You lie, you deceive, you take money—no!" von Hellmann threw his hands up in frustration. "I am going no further in this. You know what I think of you."

"And you know what I think of you," she said. "Is that all, then? Is this the only reason you invited me here? To harass me?"

"No… there were one or two other reasons."

She smiled courteously.

"That trumpet trick…" he began.

"The one you could not explain," she said nonchalantly.

"Yes, the one I could not explain." Von Hellmann licked his dry lips and took a sip of water before continuing. "I will pay you one hundred dollars for the secret."

Madame Priestly laughed, and turned her head a little to one side, smiling to herself. With the sunlight falling warmly on her face, even von Hellmann admitted inwardly that she was beautiful. In another time, another place, he might have welcomed her as a partner rather than as an opponent.

Her smile changed from curiosity to satisfaction.

"No," she said simply.

He hesitated for a moment before offering, "Five hundred."

She raised an eyebrow.

"No," she said with relish.

"Dammit—one thousand dollars."

She scoffed.

"You *are* a monster," he said, defeated. "I always knew that, of course. Oh, well. There is one other reason I asked you here today, and that is to tell you that I am not so easily fooled as Detective Richards."

"What do you mean?" the medium asked innocently.

"I know it wasn't your brother who had those thugs attack me—that was you."

She turned her gaze back out the window.

"He wasn't even your brother, was he?" von Hellmann pursued.

"No," she replied quietly. "He was a confidence artist I picked up in Denver a couple of years ago. He made a specialty of three-card monte, among some other things. We each needed a partner—unchaperoned women are not admitted to society, and I have the social graces he so sorely lacked. I sent ten dollars to a spiritualist church in Philadelphia and he was made a minister. But he was a stupid oaf, I found out later, and nearly cost us both our liberty several times. He was stupid enough to be dangerous. Hiring those thugs was just the kind of harebrained trick he would have pulled."

"And if I had backed down and he'd been arrested for it, it would have gotten us both out of your way."

"I didn't need him anymore—I had Hornbeck."

"A wealthy patron."

"A very wealthy patron, and a rare sucker," she said coldly.

For just a moment, as his hand curled almost unconsciously into a fist, he thought he was going to strike her, thought the old contempt he felt for her was about to slip its leash. He wanted to poleax her out of her chair and send her sprawling across the floor, but he swallowed his anger as she rose to leave.

"I must be going, Professor," she said. "I thank you for a very interesting afternoon."

"Just one more thing, Madame," he stopped her. "I have never said this to anyone—anyone at all. I have made a career out of exposing charlatans and challenging mediums and their outlandish claims..." He fumbled embarrassedly with his white cloth napkin. "But through it all, I have always held out the hope that there was at least a kernel of truth in it all—that although I have never seen it and have only ever found fakes and frauds in my investigations, I believe the dead can speak to the living..."

Madame shook her head and said, curtly, "No. It is all false. The dead do not return, and they do not speak. They are gone."

She turned on her heel and left von Hellmann sitting at the table. As she vanished through the doors, he knew that he would never see her again.

Chapter XXX

THE PASSING DAYS ADDED UP to weeks, and the passing weeks added up to months. The Columbian Exposition closed in Chicago, its flags at half-staff to mark the assassination of Harrison, the city's five-term mayor. The William K. Vanderbilts sailed for India in November and already there were rumors of strife aboard the yacht, Valiant. In December, Conan Doyle revealed that Sherlock Holmes had plunged over the Reichenbach Falls, locked in single combat with his nemesis, Professor Moriarty, the Napoleon of Crime.

It was snowing in Newport and the New Year was only a few short days away. Miss Brooke sat at her desk, sipping a cup of steaming cocoa and looking absently out her frosty window. A framed picture of Nellie Bly smiled up at her from the desktop, half-lost amid stacks of newspapers and piles of clippings. Miss Brooke had been reorganizing her notes and files from the past year, and had spent the last half-hour in a reverie over the pages of the notebook recording the struggle between von Hellmann and Madame Priestley.

The whispers and the rumors had not stopped; while so many other seasonal visitors were now only half-recalled ghosts shimmering in the memory as with the heat of summer, the professor, the colonel, and the medium still somehow haunted the snowy streets.

Blithewood House had very quietly gone up for sale after the end of the summer season; Hornbeck explained to his house agent that he would not be returning to Newport, and wished to be rid of the old house. Miss Brooke had heard that upon arriving back in Manhattan, the Colonel had locked himself up in the old brownstone and would accept no visitors, other than his children, his sister, and the occasional spirit medium. It was said that he did not sleep well at night.

Professor Erasmus von Hellmann, planning an extensive world-tour, died suddenly at home a few days before Christmas. The obituary atop one of Miss Brooke's piles of clippings listed the cause of death as heart failure, brought on by what von Hellmann himself had described as a very trying summer. The funeral was well-attended, at times seeming like a who's who of the variety theater. Hope, his surviving niece, thanked those in attendance and said her uncle would be missed by one and all.

In the weeks following the funeral, nearly a dozen spiritualists claimed to have received messages from him, in which he repudiated all his former claims. The Uncanny Esperanza , now the keeper of the von Hellmann flame, dismissed this as cheap publicity stunts blaspheming her uncle's memory.

Miss Brooke discounted a number of the stranger rumors she had heard circulating: that Hornbeck was on his deathbed and confessing to some sort of elaborate hoax hatched with Madame Priestley; that von Hellmann's ghost had been seen backstage at the Casino theater; that some member of Hornbeck's staff had been a Scotland Yard detective, sent to gather evidence against Madame on a murder charge....

And about Madame Helene Priestley herself, Miss Brooke had heard nothing, as if the medium had simply vanished, melting onto smoke like a spirit at sunrise. Back to the Summerland. Gone.

Miss Brooke snapped the little notebook closed, replacing it on its shelf. She smiled at the picture of Nellie Bly and crossed the room to the window, watching the snow swirl past, the gray clouds hiding the winter sun. She wondered what new spirits would haunt Newport next season, what fresh sensation would occupy the old town when the summer colony returned, new faces mingling with the old, and the verdict forgotten and filed away in dusty law books.

Historical Note

A Brief History of Talking to the Dead

Ghosts and spirits and life after death must be one of the oldest, most deeply-held human beliefs. Most world religions have some concept of an afterlife, and long before the pharaohs left for the next world laden with their treasures, Neanderthals buried their dead with food and tools, indicating they may also have envisioned death as a journey, bound for some unknown destination. In dark Victorian séance chambers, the idea that death was not the end came back with a vengeance. Spiritualism, the social, political, and philosophical movement of which the séance was the centerpiece and the sacrament, swept through the English-speaking world.

It began with two little girls in the village of Hydesville, NY, near Rochester. This part of upstate New York, known as the "Burned Over District," had already been the scene of numerous religious revivals and revelations—Joseph Smith, just for one example, supposedly discovered his Golden Tablets nearby, launching the Mormon Church. Now an even stranger event was at hand. In March of 1848, John Fox and his family were kept awake night after night by strange rapping noises that echoed throughout their small cottage. The raps seemed to have no earthly source, and seemed to center on the family's two young daughters, Margaretta (often called Margaret, or Maggie) and Katherine, (called Kate or Katie). Sources disagree about their actual ages, with most placing them around 8 or 12.

On March 31, 1848, Kate, addressing the empty air, called "Here, Mr. Splitfoot, do as I do!" And she snapped her fingers three times.

And got three raps in response.

She then made the motion of snapping her fingers twice, without making any sound, and still got two loud raps in answer.

"Mother!" she gasped. "It can see as well as hear!"

"Is it a disembodied spirit that has taken possession of my dear children?" Mrs. Fox wondered aloud. And a flurry of raps answered.

If Mr. Splitfoot—the Devil himself—had truly been raised in Hydesville, nobody seemed too worried, and soon people came from miles around and paid twenty-five cents to have a séance at the Fox family cottage. The spirit in residence rapped out people's ages, the number of children they had, and answered simple questions—three raps for yes, two for no. Someone discovered that if a sitter recited the alphabet, the spirits would rap at the appropriate letter, and now whole messages could be spelled out. Letter by letter, the spirit revealed that in life he had been a peddler named Charles Rosma, who had been murdered by a previous tenant and buried in the cellar.

Word continued to spread, reaching nearby Rochester, where Leah, the eldest Fox sister, lived with her husband. Leah is usually painted as the villain, as a domineering schemer taking advantage of her impressionable younger siblings. Whether or not this is an entirely accurate portrait of her (and the evidence suggests that it probbably is), Leah quickly decided to take the show on the road. Katie and Maggie soon gave their first public performance at Rochester's Corinthian Hall. Believers, skeptics, and the simply curious thronged the hall to hear the mysterious spirit raps.

Not everyone was convinced, and strange theories were offered—including that the sounds were somehow produced by objects hanging from the girls "inexpressibles" under their clothes.

But an all-female committee who searched the girls discovered nothing. Doubters were left scratching their heads.

Early nineteenth century audiences were well-acquainted with a wide variety of travelling mesmerists, itinerant preachers, and wandering medicine shows, so two little girls claiming to contact the discarnate probably didn't seem particularly unusual. Staging their first performances in a public—and therefore secular—venue meant that this was not necessarily religious in nature, and no one denomination could claim the spirits for their own. While an evening with the spirits certainly could be religious experience for some, it didn't have to be.

Word continued to spread, and soon Horace Greeley, the newspaper editor famous for his advice, "Go West, young man!" brought the girls to Manhattan and installed them in a hotel. Soon, the cream of New York society was attending séances with the sisters. Harriet Beecher Stowe, author of *Uncle Tom's Cabin*, went to séances there. Julia Ward Howe, who wrote *The Battle Hymn of the Republic*, also visited the young mediums, as did James Fenimore Cooper, author of *The Last of the Mohicans*. Commodore Cornelius Vanderbilt, the millionaire, attended séances to get stock tips from the Beyond. But in addition to well-heeled celebrities, regular folks also attended séances as the movement became a craze.

As tambourines shook their way across tables that levitated while raps sounded from every corner of darkened rooms, séances began to attract a broad range of liberals, radicals, freethinkers, and reformers, including suffragettes, abolitionists, and temperance crusaders—those who, according to most versions of the story, found conventional religion unsatisfying and thought the mysteries of the séance were much more appealing. Women were deemed "spiritual" (rather than "intellectual") and so of course were naturally mediumistic, which led to a great number of women giving séances or entering a trance and allowing the spirits to deliver lectures through them. Some of these distaff trance lecturers were probably the first women many had heard addressing the public from a stage, and some of those talk went on for hours.

Victorian Spiritualism was also very much in keeping with the overall optimism of the age—the Fox Sisters and other mediums spoke of an afterlife where all were welcome, all were equal, and all were enlightened. Every soul would find its perfect "spiritual mate," even if they had missed one another in this life. In the "Happy Summerland," as they called it, everyone would spend their days wandering the beautiful landscape, deep in conversation with Aristotle, Ben Franklin, or Jesus. There was no Spiritualist Hell—borrowing a page from the Buddhists, anyone not quite ready to enter paradise was sent back to Earth to try again later.

The movement also tapped into the scientific spirit of the age, offering empirical evidence of its supernatural claims. Skeptics entered the seance chamber and were converted by the evidence of their own eyes, and séances became a weird amalgam of science and religion as spirits forms that appeared had their temperatures taken and their blood drawn for analysis.

Early opposition came mostly from conservative Christians who considered it all blasphemy and impiety. Being the golden age of the pamphlet, we find such titles as *The Infidelity of the Times as Connected with the Rappings and Mesmerists;* and another entitled *Ancient Sorcery as Revived in Modern Spiritualism Examined by Divine Law and Testimony;* and (your author's personal favorite) *The Spirit Rappings, Mesmerism, Clairvoyance, Visions, Revelations, Startling Phenomena and the Infidelity of the Rapping Fraternity Calmly Considered and Exposed.*

In 1852, a Mrs. W. B. Hayden of Boston crossed the Atlantic to hold séances in London. Rumors began circulating that Queen Victoria was now attending séances. Charles Dickens was unimpressed, remarking in a letter to a friend that, "I have not the least belief in the awful unseen world being available for evening parties at so much per night." English magician John Nevil Maskelyne was perhaps even more blunt when he tsk-tsked, "Oh Yankee Doodle! Inventor of wooden nutmegs and new religions, how easily are you Barnumized!"

Back in America, the land of Spiritualism's birth, the matter was taken up for debate in the Senate in April, 1854. A petition was submitted calling for the formation of a scientific commission to investigate the mysteries of the séance room—"believing that the progress of science and the true interests of mankind will be greatly promoted by the proposed investigation." Unsurprisingly, the proposal went nowhere, and drew laughter when one senator suggested it be referred to the Committee on Foreign Relations. We can assume that the 15,000 people who signed the petition did not find it quite so funny.

Just as there were newspapers advocating for and editorializing upon abolition or women's suffrage, so too were there newspapers devoted to the Spiritualist cause. Perhaps the best known was the Boston-based *Banner of Light*. The *Banner* carried reports of otherworldly manifestations and apparitions, editorials and essays dictated from trance mediums, and ads and listings for a variety of psychics, healers, spirit mediums, and similar occult entrepreneurs. The *Medium and Daybreak*, published in England, covered similar ground over there.

The movement that had started with two little girls in a modest cabin in upstate New York had grown into an international phenomenon.

In the 1880s, no less a person than William James, the Harvard professor who would write *The Varieties of Religious Experience*, sat with Mrs. Leonora Piper, a Boston medium. Mrs. Piper, a direct-voice medium, was evidently able to deliver messages from James's deceased son, and James was deeply impressed. The father of American psychology was no easy mark; he was well aware of various sly subterfuges, but still wrote, "When imposture has been checked off as far possible, when chance coincidence has been allowed for, when opportunities for normal knowledge on the part of the subject have been noted, and skill in 'fishing' and following clues unwittingly furnished by the voice or face of bystanders have been counted in, those who have the fullest acquaintance with the phenomena admit that in good mediums *there is a residuum of knowledge displayed* that can only be supernormal."

Soon, the inevitable happened, as spirit mediums were caught cheating, and faking their manifestations. Full-form apparitions proved to be the medium, swathed in yards of cheesecloth daubed in phosphorescent paint. Spirit photographers were caught using double-exposures to produce those "spirit extras" that appeared in their photos. Mediums claiming to have psychic knowledge were found to have more mundane sources for their information, such as researching their sitters weeks in advance. In 1891, an anonymous author published *Revelations of a Spirit Medium,* a how-to manual that laid bare the secrets of the séance chamber. From slate-writing to table tipping to spirit raps, the very earthly methods were explained and described in detail. It is a rare find today because, according to legend, outraged spirit mediums bought up and destroyed every copy they could get their hands on… but probably only after reading it thoroughly and taking notes.

The rampant fraud perpetrated in séance rooms eventually prompted Katie and Maggie Fox to come forward in 1888. The two little girls who had started it all were now destitute, middle-aged alcoholics who had led lives of misery. Maggie denounced Spiritualism as "a fraud of the worst description." The whole thing had started as a prank to frighten their poor mother, she said, and the spirit raps were produced by the two girls cracking the joints of their toes. Kate tearfully confirmed her sister's story. In a public demonstration that was a strange mirror-image of the one that launched their career and the movement itself, Maggie stood in a crowded auditorium and cracked her toes for an astounded audience.

"I do this because I consider it my duty, a sacred thing, a holy mission, to expose it," she declared in a written confession. "I want to see the day when it is entirely done away with. After I expose it I hope Spiritualism will be given a death blow. I was the first in the field and I have a right to expose it."

Kate and Maggie placed the blame squarely on Leah. They insisted that she was intent on making money from the very beginning, being well aware of what was going on. She had bullied, threatened, and manipulated them their whole lives. Now stepping out from under her thumb, they hoped a confession would finally end the movement they had inadvertently created.

It didn't work. Spiritualists around the world dismissed the confession, citing Maggie's alcoholism, poverty, and/or recent conversion to Catholicism as reasons for doubt. She even got hate mail.

"Hundreds of thousands have believed through you and you alone," a woman wrote from Boston. "Hundreds of thousands eagerly ask you whether all the glorious light they fancied you had given them was but the false flicker of the common dip candle of fraud—the disclosures you make take from me all that I have cherished most. There is nothing left for me now but to hope for the reality of that repose which death promises us."

Maggie planned a lecture tour, exposing the frauds of Spiritualism, but it never came together. People will pay handsomely to talk to the spirits, but not to hear that it's all a hoax. When the lecture tour failed to materialize, Maggie reluctantly returned to mediumship, the only life she had ever known. But her confession had made her anathema among Spiritualists, and she was now shunned by those who had once supporter her and flocked to her table, including her wealthy patrons.

The Fox Sisters all died within a few years of one another— Leah in 1890, Kate in 1892, and Maggie in 1893—all alone, all penniless. While claiming to be in touch with the spirit world, their earthly lives had been miserable—Maggie admitted in her confession, "I used to say to those who wanted me to give a séance, *You are driving me into Hell.*" We can only hope that, if there is an afterlife, they were able to find the peace that was denied them in this life. While the mothers of Spiritualism are dead and buried, forgotten by some believers and held at arm's length by others, the Spiritualist movement lives on and, as it speaks to one of the oldest human beliefs, it always will.

From the author

YOU DON'T WRITE A BOOK ON YOUR OWN. At least I don't. Gratitude is due to all of the following splendid people:

First and foremost, my wife Judith, who puts up with a whole lot.

Dan Ciora once again acted as legal counsel.

Paul di Filippo, fellow traveler in antique lands.

Leanna Renee Hieber, who sat up late at night reading,

Peter Mooney, who knows more about Gilded Age Newport than the people living there at the time.

Rob Proscia, who thoroughly audited the manuscript.

John Teehan at The Merry Blacksmith Press, for giving me the chance.

Elizabeth Wayland-Seal, ace editor with an eye for errant typos.

The long-lost Andrea Yates, who offered support and encouragement at the time.

RORY O'BRIEN lives in Salem, MA, with his patient, long-suffering wife, their Treeing Walker Coonhound, and a black cat. His previous novel, *Gallows Hill*, is also available from The Merry Blacksmith Press.

Visit www.roryobrienbooks.com

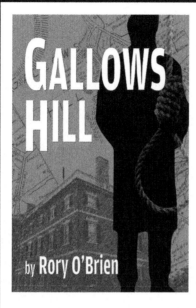

CPSIA information can be obtained .
at www.ICGtesting.com
Printed in the USA
LVOW04s1731181016
509271LV00009B/680/P